Fragile Boundaries

Fragile Boundaries

Johnny Leavesley

B

Belgravia Press

First published in the UK 2013 by Belgravia Press.

Belgravia Press
22 Chancery Lane, London, WC2A 1LS

Hardback ISBN 9780992675707
Paperback ISBN 9780992675714

9 8 7 6 5 4 3 2 1

A catalogue reference for this book is available from
the British Library.

Typesetting and jacket design by The Word Machine.

Printed in Great Britain by TJ International.

MIX
Paper from
responsible sources
FSC® C013056

For Rashid and Zeina

Acknowledgements

My profound thanks are offered to David Archer,
Zoe Butler, Drew Curtis, Sidi Hamza bin al Hussein,
Maria Leavesley, Daniel Martin, Amy Wheelton
and Hywel Williams for their advice.

*"Whoso has done an atom's
weight of good shall see it;
and whoso has done an atom's
weight of evil shall see it."*

Surah 99: 7-8,
The Koran

CHAPTER I

The day was preparing to brighten, to vapourise the park's mist and scarf trails of weakening fog, dissipating it like dry ice across the stage. It was never a place for solitude, even at that early hour. There were too many others running, gaudily dressed adherents to the virtuous addiction of the morning, kick-start jog. Through the fog's thinning veil Jayda Talhoun pounded her footfalls, resenting each person she ran past as an intruder into her private battle: the mountain of determination that she had to scale each morning to get to the paths of Hyde Park and push herself into sweat, past the sleepiness and warmth of her bed, her throat's dryness and the dull, sapping ache rising up in rebellion against sudden physical effort. Of all her London mornings, she had not failed to do so yet.

It was a fight to be a morning person. No one had demanded it of her but she had decided years ago that to create her own luck needed unusual application. There were plenty of her type at university in London — single, upper class Arab women — but she did not want to spend much time perpetuating a similar social roundhouse to that she could find in Amman. It was true that there was more freedom in London, away from the prying suffocations of family. There was space to be wild and unobserved, with no social tracking structure, always being somewhere where someone knew who you were. Well, up to a point. Parents and elder brothers might not find out who you partied with but contemporaries certainly did and embraced every event with the commentary of social media. It might not be the same crowd as at home but there were the invisible connections. Such as that medical undergrad from Bahrain she half-liked and who undoubtedly liked her; he had a cousin in Kuwait who was an old friend of one of her brother's fellow officers. There was always a connection.

To ease the irritations of rising early and getting there and to distract herself from the boredom of running, she allowed herself fantasies. In them she imagined she was powerful: a diplomat resolving a crisis, a Prime Minister advising the King or even a Chief of Staff berating generals in a war. Public roles for which women were not favoured. She considered herself in a fight for opportunities to prove herself. When she was little and playing doctors and nurses with her brother, why had she always been the nurse? 'What shall I do when I grow up?' 'Marry,' was the reply, from everyone she asked. She was offended by what she saw as the overwhelming, ubiquitous culture of Arab misogyny. Jordan had been liberal even without the violent cleansing of an Arab Spring, had always been a place of tolerance and conservative progression. No barely literate Salafi lunatics preached hatred and suppression, at least not publicly. It was a mild, uneventful sort of place, officially friendly through the financial imperatives of both Gulf petrodollars and Western tourists. Jordan was her birthplace and best chance. If she could not rise to the top there she would have betrayed her own luck. It did not occur to her whether this was feminism, but it was her struggle.

Mostly, she imagined running the family businesses with her father and brother uninvolved. The large, light-flooded corner office on the highest floor that was her father's would be her own, with the secretaries and managers responding to her directions. Her picture on the magazine cover, with four pages of profile inside. Even when, from some modesty connected to her sense of reason, she had to pause these thoughts and feel the aching rhythm of the run reduce her ambition to the immediate boredom of continuing, she reassured herself that such thoughts were necessary. At its core, Arab sensibility was the family. The man to create and protect it. The woman to be wife, mother, mistress and servant of it. Children for family and family before tribe and nation. Family for Islam and yet, even if Islam improbably dissolved under a secular sun of western affluence to a mere lifestyle choice, there would still be the kernel of the Arab family with pressure to marry, to breed and to obey. Family would one day consume her and maybe, then, she would want it. She just had to find reason to justify delaying it.

The irony was that Jayda adored her father. His expectations for her were conventionally prosaic, as were her mother's, but she could sense his weakness, that he loved her to indulgence. So a series of charming manipulations had led her to university in London and, from that, to the panting circumnavigation of a misty park at seven in the morning, four hours before her first lecture. Whether this period was a brief blip of independence before Amman swallowed her again in rounds of social trivia and then marriage to a man vetted by her parents, or was the pause before the curtain was raised to her career, she could not, if she was honest, predict with any certainty.

Heat prickled upon her sweating skin against the disappearing cool of the morning. The adhesive dryness in her throat cried for water she did not have and began to make her breaths raspingly painful. She was halfway through her usual run and it felt harder than ever before. The urge to surrender to a walk was strong, to suspend the discomforts in pausing motion, to rest, and she began to shudder to a stop. A pair running side by side, man and woman earnest in matching fluorescent skins, overtook her. It annoyed her. She frowned her ignition, clamped her teeth and powered on.

Cosy Cheshire always allowed herself the luxury of time when preparing for parties. Her toilet was no lengthier than any other self-respecting woman's but the preparation seemed to be more emotionally complicated. She loved and feared invitations in equal measure, finding them generally impossible to refuse and the signal for chasms of malaise-seeping apprehension. For this one she tried to gain control by closing her shop early again and spending most of the two hours of captured time in an indulgence of indecision about which outfit to wear. Half a dozen were splayed across the bed, all dissimilar, all her own designs. She exhaled and allowed herself the sort of earnest frown she imagined was attractive but knew gave her nothing but wrinkles. There was the black leather catsuit that advertised adventure and sexual power; the soft rose-pink imitation Chanel suit for a demure posture; a lime green matching set and flat shoes that emitted confidence; a dark, richly coloured, high collared cheongsam for an oriental pose; a billowing white dress and three pastel blouses for when she felt too fat and hot in summer and, of course, her version of the classic black cocktail dress with its suggestive curve-clinging lines and slits. The prospect of making a choice seemed overwhelming until hunger pangs distracted her again. As she stood beside the bed, in growing undecided pain, the ever-present emptiness in her belly groaned and Cosy remembered, with a cold shiver that did not seem to start from anywhere but filmed her in sweat all at once, that she must keep the scars on her arms covered. She clutched herself, rocking from toes to heels repeatedly as the shiver calmed itself away, frowning at her predicament in fear. What if she knew no-one there? What if no-one new liked her? What if she had to return home that night with the haunting sense that it had all been for nothing — her preparations, her faux confidence, laughter and smiles, to stumble from a taxi half-drunk and alone, returning to a dark, untidy house? Waves of nausea began to crinkle throughout her from the weakness fuelled by virtually no food all day, so she gulped air several times and forced herself steady. After a smile at her self-control she began hastily to take off her clothes, dropping them forcefully behind her as if they disgusted her. Only a breakfast apple and several sugared mugs of coffee had passed her lips but still her belly felt slightly swollen.

Naked and suddenly conscious of the exposure she rubbed herself randomly with her hands. Turning to a full length mirror she examined her face, searching for any immediate truth. Whether her mood was now fear, boredom or both she could not tell. A default narrative of self assurance advanced within her allowing her arms to drop from their hug and place themselves upon her hips, giving a more confident, critical posture. She was, she thought, still pretty. Still blonde but with browning roots, her skin not fresh, but there was enough of an outline of past beauty to yet give her a chance of filling the great void at the centre of her existence, the absence of someone to share it with. So, sighing within, she had to go to the party.

Her eyes rested their critical gaze not on the flat slimness of the torso reflecting back to her but on her knees, the wrinkled knolls of which were blotchy pink and strangely incongruous upon the mainly clear alabaster of her skin. They revealed her age like the backs of her hands. She needed to summon her reserves of bravery and glanced to a half-full bottle of vodka and glass by her bedside lamp. The thought of taking a drink reminded the pinpoint of her Adam's Apple of the reflux of bile that was likely to erupt from within after swallowing but she needed to create some layers of courage before the party began. She paced to the bathroom next door, her toes appreciating the carpet's depth with each ponderous step, her nakedness feeling free and daring in the walk, to place herself kneeling delicately astride the glaring ceramic of the lavatory, one arm steadying the seat and her toes now flexing an arch to tip herself forward as the other hand, with mechanical grace, reached into her throat to tickle out a small convulsion of puke.

CHAPTER II

There was a sweet lift of cooling breeze, unexpected and sudden, through the open window of Jad Talhoun's study. The day was already hot. A wave of jasmine, baked thick as if it had been heated in confinement, rose and surprised him, dissipating his concentration. Having finished his task he placed his pistol with careful precision to one side of the desk on top of its case. Stripping down and reassembling the weapon he kept at home was a ritual he repeated every Friday after breakfast as the weekend started. His was a collector's edition Pietro Beretta 92 F, its handle polished mahogany, its screws brass, its barrel not yet fired in anger. It was an expensive tool for a home security policy, one he liked.

Jad took a cigarette from a red lacquer box upon the desk and walked to the window. The leather surface of the desk behind him was overlaid with neatly spaced sheets of paperwork, the weekly reports and financials from his companies, spread out and then ignored. The jasmine was still strong as he exhaled his first drag in a plume. Looking upon his garden with mild curiosity, he regarded with a proud smile its grass, green and coarse-leafed. Most Amman villas squatted their expanse upon all their allotted space, leaving little but paved driveway to breathe around them but Jad's father had built this mansion when the surrounding land was dust. Sprinklers whirred their continual clicking mists. Dense shrubs hugged the perimeter, colours of mainly variegated greens and yellows forming a controlled, angular jungle bordering the lawn's ordered lines. Behind this fringe was a whitewashed wall, 12 feet of even brickwork topped with embedded broken glass. The city beyond the wall, subdued because it was a Friday, hazed its immediacy behind a fat, blurring heat. Flat-roofed white and sandstone buildings and the glass stumps of offices seemed to warp in baked vision. The surrounding sounds travelled softly to mesh in a blanketing backdrop of urban noise. He could identify nothing that could give off the scent but still he stood there, raising his eyebrows wide in contented interest and smoking with relaxed ease.

The door behind him opened softly, turning him in response. The new weekend maid, whose name he could not remember, bobbed herself in and avoided his gaze. She placed down a tray trembling with Turkish coffee, water and unwanted biscuits. Thoughtless as to what papers she had covered she slipped out as quickly as she had come, leaving the door ajar but with a backward glance at the pistol, its smooth dull metal enhanced in an arrow of sunlight.

His family was elsewhere: his wife visiting friends, his eldest still in his room, his spoilt daughter abroad and the two youngest playing together on the top floor, half in argument, their urgent sounds reaching him muffled. On a bookshelf behind the desk rested a framed photograph of him seated outside with his daughter, Jayda, draping an arm over him, her smile beside his, her face presenting a beguiling freshness. He missed her. She had now been in London nearly three months. When he stared at the picture it seemed to him an ungraspable surprise of nature that his genes had contributed to a creature of such beauty.

When Jayda had proposed that she study in London he had realised it was her way of escaping, although that explanation was avoided. Despite his hesitations in granting consent she had been, as always since her earliest smiles, too persistent for him to resist. Whilst he loved his wife with the honour and respect that every family man should, Jad adored his eldest daughter foremost. For him such concepts as romance and uxorious love were weaknesses to be shunned by an impregnable masculine facade. Not that his Zena seemed to be unhappy. They had been pushed together at an age when they were little more than children by two sets of parents whose consideration for their happiness was, initially, marginal. Happiness was expected to be found within the formula of marriage which the parents, the unquestionable authority, had decided upon. For Jad, the overwhelming reason his marriage was successful was because he had children. The purpose of his marriage was for his children. As for his wife's happiness, whilst he would, if asked, declare it he could not be certain because they had never spoken of it. Whilst he did not regard himself as inconsiderate to such things, marital happiness and his own equilibrium were secondary, self-indulgent byproducts. Jad Talhoun was a man of position in Jordan but even more important to him than any status his businesses gave him, it was crucial to Jad to be a paterfamilias: a loud, loving, opinionated, generous, ursine, self-generatingly kinetic bubble of a man. Real men were family men.

The particular combination that was Jayda's character surprised and delighted him. The friendly brightness of her optimism usually pleased him, but it was the shocking unanswerability of her intelligence that was foremost in plying his emotions and prejudices. She had a tendency progressively to traject towards whatever ambition currently burned within her. It was a simple approach that he approved of. Her beauty he was proud of and the elegance of her movements he absorbed without noticing but they formed the subliminal essence of his adoration. Despite his paternal longing whilst she was away it did not occur to him to ring or text her, even though there was only an hour's difference at this season, even though he loved to talk to her and hear her soft, expressive tones, sensing sometimes through the babbling trivia and disproportionate worries of her concerns that he still mattered to her emotionally. It was deflating if she rang the house and he missed her but he would never impose himself. Above all, he wanted to feel needed.

Whilst still facing out to the garden Jad knew from an almost imperceptible alteration in the air behind him that someone was filling the doorframe. He turned to see the tall angularity of his son, hesitant on the threshold.

'Sabah al Khayr,' welcomed Jad.

'Ahlan.'

'Well, have you been thinking on my suggestion?' He moved inwards to behind his desk again, liking its physical barrier as an aid to the formality he needed, and stubbed out on a glass ashtray.

'Yes, Baba,' started Jamil at a volume louder than he had perhaps intended. 'I think I should like to go tomorrow. It would be useful for me to meet the insurance people.'

Jad blinked surprise at his son, not at the decision, which was what he had anticipated, but at the reason stated.

'Jamil, seriously? Would you not be going because you want to see Jayda?'

Jamil was a big man, like his father, but not yet thickened out. Only the cratered bags beneath both their eyes seemed to give similar physiognomies. Even their moustaches were different: Jad's a bushy greying tuft, his son's a thin black definition of self-consciousness. The son seemed exposed and nervous. He walked over to the window to look out as his father continued, 'Bijadd? Would not seeing Jayda be a better reason?'

'Perhaps, but the work needs to be done as well.'

'Of course.' Jad felt wryly amused. His son's foibles had long ceased to frustrate but now gave quiet entertainment to him in the natural course of their daily frictions. He knew that Jamil, his proud, awkward, shy, blustering, unmarried son, must miss his sister with unusual intensity. 'You could find out how she really is. Whether she is studying hard. Whether she has a boyfriend that we need to worry about.'

'Yes, I will.' Jamil hastened away with a couple of long jerky strides, avoiding his father's gaze, desperate to be away. 'I will make my preparations.'

Later that day Jamil was late for the Jummah Prayer despite his rigorous attention to motorised speed. This was something that particularly irritated him. Tall, ramrod, gangly but dexterous, he appeared stiff because that was how he felt comfortable. Driving fast had become part of his identity, his masculinity. Captain Talhoun had commanded tanks, Chieftains and Challengers in the 40th Royal Armoured Brigade, but now he drove his black BMW around Amman as if he still had the same sort of firepower. At least he could adjust the seat to meet his frame.

The sidewalks around the King Hussein Mosque were blocked with parked cars and so he had to park several streets away. A cigarette stitch tightened his chest and beads of sweat clammed his underarms as he ran in. The Adhan had abruptly ceased being broadcast from the minarets when he parked and it was nearly a further five minutes of jarring his footfalls in a jog before he entered the courtyard.

He had been delayed by news which disturbed him in a way that surprised him. Every Friday morning Jayda rang from London and gabbled to each of them in turn. Today she spoke to mother first and mentioned she was going to a party the next night. That was, of itself, nothing, but it reminded him that with each passing week that Jayda was away in London, the further away she was growing apart from their influence. He had felt chilled and left the room for his own without a word; he smoked and felt the apprehension of not knowing but sensing an impending disaster. The nexus of his emotional ley lines felt strained. Five unenjoyed cigarettes, one after the other, had given no insight or challenge but enhanced the biting grey colour of his mood. He had managed to get to his car unseen.

Shoes and socks hastily discarded, he could hardly rush the ablutions. He crouched on the stone bench before a tap as he muttered the Bismillah in panting breaths whilst washing his hands, over and over like a preparing surgeon late for an operation. Then, leaning forward, he took in water to his mouth, swilling and spitting out three times. His nose hurt with the unnatural snorting of the water, cupped from his hands, three times up. Three times more he filled his cupped hands and dunked his face with messy, blasting splatters. There was no-one behind or alongside him to worry about. His right arm washed to the elbow, then the left, each the three times. The ears with his fingers and then the culmination of this ritualised, compulsive cleansing: the washing of his feet up to the ankles, thrice, beginning with the right.

The dust of the desert now washed from him he paced with undignified haste into the main jamaca. It was, inevitably, crowded but was momentarily hushed. He joined the back row of the ruku, each bowing in their carpeted, proportioned, windowed space, in rows across the large expanse of the domed floor, a regulated community of humility.

Despite his rush he was less annoyed with his own faults than he was with the rest of his family. At least he was bothering to attend prayers. He realised that he was not perfect but his attempts to be devout were coupled with his understanding of duty, identity and honour. That his parents rarely came to the mosque and, indeed, rarely prayed at all counterpointed his own pride that he did so. There were days, weeks even, when he did not observe the five daily prayers, either at home or office and there were periods when he did; periods, usually, when he was troubled. Once, on an RJ flight home from London as he had crept, bleary and tired, to the front toilet cubicles he had nearly stumbled over the flight security guard bobbing his devotions at the ruku. The sight of the devotion, inconveniently observed, immediately jolted him from turpitude so he shuffled across the gangway past chattering hostesses, ignored the pressure upon his bladder and sank to his knees in the small space in front of the opposite loo to join in the prayer. Impure with alcohol from the flight meal and not having ritually washed he nevertheless felt an overwhelming urge to observe prayer, the intonations rhythmic, natural, wholesome and reaffirming, the structure reassuring and allowing him to pray without reflection, without troubling the inchoate worries that compelled him.

'*Samia Allahou liman Hamidah,*' intoned the congregants and from somewhere hidden in front on his Dakka the imam incanted the reply, '*Allahumma rabbana wa Laka.*'

The imam intoned a reading from the Koran and, as so often, Jamil's thoughts wandered now to his own mix of prayer and prejudice as he knelt facing the rows of male backs, all silent and attentive, though shifting continually like small opposing waves.

'Allah Almighty, Specifically Merciful Lord, forgive my sins,' he prayed. 'Grant me a wife that I may honour you with children. Grant me prosperity that I may honour you with charity.' And then, with a shift of thought and intention, with no distinction in Jamil's mind as to degrees of purity of intent or appropriateness, he carried on, 'Almighty Allah, guide Jayda to find love, honour and respect with a Jordanian husband, a true, good Muslim, and bless her with many children.'

The prayers developed into the sermon and Jamil allowed his mind to rest, kneeling, observing the sunlight cast down from the dome's open edges upon the assembled rows of men. It is a peaceful transcendence, the contentment earned from pious observances of regular prayer and Jamil felt a rare moment of untroubled ease but the imam's tone was rising in stridency, itself unusual.

'No matter how knowledgeable I am, not if I were the greatest and most insightful imam in the history of Islam could I condemn anyone, any infidel, any seemingly unclean and evil man, a takfiri. And why not? Because I am not Allah. Only Allah Almighty, the Beneficent, the Merciful, the Wise, the Just, can do that.'

The very worst that could happen would be for Jayda to fall in love with a godless man whilst she was away in London. If it were an Englishman he would most likely be an infidel and apostate, a kafir. As a stream of light rayed its bright column from the dome and shifted all other perspectives into shadow, Jamil squeezed his eyes shut away from the beam and prayed again that his sister could be guided to Allah; but the thought most acute to him at that moment was that such a temptation would appeal to her.

He was his father's son, he told himself. Babu may not be pious or as observing as he was, but he knew that their prejudices coincided, if only reached by different paths. Jayda was the child and beauty of the family, to be protected and guided by them both, to God, to marriage, to her future.

CHAPTER III

William Clive did not pay much attention to where the cab was going but somewhere in Chelsea it turned into a mews. Light and conversation bounced out into the evening's thin greyness from a boxhouse halfway down the row. Mostly he disliked parties, although he would never admit that to anyone. Nervousness did not cripple him, it was just that he hated the self-conscious knowledge of being on display, of having to perform, of wanting to perform and be liked and being nervous about it, like stage fright. Not that William actually had any particular party performance beyond being himself. For that reason he always avoided dancing.

He felt his palms sweating as he hesitated before the door when it was abruptly opened by a small grinning blonde woman who, with the upbeat vowels of the thoughtless, shrieked a cheerful, 'Hello!' and then paused, smiling insincerely as she realised she did not recognise this possible gatecrasher.

'I'm William Clive,' he said hopefully. She had crow's-feet that crinkled into laughter lines and her thirty-something skin had seen too much sun. Only her grin was now filling the pause. 'Oh, I'm Frances Clive's brother,' he added.

'Yes, of course. I'm Samantha. Come in — you'll make a draught.' She closed the door behind him, pearled again, and then slipped into the crush of people that filled the room.

Just inside he paused and saw that the whole of the ground floor was one room. In front of him were some steep wooden steps to the next floor, on either side of which the room expanded and a mix of suits and long hair above bare shoulders filled the space. Someone had smoked a cigarette, which gave out, he thought, a vague sense of sin. The walls were white with, from what he could see, no pictures. He decided he needed a drink for a prop.

William knew that he had to go to as many parties as he could, even when, as tonight, he was tired and bored. Overall he liked himself, comfortable in his habits and confident with his poses and attitudes but he was, even if he could barely acknowledge it, lonely. A bachelor in his early thirties, nearly young but not youthful, habitual but not yet atrophied, he was self aware enough to realise that he had become too old to be considered by some of the younger women he knew. As he stared at the ceiling in the small hours a conscience, possibly hormonal, often forced its way into his thoughts. He did not want to be a bachelor forever, even if he had no clear idea of who for a companion or what sort of relationship he wanted. He had even had these yearnings whilst lying next to naked, sleeping girlfriends but he had not found who he was looking for. It was this which had propelled him towards another loud room full of mainly strangers, this and innate ambition for what he knew were the usual vanities: money, status and popularity.

It took him longer than he thought it would to snake through the crush to the kitchen area in the search for a drink and then, as he paused to find a way through, he realised he was being stared at.

Of two blonde women who were bantering by the fridge, William realised that one of them was the Samantha who had opened the door to him. The crowd obscured who she was talking to until he was beside them.

'Oh, hi!' she trilled out to him and then turned, revealing Cosy. 'That's him?'

'Yes, that's him,' replied Cosy, quite loudly. 'He who flirts shamelessly with you when you first meet him but then never returns calls. A bastard and a jerk, I suspect.'

'Yes, sorry Cosy,' said William, without thinking. 'I've been away and busy.' Not for the first time the self-regarding nature of the nickname struck him as he addressed her. Her hair was messy, in a cropped pageboy style. Despite her opening insult she was coy, her eyes, wide but impassive, steady upon him as she adjusted herself with a single, soft roll of her shoulders. He noticed that, above what seemed to be slender legs and a lime green skirt was a slightly swollen belly, incongruous for being there amidst her slim, small frame. Looking at her eyes again which were by now in the greedy way of the superficially busy, flicking him up and down, he thought, within the same half-second, that this woman was either permanently scatty or on a cocaine high. Cosy Cheshire. They had met the weekend before at a party his sister had arranged. He had liked her and remembered flirting, but not much else. The next morning had yielded an unignorable hangover, the regret from which was purely dehydration rather than any dimly recollected embarrassment. She seemed a forward sort of woman and normally he liked that, yet it was the earnestness brimming out from behind that made him hesitate. Samantha nodded to both of them and slipped away.

'So, what is it you do again?' Cosy demanded, her eyebrows slightly raised in a feint of interest, resting her sight slightly above his.

It occurred to him that this might be her way of giving genuine attention and despite being possibly mad or high he still found her attractive. He felt a tinge of sympathy and smiled.

'I'm an insurance broker.'

'One of those Lloyds suits?'

'Yes. Sorry,' replied William. 'I remember you though – you design clothes and presumably sell them.'

She grinned at him so he thought it polite to affect a smile in return. William noticed her nose somehow tweak between the lazily focused, wide eyes and watched the curves her mouth made as she smiled. He could sense that this woman was used to being spoilt and indulged, probably from when she was very young.

She had a spark of freshness that began to be attractive but he still did not feel hooked. Her atmosphere was alien, though intriguing. When he realised this he felt a daring ease in wanting to say what he thought.

'You're slightly mad, aren't you?'

'Sorry?' Her eyes moved even wider.

'Well, endearingly off-message.'

'Yes,' she said quickly. 'Do you snog?'

'What?' spluttered William, surprised offguard, 'Umm, well…' He was a moral man of sorts, he often told himself. He went to church, prayed occasionally to say sorry, but he also drank, sometimes smoked as a prop, and wanted sex as much as the next man. He wanted love as well but until then just sex would do. She was smiling at him now and her eyes bounced with pleasure at his reaction. He had the wit to realise that this was either a tease or an invitation that he should not decline too early.

'Err, well, only teenagers from nice families do that, don't they? I'm not averse to it, mind.'

'I haven't snogged for ages,' she continued, now gazing at the crowd but still addressing him. 'I used to think it the pointless part of the sex thing, but now I think it the best bit.'

William instinctively wanted to extend this avenue but felt hesitant in the face of what seemed to be an unhinged proposition. He affected relaxed casualness. 'Tell me, does your attitude to it affect your designing?'

'Oh no. How could it? Look at this.' She spread her

hands over the front of her thighs, slightly stooping to do so. When she regained her posture William saw she was celebrating her skirt, upon which were elaborately embroidered daisies in a circular pattern. Her shoes were also lime green.

'You made that?'

'Umm,' Cosy assented, her lips half smiling and half nodding. William looked at her again, now not sure whether he fancied her and unsure whether or how he wanted the conversation to continue. She held his eyes with what he thought was a soft gaze although it made him blink and all he could think of was, 'It's, err, very good. Did you hand-make it?'

'Sort of.'

She must have inched closer to him. The lines around her eyes looked kind. The slimness of her so close to him did not impose but seemed to yearn for contact. He moved his sight from her eyes to her lips. They were small, poised and almost pulsing.

A besuited man opened the fridge behind her, jolting both of them as he pulled out a bottled beer. William used this to step back but then curved around her to reach the fridge himself and took out another beer. Their faces came very close without touching. He closed the fridge door and realised that he was now holding two bottles, not having finished his first.

'Silly,' said Cosy quietly and lowered her head in a definite coquettish manner. She clearly wanted him to like her.

'No, err, this is for you.'

'No thanks.'

'Oh.' Awkwardness descended. He had to escape and looked around the room, thinking inattention to her would provide an escape but she was sweeping the room with her eyes as well. Mumbling an intimate valedictory with bowed head, which William did not fully hear but smiled at anyway, she then slipped away. He supposed he felt relieved but then there was the awkwardness of a conversational vacancy as he could see no one else he knew.

Then, abruptly, there was a shift within him. A few seconds echoed past within which all background noise was muffled before he could understand what it was upon his senses. There was a woman on the other side of the room. She was utterly unignorable; a life-alteringly beautiful creature. Her oval olive face was the only clear thing tunnelled in his vision. Dark eyes and eyebrows and silky dark hair sailed a glide as she turned her head, her lips revealing a cheerful, white, knowing smile. She wore a white blouse with style, the sleeves rolled up casually and held red wine as she listened to her neighbours with a tilt of her head. She was undoubtedly an attractive woman but her very foreignness meant that to raise her higher needed a conscious decision to fall for her beauty. William was compelled to make that decision in the instant he saw her. Clarity seemed to radiate from her because his eyes were blurred to everything else. He suddenly felt ill. A lump hardened and dried at the top of his throat and simultaneously a seed of nervous fear rapidly accelerated its growth to shudder throughout him in a nauseous wave that made him, without knowing it, rock between his toes and heels. He had to talk to her.

The party was by now even more crowded. Loud jazz was an unlistened-to, heavy backdrop and on top of it conversation noise curled up and waved through the room like sea breakers. The immediate slam on his perceptions was a shifting, braying, drinking sway of people blurring around the margins of his focus, still upon her.

William angled himself to squeeze through as he worked his way through several progressing hesitations across the room. His mouth was dry and sticky. The palms of his hands perspired. He tried to picture what his character might look like if it could be seen: another middle class, minor public school wannabe in a suit, anonymously corporate, not ugly yet not handsome, clean cut but with habitually masculine sloth, and suddenly besotted and nervous. Having no certain idea of what to say or do when he arrived he felt huge, clumsy and numb with the embarrassment of it. She was part of a small circle, their backs excluding newcomers. She laughed at something just said to her and stroked a hand through her hair. The way she did that, as an affirming display, told him self-confidence was clearly a characteristic. Her laughter sounded soft, smothering over the din as his focus concentrated on her. An old, pinstriped man frowned as he pushed his way in front of him, momentarily blocking his view. He sensed Cosy talking excitedly and close to Samantha off to his right. The whole room seemed to consist of twosomes, pairing and splitting constantly, rearranging the crush. A small sourfaced Filipino maid in standard white blouse and black skirt interrupted her group and refilled glasses with bad grace.

The phalanx of backs before him made him hesitate and, thinking that to get out his phone would be too obvious an affectation, he felt momentarily at a loss until deciding he would be comfortable in taking time to observe her. She seemed tall, her slimness emphasised that and everything else about her. Raven hair tousled above and below her shoulders. Drainpipe dark jeans tapered from her hips to felt canvas shoes. Another joke erupted into laughter amongst the group and with that she shifted her weight to rest upon one hip. It was a movement so fluid that it seemed to William to have enormous latent energy and sensuality.

He was staring. There was no available breach in the wall and so he armed himself with a drink from the Filipino, sidled to a near corner, and petrified.

'William!' It was Buff, an old friend, looming tall and over his shoulder. Buff was enormous and bumptious. He did not want to engage but had to smile hello. 'Meet your host — Julian Green.' Buff, fluid with the lightness of drink, clicked his heels together and bowed ridiculously to give space to a man of short, stocky build, who pumped out an extended hand.

'Hello there. You're obviously a marvellous man!' broadcasted a deep voice above the handshake. He had a full round face, with fat, round glasses. His fringed hair was dark with twists of grey and his skin was lightly pitted. The grey suit he filled as if he were bursting from within, peacock-blooming his chest with a deep breath.

'Heard a lot about you,' the man lied. His voice had projection, even above the din and each of his rapid, short phrases was bordered by a tiny pause, emphasising it as a bullet of conversational energy.

'Hear you're in the City. Very wise. More chance of making shedloads. Unlike me. Politics is a poor cousin,' said Julian.

'You work in politics then?' William felt obliged to ask something.

'Absolutely mate. I *am* a politician. An MP. All I try and do is change the world.' The words came out rapid-fire. 'You got a fag, pal?'

'Errm, no, sorry.'

'Here,' said Buff, presenting a red packet from his coat. He was a large man but made trivial movements with the impression of great dexterity. They took one each and the conversation took a momentary pause as a light was waved about.

'Well, see you met Lady Caroline,' continued the politician.

'Cosy?'

'Yep. Daughter of an earl. Friend of Sam's. Mad as a hatter. Completely asexual.'

'Asexual?' William began to wonder who was the more unhinged, Cosy or Julian.

'Yeah well, suppose so,' said Julian. 'She's too bonkers to have relationships. Still, be nice to take her from behind — more give and take that way, especially with titchy girls.'

'Sorry?'

'Sorry? Sorry what?' jabbered Julian, his finger pointing and a broad grin emerging, seeking an enemy for ribald confrontation. 'You got a problem with that particular sexual position? You got a problem with achieving satisfaction via that physical mode?'

'No. I never said anything...' William's discomfort was evident.

'Buff, you got a problem with the canine copulation position? Of riding the beast with two backs?'

'Not at all,' said Buff jovially and patting his belly. 'If they can take the weight!'

'No, really William,' Julian continued in a more modest tone, 'Cosy's a truly sweet girl. Genuine toff. Friend of Sam's. It's just that...err...' He seemed to be struggling.

'Well, you are a politico,' rescued Buff.

'That's right pal!' jumped Julian, in another swing of emphasis. 'A politico potentate extraordinaire — so I've got to know about these things! Anyway, must be off. Good to see you. *Sound* man. Party on!' He patted

William on the shoulder, drew deeply on his cigarette and moved on.

'Nice chap, isn't he?' said Buff, without irony.

'Is he important?' replied William, not able to see any connection.

'Seems to think so,' chuckled Buff and then, noticing William's face, 'I was up at Emma in Cambridge with him.'

All William cared about was the woman just yards away but Buff was too close and massive in presence, blocking all view and eager to be heard.

'Do you know about his better half, Sam Fifoot? Well, she used to work for the Tories until they sacked her. She's *desperate* to get married you see, so she kept on asking persistent questions about people on their database and trying to access it. They thought she was spying on their donors but she was merely hubby hunting. Now she's with Julian Green.'

'Hmm.'

With a hesitant wobble of his head Buff recognised that he was not being listened to. He did not mind much and shrugged his shoulders as he turned, aligning them beside William to see who he was trying to stare at. 'I love exotic girls.'

'Me too,' said William, his eyes having found her again.

'Like that Arab girl over there. One of Julian's ex's. She's stunning.'

'Oh, God.'

A quick ache pained William somewhere near his soul. Julian Green, on current evidence, was simply too much of a preposterous egoist to merit a relationship with someone so beautiful. It was completely inequitable for that man to have known her.

'Hello boys.' It was Cosy, head tilted down, eyes wide and poised up. Buff smiled in reply but William mumbled a noise and abruptly turned, escaping.

Like everywhere else there the upstairs bathroom was austerely bare: clean white tiles and polished chrome fittings. The house was probably rented, he assumed, looking at himself in the mirror to alter his hair, wanting to feel handsome. Perhaps, he decided, some drink would relax him and enable an approach to the Arab girl, somehow being engagingly charming. The door opened. William nearly snapped his neck retreating from the mirror in horror that he had not locked it.

'You needn't bother — you're handsome enough.'

'Hello Cosy,' he managed, reddening.

'Have you a cigarette?' She was smouldering in the doorway in a rather fetching, girlish way so he averted his eyes to the floor tiles and patted his suit coat.

'Errm,' he murmured and looked up. He then realised, too slowly, that looking at her eyes was encouraging her. 'Errm, no.'

'Oh dear.'

'You needed this loo?'

'Yes,' she said and took a step closer to him. She started to smile.

'Oh God,' he muttered, sensing what was going to happen and not feeling able to prevent it. Her small lips parted and her tongue darted inside his mouth with a hot palm crumpling the rear of his hair. It was rude, eager and slightly arousing. She ended it quickly, coming up for breath.

'Oh,' said William, feeling his ears glow scarlet.

'Thank you,' she chirped, wiped her mouth with her palm and grinned. 'Well, go away then — I've got things to do'.

Downstairs, he quickly found and gulped another beer and decided not to think about what had just happened. It had been a random coalescence from which, he told himself, there would be no collateral ill. He sought out the beautiful Arab woman, eyes darting, wanting to apply himself and needing to somehow redeem some virtue. He told himself he would feel no guilt if he forgot about what had happened and now ignored Cosy but in the crush he could not see anyone he knew so, for want of something to do, he pushed through to the kitchen again and took another green bottle from the fridge.

She was close by, nodding at another man. His mouth went suddenly parched and sticky when he realised she was close enough to touch but he shifted himself adjacent to them, unignorably, and then felt ineptly mute. He had to butt in somehow, something he hated doing.

'Fascinating,' the man was saying. 'I have a cousin who's an economist, who could probably help you.' William could not help noticing that he was tall and well tailored.

'Hi!' tried William.

'Err hi,' replied the suit stiffly. There was a pause. She smiled a little as she noticed him, kind but uncertain. It was clearly a safety response to an awkward moment. Immediately he felt brave. The man relieved the situation a little by offering his hand and announcing his name, which William promptly forgot.

'Are you a politician as well then?' asked William.

'God no,' he said, bearing himself up. 'I'm a financier.'

'Sexy Arab Girl!' boomed the now unmistakable voice of Julian Green. She paused and winced as she turned to him. That voice had been a permanently audible sound throughout the party. 'God you look like an angel!' he continued.

'Thank you,' she replied, deadpan with a foreign lilt, then giving a weak smile.

'Who are you?' said Julian, abruptly addressing the banker.

'Simon Church.'

'Church! Angel! Marvellous,' continued Julian, swaying and oblivious to any ill effect he was creating.

'Julia, you're drunk,' she said in a tone that accepted its inevitability.

'My party. Well, Sam's, but my drink. Anyway, I'll pray it all off at Mass tomorrow.'

The banker looked affronted, frowning and staring. Her eyes glazed over completely. She had clearly been here before.

'Where do you go to Mass?' asked William, his curiosity roused.

'Absolutely pal. I go to a Simon here, ha, ha, just behind Sloane Square. Incense. Latin. Minor European royalty. Politicians. *Smart* people.'

'And tramps,' she said. 'There were tramps when you took me.'

'Do I sense a spasm of criticism? Do I detect some reservation at stylish worship of the Almighty?'

'No Julia, I merely said...'

'Yes, yes, yes, yes, I heard that.' Some sort of point having been scored off him, Julian plucked his breast and, his voice even louder, 'Must circulate. Keep in touch Arab Sex Bomb! Church, come here. Meet Nina. Nina, hi there!' He grasped an unsuspecting brunette by the elbow and the financier was sucked into Julian Green's next round of bombast. As he turned, Julian glanced over his shoulder and, as a gesture for William alone, flicked his eyes toward the Arab girl and ran his tongue swiftly over his top lip.

'You called him Julia?' asked William.

'Oh, I do it to annoy him.'

'I'm William.'

'Jayda.'

How she spoke was partly irrelevant since he was already emotionally committed to finding it intoxicating but he absorbed the way she widened her eyes and innocently bobbed her head before the words came out, as if she were earnestly struggling for them. Suddenly he had a horrid thought. 'Jayda – is that, are you, an American pop star?'

'What? No!' She gave a happy laugh. 'No, I think you are confusing me.' She laughed again. 'I like that though.'

'Oh.' He felt a little stupid but managed, 'Does *Jayda* mean anything?'

'It means Strength. Strength and Honour. What does *William* mean?'

'It means my parents didn't have much imagination when they had me christened.'

'Really?'

'Err, well, no.' William felt his confidence rise. She seemed engaged. As well as everything else about her beauty, the voice was captivating: soft and lilting but speaking an internationalised English that came from everywhere and nowhere. She held herself assuredly, with the quiet unassuming confidence of those who perhaps realise that they are truly beautiful.

'How do you know Julian Green?'

'Oh. It's embarrassing. It's over now. Over very quickly but he pesters to stay in touch. You?'

'My sister Frances knows his current girlfriend, Sam.'

'Where are you from? Are you an Englishman of the same type as Julian?'

There seemed to be many ways he could answer those questions. He sensed he should at this juncture be convincing, different and bold. 'I'm certain I'm not. However, if he found you beautiful and interesting then I'm with him there but more so.'

Her eyes had widened. He moved from gazing at her lips as he spoke to holding those eyes with his own. They were very dark, brown with the darkness of black tea, and absorbed all that he was exposing. 'I'm from Pimlico and a quiet, pretty market town in the Midlands. I work in the City, wear a suit most days but am actually wild, romantic, passionate and striving for world domination.' These were lines he had used before but he suddenly realised they had only been polished for this moment.

She was smiling wider now, teeth noticeably bright. 'Maybe you are different. Maybe not.'

'What do you do?'

'I'm studying Oriental History at UCL.'

Suddenly, he thought of a plan to be able to see her again, to impress her away from here. It was not much of an idea but it was, it seemed to him, better than having no structure to his talk.

'Have you seen much here, outside London?'

'No. I've not even seen all of London yet. I've only been here a few months.'

'Well, you must. Britain is small enough to get

round. You must see Edinburgh and Dublin. Don't bother with Cardiff. You must see some English cities, smallish places with cathedrals. London isn't an English type of place; just an international, capital mess. And you must see the countryside. It's what England is, at its core, even if there isn't as much of it as there used to be.'

'Well, perhaps.'

He plunged on. 'You'll have to let me be your guide.' He was so enthusiastic that just to talk to her had set him off grinning. Then he stopped, feeling stupid at sounding too keen, and to his immense delight then saw she was grinning back. It was going better than he could have wished. One thought rose up that instant and the fear of it held his smile in a nervous freeze. She was so clearly a person of such overwhelming attractiveness and niceness that maybe she had already decided she wanted him for nothing more than friendship. That would be unbearable. Did women decide that sort of thing, whether or not to desire someone, instantly, the way that men do? Or later, as they get to know you? For a relationship as pregnant with potential as William intended this to be, it was a terrifying prospect. He simply did not have the confidence to reassure himself that he would not mess it up.

'Where are you from? Please don't say Birmingham.'

'I'm from Amman.'

'Oman? Ah yes, in the Gulf.'

'No. Amman. The capital of Jordan. People always get that wrong. It's so irritating.' She glanced away, annoyed.

'Jordan. I don't know it.' And then, too eagerly, 'but I'd like to.'

This time she shook her head and then, to his relief, with a slight smile simultaneous to a blink of her eyelids and a world-weary exhalation through her nose, 'Look,' she clipped, 'I need to visit the toilet. Please speak to me again, though, later. Oh, do you know where it is?'

'The loo is first left up the stairs.'

She smiled, paused, then left. He could not take his eyes off her until she disappeared.

Half an hour and three or four drinks later William realised that the financier was quite keen on Jayda and had her trapped again. He attempted to rescue her a couple of times but did not succeed, both times feeling stupid. She had noticed though and smiled. The smiles told him, somehow, not to worry about his rival, that she knew he liked her and that it was fine he had come back. He felt a little more relaxed at that until the drink he had gulped down made him worry whether he had misinterpreted something. Even, or perhaps especially, amongst the press and noise of the crowd he then felt a void that needed filling. At the higher end of his motivations he knew he had to interrupt again and somehow get her number. Then, bored and becoming restless in thought with each drink, he suddenly wanted to talk to Cosy again. He had not wanted to think about her but had to when, moments earlier, her darting eyes clocked him across the room. Remembering her small, eager mouth he thought what a fine thing it was to be able to remember, that one had kissed the daughter of an earl. Maybe it would make Jayda a little jealous to see him talking to her. Moving around the room with a purpose, he found her sitting on a sofa in conversation with another suit.

'Cosy?'

She turned and William looked at her and knew what it was he wanted from her. In that moment, weak and fuelled with drink, he could not care less. 'I so enjoyed our conversation upstairs earlier. I've been thinking about what you told me and I wouldn't mind if we could continue the conversation upstairs in private.'

Her little eyes sparkled.

'I couldn't possibly.'

'Why?' said William, just knowing she did not mean it.

'Because this is my new true love.' The man next to her raised his eyebrows. Cosy noticed this and added, 'Bernard has said I can design his ties for him.'

'I have?' said the Bernard.

'Yes sweetie. I'll ring you about it in the morning. Come on Willie.' She grabbed his hand.

Two minutes later, again in the bathroom, with his legs between hers and with his right hand fumbling for a bra strap, William wondered whether he could grow fond of Cosy. It struck him suddenly how easy it was not to enjoy sex, how Julian did not seem to know people at his own party, how preposterous Cosy seemed as a person and, then, how Jayda looked downstairs, chic and unignorably alluring. Jayda. The name was lovely. He had to concentrate to freeze the thought away that what he was doing was wrong, even though he knew that he would always remember these two absurd, greedy trysts, and remember them as lust coloured with guilt.

'Here, let me,' said Cosy impatiently. 'Now kiss them.'

CHAPTER IV

Jamil ran a hand across his thin moustache and stubble, then frowned deeply, both to block out the sun and because his way was impeded by the usual rust- and dust-battered truck in front of him. Abdul, the pensioner old houseboy, sat beside him enjoying the suburb-to-desert views out of the window and would, no doubt, be respecting speed limits as he returned to the city with the black BMW once Jamil had accelerated himself to the airport.

Jamil, however, liked to drive fast. With a lurch he pulled left into the oncoming lane, floored his foot to the satisfying, whining, deep throbs of acceleration and swiftly muttered a prayer for the approaching car to brake a little as he slid past the fuming truck. He slammed the wheel back right once he was clear, to the sounds of horns, sudden then fading, from car and truck. Abdul continued his silence with a petrified smile. He had been a passenger before and had learnt to clutch his seat and intone prayers in his head.

There was enough time. It was just that Jamil enjoyed speed. Satisfied now, he eased up a little, pulled out and lit a cigarette and turned on the radio, low. 'Habibi da!' blared out a song continuously, the music thin and rhythmic but subsidiary to the repetitious chants. He bobbed his head in time, past the approach checkpoints and palm trees, until suddenly slamming the car to stop with a juddering, convulsive wave at the International Terminal. Outside the car Abdul continued to smile with what teeth he had remaining and handed Jamil his bag whilst accepting car keys with the other hand. Jamil nodded and, without word, turned on his heel and strode into Departures.

William had never had a landline in the flat but, as he paced throughout each small room, searching, he wished he had. Eventually he found his mobile in the bathroom. Cosy had texted him late last night, 'When are you free?' He had, as usual, drunk more than he had intended and could not remember many details of the last part of the night beyond the simple void of Jayda's absence when he returned downstairs with Cosy. The battery power was low. The charger lived in the kitchen adjacent to the toaster's socket. He plugged in, dialled and circled the small space with a pace that confirmed his nerves.

'Frances, it's me.'

'Huh?'

'Yes, me. Sorry if I woke you but do you have a number for Julian Green and his girlfriend Sam? Or rather, I don't suppose that you know and have a number for Jayda, the Arab girl who was there last night?'

'Huh? It's 8.00 o'clock, William.'

'Actually, it's 9.00.'

'No. Go away.'

'What? Isn't Sam your friend?'

'Oh sod off. I'm asleep.' There was a shuffle of linen. 'Why don't you Facebook her? I'll text the number.'

'Is that for Sam or for...?' The line went a tonal buzz.

It was over an hour of feeling thin and dehydrated before he received a text and it was just a number. He wrote it down and then dialled as quick as he could, making mistakes. Cursing, he paused, breathed out and tried again, pressing each number with certainty.

'Hello?' It was an English female.

'Hello. Oh. Errm, is that Sam?'

'Yes. Who are you?'

'Oh, I'm William Clive. Frances's brother. I was at the party. I'm sorry to pester when you must be clearing up and everything. I met, err, Jayda last night and we agreed to meet later on today but I've lost her number and I was wondering if you have it.'

'Oh. Well, err, I don't know. Julian might...Julian!'

William could sense the annoyance he was causing.

'Julian! It's one of your friends. Wants that woman's number. Speak to him.'

'Who?'

'A man. Oh. Hang on, William Clive?'

'Yes?'

'Cosy just rang me, asking after you.' Her voice

had changed to a very suspicious tone.

He had to think and say something convincing very quickly. Prickles of heat suffused his temple. 'Oh good. That was going to be my next question to you but I was a bit, you know. Anyway I was going to ask you if you had her number as well.'

'Yes, Cosy said that you'd already swapped mobiles at the party but she wanted to know if you had a landline.'

'Oh. Yes. Ahh…' He then got a hold of himself. To admit he did not have one might seem like a lie so he trotted out a number, which he realised as he was halfway through was his sister's so he gave, stumbling again, other last digits. 'Thank you. That's great. Great. I really liked Cosy. Umm, anyway, I was after Jayda's number and I was wondering if you or Julian?' Silence and suspicion throbbed between them.

'Don't you have Cosy's number?' blanked Sam.

'Seemed to have lost it, I'm afraid, along with Jayda's.'

'Julian!'

The line gave noises of words beyond a muffled handset. William wished that he had never met Cosy. His aching temples and nauseous quivers were other physical signs of the excess but this felt like some sort of moral lesson, choking him with shame. He was just going to ignore it and sprint towards a fresh start.

'This is Julian Green. Who are you?'

'Oh. I'm William Clive. We spoke a bit at your

party on Friday night, err, last night.'

'Yes. Hmm.'

'Sorry to trouble you. I was after Jayda's number. You see, we arranged to meet tomorrow at the British Museum and I need her number.'

'If you arranged to meet her you won't need her number. Just turn up and meet her.'

'I, err, we, well we didn't arrange the details so I need to speak to her.'

Julian Green breathed heavily, then coughed. Sam was saying something. William could not hear the words but could tell that it was unsolicited and opinionated advice. He sensed that failure was accelerating towards him, about to hit him hard.

'I tell you what Clive, you see, I have to protect Jayda. I know the family well. Old, big, Levantine and Jordanian mercantile, trading concern. Her father asked me to look out for her whilst she was here in London, so I've got to be mindful of that. I'm going to ring her before I go to Mass tomorrow at St. Mary's, Bourne Street at 11.00 o'clock. If you're there – it's behind Sloane Square – and if she says yes – you'll buy me a pint in the pub afterwards whilst we're both in a state of spiritual grace and I'll give you her number. But if she says no – and by the way I might tell her that you sucked Lady Caroline Cheshire's tiny tits in the loo last night – then I'll buy you a pint, because it will amuse me. Alright? Jolly good. I think that's clear. Goodbye.' Agony and God filled his mind as he walked. St.

Mary's was behind the southern side of Sloane Square and he walked because he had set out early from Pimlico, earnest in intention, and there were no cabs. He had sinned. It seemed, to him, an innocent sin though. William was thoughtlessly religious. His were Anglican impulses: accommodating, lenient and comforting. Since he had not initiated and had only been lustful because another had also been lustful he had only been, to a point, politely accommodating. But he felt guilt nonetheless. It felt like a penance, attending church; a pre-ordained humiliation given the mocking archness of Julian Green's proposal, compelling him to go. The image of Jayda sweeping hair from her face and curving it behind her ears repeated itself to him continually as he walked. It did occur to him that God could have shown him someone he could love and then punish him by denying her to him. To pray for forgiveness then would be no bad thing.

It announced itself outside on a painted sign as an Anglican church before he entered its low, redbrick gloom. He was late. A choir, somewhere unseen, intoned.

'Wash me with hyssop and I shall be clean. O wash me, wash me and I shall be whiter than snow.'

A priest was circulating the aisles with perfunctory speed, followed by robed acolytes, and dunked a silver rattle into water to douse the head-bowing congregation as they crossed themselves. This was higher than Rome and seemed a strange, secret and unique little alcove of London. He hesitated to take it all in. Its redbrick vaults, barrelling above a statue of Mother Mary, Stations of the Cross and a huge gilded altar, encompassed a Christian world only distantly related in style to the bare rural parish stone churches of his experience. It seemed full but the congregants had spread themselves out in ones and twos. He walked in some more and tentatively waited to be approached but no one did, so he placed himself at the back next to the font and underneath a huge wooden canopy. This, he worked out, supported the organ. A shuffling noise behind him turned his head and William was affronted with the sight and smell of a gentleman of the street clutching a plastic bag and vibrating with seemingly involuntary tremors, his hair and beard wild, thick and matted. He wanted to move but felt glued by uncertainty. Eventually, by degrees, he relaxed enough not to care and concentrated on the priests at the altar opposite them wearing opulent red and gold robes, intricately decorated stoles and chasubles declaring magnificence.

He searched for Julian Green but could not see him. A hymn started so he stood up to sing and, a verse in, sat down again when he realised no-one else was standing. The first reading came in solemn dignity, the second was intoned by a priest in a mournful nasal that made it hard to follow, then the gospel rose everyone to their feet with a flurry of arm movements making the sign of the cross and the descent of the priestly group from on high. The priest then rose to the wooden barrel of a pulpit and preached earnestly of charity after a few knowing in-jokes with his congregants.

A little into the sermon Julian Green strode in, brogues clicking the tiles, tie strands floating across his belly and before marching halfway down the nave to a seat, genuflected like a wavering, obese swan a little in front of where William sat. He clearly enjoyed his entrance. The priest found it hard to ignore him but tried to.

Intercessional prayers came, '*and we pray for Elizabeth our Queen.*' William tried to pray but mainly thought, with a little guilt, about Cosy's breasts and her eager tongue. '*Lord, in thy mercy, hear our prayer.*' Then he imagined what she would look like, naked, in the throes of ecstasy. '*We pray for Mother Mary, St. Barnabus and all thy Saints.*' Similar sexual thoughts involving Jayda drove themselves into his vision but he clamped down on those. She was too important to slight, even in thought.

Peace be with you. After a hesitant beat he turned to the tramp behind him and offered his hand.

'Pax vobiscum,' said a booze soaked breath from the midst of the thick grey beard.

'Eh?' frowned William.

'You're supposed to say "Et cum spirito tuo",' replied the tramp in a patient tone.

'Oh. Peace be with you.'

Everyone fell quickly to their knees. Being

upstaged by a tramp quietened William's fantasies. The Celebrant began to sing his way to the Mass's crescendo, incense rising and incensor clanking. He began only now to concentrate in prayer.

'God, I am sorry. I have sinned in lust, in drunkenness, in sloth and many other things. I am sorry. I do think I could love this girl, Jayda, though. I could be good. I will be good. Please help me. Give me a chance. Please help her love me. Amen.'

The congregation suddenly murmured in a low but distinct wave, '*Lord, I am not worthy to gather up the crumbs from underneath thy table but say the word only and my soul shall be healed.*'

He queued up between strangers, shuffling forward to kneel and took the bread and wine into the relaxed vacancy of his mind. As he walked back it occurred to him that she was probably a Muslim. In addition to whatever he did not understand about Christianity, and there was plenty, there might be Islam forcing itself into his life.

The ceremony seemed about to end but when the priests and acolytes trained away from the altar and the congregation stood, they faced towards a statue of Mary holding the infant Jesus and, with organ blaring a lifting sound, sang the Hail Mary with more gusto than seemed appropriate.

Suddenly the noise ended and people ambled out alone or in small clusters. William strolled with the tide into a sunshine outside so contrastingly bright with the comfortable gloom of the interior it blinked him into a daze. A heavy hand impressed his shoulder and Julian Green's bellow was by his ear. 'There's a good little pub here. Follow me.'

The Fox and Hounds was small but bright and crowded.

'We'll have two pints of Best,' Julian announced in the direction of a preoccupied barmaid. He leant conspiratorially against the bar. 'So, you want Jayda's number?'

'Very much so.'

Julian looked alive with anticipation, his eyes behind fat square glasses eager with the joy of being dominant. His lips were moist. The pints were pulled. Both noticed this but only William acted on it, realising the expectation for him to tug out his wallet from his jacket. Julian waited quietly until the clouds settled within the brown, thin liquid, took a gulp and then, after a satisfied smack of his lips, launched himself.

'Sam's best friends with Cosy. Cosy rings up before you did and shared the shagging gossip about you. Then you ring up a few minutes later, don't even mention Cosy, and ask for Jayda's number. So, what are you? Some sort of pussy-chasing, untrustworthy, cheating, caddish, overheated twat?'

He was leering at William, index finger pointing. William's guilt told him that maybe he had a point. It might be easy to answer in kind rather than contrition but this was no circumstance for a trial of debating strength. Julian was clearly a bully. He took a breath and resolved to be firm but the tone of his voice came out more wavering than what he intended.

'Look, I'm sorry if it seems that way. It's not meant to. I met both Cosy and Jayda at your party. Cosy's fun but I met Jayda after that. I can't imagine Cosy likes me that much. I'm not her type. But Jayda…'

'Not her type? According to Sam she's pretty keen on you. And you should think about it. The family has a rather good grouse moor, actually.'

'But Jayda…'

'Jayda what? Jayda another shag? Another notch on the belt? Fancy a bit of a hit on a heathen? Salacious sex with a Saracen? A bit of concupiscent curdling copulation with an Arab concubine? Get lost William Clive, you're just a male slut.'

'Well, err, I don't like the way things happened on Friday but Jayda is different. Different to anyone else there is.' William searched but could not tell as to whether Julian's incredulous expression was mocking him or genuine in surprise. He had to do better. 'I've no idea as to whether anything would happen. I just want her number to see if, to see if…' He hated this, hated to have to come begging. Julian was staring at him over his raised pint. 'Whether she wants to be friends.'

Julian gulped his beer deeply. 'Tell you what pal, where d'you live?'

'Pimlico.'

'Good. My constituency is south of the river and

my majority is not what it should be. You join the association, undertake to do a couple of leaflet drops on my biggest council estate this month and I'll give you her number.'

'Leaflet drops?'

'It's how local politics works, pal. Spreading the message and reminding the marginal voters I have a presence. Of course it'll cost you a membership fee. Fifty quid a year from a man like you. Deal?'

'Fifty quid?'

'At least fifty quid. You can impress me by paying more. I'm trying to help you here by making you help me justify this in my busy head.'

'Oh.' William knew his answer. There was little he would enjoy less than spending an evening shuffling from door to door amongst dirty high rise tenements, slipping political propaganda into postal flaps as dogs barked and curses followed him down the rows, echoing indifference or hostility. He had a third of his pint left and so drained it. 'OK then.'

'Good, Give me your card. I'll get the membership secretary to contact you.'

'Here it is.' William fumbled with his wallet again but he knew what he had to ask. 'Did you, did you, err, ring Jayda? Since we spoke on the phone?'

'No. Couldn't be bothered. Now, if you don't follow through on the leaflet drops, I will ring her and what I might say would rather ruin your chances with her mightn't it? Got it?' Julian nodded the question.

William nodded back.

'I like you, William Clive. I'll have another pint now please, pal.'

Jamil had had his usual one whisky on the flight and had even slept a little, but the impersonal size and inefficient bustle of Heathrow made him late, reminding him he was tired. The family apartment was in a block off Kensington High Street. He was not used to carrying his own bag and quite hated it.

His sister did not keep tidy habitation. Clothes were strewn, paperwork piled, coffee mugs abandoned, bags and shoes cluttered everywhere and in the midst of it all in the main room she stood as he came in the door, with cotton wool partitioning each freshly painted red toenail.

'Hello brother.' Jayda did not sound welcoming. 'Good flight in Crown Class?'

'Not bad.'

'I have to fly economy.' She had the voice for a fight but then turned to stoop over her toes to glide on another layer.

'I run a business. You are a student.'

'So, Baba sent you out to spy on me? How long are you here for?'

'Two or three days. I have to attend to some insurance matters for him.'

Mostly, he liked his sister. He used to adore her when she was a child but as she had grown and exerted the willpower of her own personality this became tempered by annoyance. The reality was that, frustrated by her independence, he had clamped up any candid engagement with her years ago. She barely obeyed Father, let alone him or Mother. Women should take the advice of the men of their families, which was the modest and correct attitude to take. They were modern. There was no need for hijabs or chadors, house arrest or continual chaperoning but his view was that women should take instruction, obey their men and look after children and home. Prosperous, urban and holidayed, the circles they socialised amongst in Jordan were liberal and tolerant. No warped Islamic logic dictated against emancipation or vocation for women in their world but Jamil knew, from a thousand cigarettes with his soldiers by their tanks in the desert heat, that the Arab Street choked its tolerance on the dust thrown up by the heels of a woman escaping hearth and home. It insulted their masculinity.

Jayda was a modern Abdoun Ranger turning into an internationally aware, unspecifically ambitious woman. He realised that she wore her beauty lightly, natural in the way she held herself as if unaware of its potency and, if he were honest with himself, it unnerved him slightly.

When he married — and that would be soon he hoped, for he was in his late twenties and his bachelor status was becoming embarrassing — Jamil needed to marry someone like Jayda but much more like his mother.

'So, bint, are you studying hard?'

'Harder, no doubt, than you ever did.'

Jamil walked into the main bedroom and saw from the doorway that she had made it her own. He exhaled air loudly to show his annoyance and turned to stride to another.

'I hope this one is clean.' He realised that his tone was harsh but could not help it.

Jayda concentrated on removing the cotton wool from her toes then, without looking at him said, 'So, are you making money for Baba?'

'Yes.'

'I think I should be able to run the business when I graduate. I'll have a degree. It's more than you have. All you ever did was play around in tanks with other little soldier boys. Playing with their big toys.'

She was not looking at him but he could tell that she was defiant, her eyes narrowing, nostrils flaring and colour rising in her face. He had seen it many times before. It set him off.

'You know nothing. You don't even know what businesses we have. You need to be practical in business, to understand finance, to be able to make decisions. You're not even practical enough to keep this apartment tidy. It's a disgrace.' That felt nicely powerful. He had countered her without hesitation and changed the subject.

'Jamil, you're such a jerk. No wonder you're not

married yet. Every girl I know thinks you're a brute. Every father of every girl you might be introduced to will think you a jerk. Or weird. Or a homo for not being married yet.'

He paused to regard her fully and saw her as before, his angry little sister. Even though the apartment was messy its air was clean. Jayda did not often smoke. He opened up his soft pack and lit a cigarette, extending the pause to inhale deeply and exhale the smoke towards her. 'Actually I'm a great guy. And macho too. It's nice to see you too. Now, why don't you go into the kitchen and make me some coffee? I'm tired after my journey and it would be hospitable of you.'

'Sod off, jerk. Make it yourself. I'm off to the library to study.'

'You're going off? I haven't seen you for months.'

She was now gathering books and papers into a leather satchel, moving with purpose. She turned in the doorway. 'Yes, seeing as you are being so friendly. You can tell Baba that while the apartment may not be immaculate – he doesn't give me enough money for a maid – I'm working hard on my career.'

Jamil found himself staring at the door's paintwork once she had rushed through it and then realised that the empty apartment seemed a husk of an auditorium for his fatigued restlessness. Cleansed white in colour thoughout, cluttered with feminine effects, it was emphatically silent after her slamming exit. After a few minutes he left for a coffee and, descending to the quiet street in search of a cab, thought that he would browse the antique shops south of Sloane Square. It was only when the cab dropped him off that he remembered that the first day of the Arab working week was the western day of idleness.

Anger was never far from Jamil's grasp. Not understanding where it came from or how to control it, he had long ago reconciled it as a source of strength that changed irritation to cogency. Whilst he was capable of reflection and discipline this deep store of gall gave him, he reasoned, the freedom to feel, not think. What displeased him was how poorly he had communicated with his sister. What angered him was that he should have remembered it was a Sunday and what that meant. He shunted from one glass frontage on the street to another, each time cupping his hands and peering through with a curse. Outside one shop he slapped the glass with his palms, twice, hard. The noisy shudders convulsed to him and a passing couple, who stared as they continued on. Embarrassed, he turned on his heel to cross the road, to escape. He had not planned to buy anything, nor to view with any purpose but the inability to enter now enraged him and he had to leave. Somewhere behind him was Sloane Square. He would regroup his thoughts and find a cab from there. Down a sidestreet of cream moulded stucco fronts he strode, staring only yards ahead of his feet, his silent spleen bellowing echoes in his head with the hammer of his heels on the pavement.

William now had Jayda's number on his mobile. He left Julian Green in the pub talking to another congregant as soon as he could slip away. The door swung behind him. Buoyed by two pints he almost skipped around the cluster of pavement smokers and hurried his way towards the Pimlico Road. Shuddering with relief as he settled down, throwing off the strands of the ordeal with Julian, he looked at the sky and stretched his arms, then glanced at his feet to check their pace and ran a burst of twenty yards with his eyes closed to shake off the contaminant drops of atmosphere from the crowded pub's clammy heat. He wanted to be back in his flat and composed for the call to her. He adjusted his rhythm to a quick walk and noticed the crouched pace of a tall unshaven Arab, wearing black leather and a scowl, approaching him. The Arab glanced up, saw him but, with eyes down again, continued his speed, expecting him to move. William did alter the angle of his walk a little but not enough. Their shoulders slammed hard, unsteadily pirouetting both around to face each other.

'Sorry, I…' William hesitated, waiting to gauge a reaction and apology.

'Damn you! Idiot!'

The smokers outside the pub had not yet noticed.

'Well, hang on. You weren't looking either.'

'Damn you! Fool! It is I who had the right of way. You should have moved.'

William could see his flowing rage, his fists and

eyes darting menace. The Arab looked a caricature of misunderstood fury, his stance still crouched, ready to pounce. William's posture was instinctively open. This was Belgravia, where casual violence was long extinguished in historical past. He stood, open, his palms wide. 'I'm sorry, but we both might have made a mistake. Not looking where we were going.'

To Jamil, William's puzzled brow looked more like patronising sympathy and contempt. He did not think or know why he did what he did. Adrenaline controlled him. He pushed William on the shoulder, spitting out the word, 'Jerk!' William staggered back, aghast and looked around him as if to appeal to any passing judge, but there was none.

Jamil, his heart pumping loudly in his ears and his mouth suddenly painfully dry, clenched his right fist and followed on to the Englishman. He grabbed his throat with his left hand, squeezed it, and punched his right, twice, into the stomach. He stepped back to view the effect – the Englishman doubled up, emitting a deep whine and coughing splutters – and then remembered a basic rule of combat: that his violence should be so overwhelming and sudden that he could safely walk away. He moved to the side, to aim further punches and stepped up to deliver them, his fist raised high. Air flushed past and the pavement impacted hard on his arm and shoulder. A pain thumped suddenly without delay and its surprise was total. William had balletically swept his right leg behind Jamil, collapsing him at the knees. Without hesitation William kicked and kicked again, hitting somewhere, anywhere, on the torso.

Despite finding himself surprisingly dominant, his foot impacting heavy, soft dents, fear was overriding William's senses. He stopped, not knowing what to do or say now, with the Arab rolling at his feet. Saying nothing, he suddenly declared a quick victory to himself and span around to walk, as swiftly as dignity would allow him, away down the sidestreet. He heard the muffles of his opponent rising to his feet and looked over his tweed to confirm. Then he ran, coughing still, the bruising on his stomach jarring in a cutting stitch. He ran left, down Pimlico Road, his thought being to run, if he could, to the police station on Buckingham Palace Road, but when he panted up to Orange Square the urge and threat had gone, leaving him panting stupidly, stared at and shivering in shock.

The fall had stunned Jamil. He regained his feet soon enough but the heat of his need to fight had gone in the impact of the pavement. The English jerk was walking away fast and his impulse to run after him and spit rage in his face hesitated when he glanced behind him and saw a crowd on the pub's corner, glasses and cigarettes in their hands, staring greedily. Then the Englishman was running away, too fast to catch easily and so the greater challenge was then to stroll past them, composed despite the pain, meeting as many eyes as dared to look to him, finding a way to Sloane

Square and a black cab to anywhere.

Back in his flat William shivered and felt disturbed, dirty and confused for hours afterwards. The unexplained violence of the moment tainted him, it seemed, irreversibly. He sat in a chair, rocking himself uncomfortably but without the ability to stop until he began to feel nauseous, then wandered around listlessly and smoked half a cigarette, leaving it to burn itself to a tube of ash whilst he fixed himself a gin and tonic. Halfway through that, on an empty belly, he began to feel more stable. It occurred to him momentarily that, given his rare churchgoing and the blessing of his uncertain victory in achieving the phone number, he should consider forgiveness. The Arab had reacted the way he did because something had been misunderstood. But he had defended himself and had won. God had consented that, perhaps. Relaxing into fantasy and imagined bravery, he should have kicked some more so that he need not have run away, kicked again to bruise, slammed in aimed shots at his groin to crumple the Arab in agony and stamp on his head till blood had trickled out of his mouth.

CHAPTER V

William dialled the number, ready with opening words and intonation, but it transferred to her recorded voice. He hung up, then rang again, reverent to her soft cadences, picturing her saying the words, and castaneted the phone shut again. The third time he left a message, trying to sound far more confident and warm than he felt.

'Jayda, hello. It's William Clive. We met at the party on Friday. I was the nice, charming chap in the dark blue suit. Not the arrogant, blonde man in the pinstripe suit. Julian Green gave me your number. Hope you don't mind. Err, well, I remember offering to be your travel guide to the British Isles but, umm, I could show you bits of hidden London, if you'd like. Anyway, as a start it would be good to get together. Even if you don't need a travel guide, I'd love to see you. I need to, errm, I need you to, well, I need to prove to you that I remember there's a difference between Amman and Oman. See, I can read a map! Well, hope to hear from you. Bye.'

He dropped the mobile into an armchair, put his head in his hands and moaned.

When she left the library in late afternoon and looked, paused upon its steps, at the sky Jayda saw that clouds now concealed the earlier brightness of the day. She was not yet used to the English weather's daily microclimatic mood swings and, thereby, they seemed to affect her own. Anger and an absence of a planned alternative had forced her away from her brother. Boredom with her work and herself seemed to be about to meander her back to him. She pressed on her mobile, glazed her eyes in surrender and started for the Tube.

Dropped into the depths of her bag the mobile chirped an alert when she was a few paces on. She searched for it as she walked, irritation creeping with each step until she grasped it and paused on the pavement to listen. Initially she did not know what she felt or wanted. No obvious emotion reacted to the Englishman's message apart from a vague recognition that his voice seemed pleasant. She remembered him, of course, but with neutral emotions. That she immediately felt nothing about a presentable man wanting to take her out slightly puzzled her. She walked on.

With their particular blend of Arab values, western savvy, loyalty, liberalism and sheer humour, Jayda and her friends had long ago decided that Jordanians were the finest countrymen of any in the world. But not in fulfilling every impulse. Marriage was still socially compulsory but love and sex were from separate worlds. They happened in Jordan, of course, but to Jayda seemed to happen elsewhere, in spheres of different priorities. She knew of them but did not really know them. As a teenage girl she once thought that she knew about love, as desperately felt as anyone who had felt anything before; but that, complete as an episode, was itself unattainable in terms of her being able to understand or remember. Marriage as an abstract concept did not attract her, though families did. She knew girls who were already married and rather looked down on them for surrendering their independence to the first suitor who had declared an interest or who their parents had suggested. Sex had, for years, seemed somewhat disgusting and as something purely recreational still seemed alien. She had done it precisely twice, curiously, nervously and disappointingly, with the same boyfriend in their last term at the University of Jordan. He had wanted to, insisted and persisted. It had not been for love but she assumed that they would marry very soon anyway although that union would not have been for love particularly, but convention. In that sense she would have been no better than those whom she now sneered at. Then he shamed her. His parents arranged for him to marry a Damascus girl and he did. She felt as if a vital part of her had been abused through her own unwitting choice. Before she had met him she had taken a haughty pride that no-one had conquered her, nor been privileged with her intimacy. These mistakes, natural enough, gnawed at her core without concession. She had been sleepwalking, consciously but unreflectively, into the stridently conformist pattern of many of her peers towards matrimony and motherhood. After the last crisis telephone call, poignant but banal, from which she confirmed her fate, she had shouted and then cried. She had used the doorlock to her room for the first time. Her mother, full of hope for a marriage, had warbled sympathy and love. Her father and elder brother, full of a nightful of whisky, had threatened to kill the boy but had done nothing but bluster. Once a month had dripped miserably away she realised the daring, beautiful simplicity that she did want marriage and children, only not now and not by any impulse but her own. Therefore, conquering her past by resolving the future, to forget, and to further her new certainty that she would be the first female chairman of an Amman stock market listed company, she arranged for herself, now 23 and vital, to be in London.

When she ascended from the depths of the Underground at the other side she played his voice to her again, nearing her building. Still she had no certainty as to what to think or feel but she liked the fact that someone was trying to brighten her day.

A wrought iron curtained lift clunked up two floors to the apartment. A chaos of keys, precipitously clutched, opened one of the three heavy locks. London demanded such security. She could smell her brother and his smoke as soon as the heavy door timidly revealed its space. Jamil was sat in the living room, watching motor racing and working his way through a packet of Duty Free's strongest. She walked in, dropped her satchel full of books in the hallway and paused in the doorframe. Neither spoke. Jamil would not turn his head from the screen. Jayda kicked her shoulder from the wood, turned for a handbag displayed on a hallway table, dropped in wallet, keys and mobile and slammed the door as she left, pleased with the effect that might have had. Back outside she wondered as to whether she should first get a coffee and then ring the Englishman but the knowledge that she might be self-conscious if she sensed other coffee addicts were creeping their ears to her made her ring William as she stood under the building's white portico. All she was sure about as the dial tones hummed was that she did want to say yes to a date but not to his first suggestion, whatever it was.

It was answered quickly.

'Hello?' He sounded alert.

'Hello.' She tried to seem friendly but cautious.

'Err, hello? Oh hi, it's you!'

'Yes. Me. Are you surprised?'

'Well, I, err. Gosh, thank you for calling me back.'

'No problem. I need cheering up. You seem like a good guy to do that.'

'Well, yes I'll try. I can. I will. Me and some champagne. I know a great bar that's open Sundays. What time do you...'

'No. Sorry. I can't do tonight. I'm not in the mood.' Apart from a warm but imprecise memory of his face and mannerisms from two nights ago, a conversational tweak caught her imagination. 'Did you say "gosh" just now?'

'Gosh, did I? No, I didn't. That was a cartoon Englishman. So...' He felt that he had to keep it going, light and cheery. She seemed slightly offhand. He was aware of his heart thumping noisily. His talk felt like clumsy tennis and he had to relax it. 'So, why are you sad?'

'Oh, my brother annoyed me today.'

'Tell me all.'

She made a hesitant sound, exhaling. With the heightened awareness of needing to impress resonating each heartbeat in his throat, William remembered that he had read somewhere that women want men to be good listeners. He tried to relax his tone to a richer base. 'Go on. I'm a sympathetic ear. My sister tells me that.'

She started slowly but rose in volume and pace. 'Oh, he is a jerk. Such a jerk. He flew into town today and, well, he just annoys me by just being. I come from a very old-fashioned, sexist world. He is no better than I am but gets all glory for being a man and the expectation that he will run the businesses when I know that I am cleverer and more practical and yet all that is expected of me is to marry and have fat, messy babies for some high-status, working husband, whom I probably won't like.'

'Oh.' William was digesting the key words 'sexist', 'businesses' and 'husband'. 'Did you argue about all this then? Sounds grim, I agree.'

'No. We hardly spoke.'

'Well, I don't doubt that you are capable of achieving great things. You're in London now. All things are possible here. You could make your career here.'

'You don't understand. We are a very close family. There is my father – he is – my father is there.'

'I'm glad about that.'

'He is very dominant. He is a businessman and likes to be in control. Jamil is supposed to be learning whilst working for him but that is only because he is male. He is not qualified for anything and no doubt started out with as little knowledge as me but because he is a male heir, he is to get the chance.'

'You sound pretty sore about it.'

'Well, it is madness. I am as good as he.'

'I'm certain you are but is some of this anger because he is your brother or because he is a man?' William bit his lip. As soon as he had said it he wondered whether his voice had sounded too aggressive. She stayed quiet a moment.

'Both. He is stupid and men are simple.'

'Well, we have simple needs but we can do philosophy.'

'Philosophy? What's that to do with anything?'

'All the great philosophers were men and being men they all had a need to ask beautiful Jordanian women out on a date.' This was lame and both of them cringed silently but, nonetheless, she decided that she liked the simple earnestness of his trying.

'Oh. Are you mocking me?'

'Only a little. I like you too much not to.'

'Oh.'

'Which is supposed to mean, I like you enough to want to know you better.' This, at least, was sincere.

'Hmm.' There was some warmth entering her voice.

'Do you have other siblings?'

'Just another brother and sister. They are younger. Only four of us. What family do you have?'

'Mother. Father. Divorced – as tends to happen in decadent western societies. Both remarried to people I don't mind but don't really like. And a sister, Frances. I like her.'

'I pity you.'

'Pity? Why?'

'Your family is so small and it is broken anyway.'

'True, but that is more normal over here than perhaps you may realise. Are you outside?'

'Yes, my brother is in the apartment and I'm so annoyed with him and with myself for allowing him to anger me that I had to come here to the street.'

'That's a bother. Look, you sure I can't tempt you to meet up? It sounds as if you are halfway to me already.'

'No, I'm fine.'

'Oh. Well, fine or not fine, I'd love to see you.'

'Not today.'

'Tomorrow?'

Now was the moment for her to make a choice. The freedom of being far away from home meant that there was no-one's permission to ask. 'Errm, tomorrow would be lovely but I have lectures.'

'I have work as well but can I take you out to dinner?'

'I'd like that.'

'Perfect. I'm happy now. Tell me where I can pick you up and I'll taxi us somewhere nice.'

Jayda paused for a moment to think. 'I'll be done by 4.30. We could meet outside the UCL Senate House.'

'That's a tad early for me. I won't be able to get away to meet – and believe me I want to – until 6.00.'

'Oh, errm, uh. I want to avoid going back to the apartment and seeing Jamil.'

'Jamil? What does that name mean?'

'Jerk.'

'OK, OK, you don't like him. I'm just trying to understand a little about your parents from the names they chose for you, Miss Strength and Honour.'

'"Jamil" means "beautiful" but I suppose translates as "handsome".'

'That sounds an alright thing to be called.'

'Whatever.'

'Gosh, is he really that bad?'

'Maybe not. I like the way you say quaint things like "gosh".'

'Quaint? You're teasing me now.'

'No, I do like it. I guess you say things like "jolly good" and "spiffing".'

'Jolly good is something I'd say, and will, if we get round to arranging this date.'

She laughed a small snigger so William carried on, 'I don't know what "spiffing" is but it sounds like something I might want to do with you.'

When she then quickly laughed from her belly he knew that something massively right had just blessed its luck on him. Whether by luck or love or his swing in the cycle, he knew that his time had come. Simultaneously, again doubt immediately perplexed him. He could not mention the backdrop of what had been unsettling him, the scrap in the street, incongruous and inglorious as it was. Two days previous he had never spoken to an Arab, let alone flirt with one and fight another. Now on the cusp of love or worse there was also the moral stain of Cosy, too close to the moment to be ignored, too recent to be forgotten. With the unease he felt as to his conduct and the urges he had to please her, to be light and charming, he knew all bestial aspects must remain veiled; blood and mortality beyond the garden, ignored.

After a pause, as if embarrassed for having laughed, she said, 'I don't know what you mean.' There was warmth but a nervous smile in her voice.

'I'll think of something.' There was the same smile in his.

'So, do you know where you are going to take me?'

He did not. Her intonations and inflexions had held his attention more than her words. He grasped a decision.

'The American Bar at the Savoy. 6.00 o'clock.'

'OK, I think. I've been in bars here before. Will it be noisy and unpleasant?'

'No. It's not a pub. Although a good pub is the best of our culture so you should learn to love some of them.'

'I don't drink beer.'

'There's always cider, and Guinness is like nothing else you'll have ever tasted.'

'They have them in Amman, actually. So, 6.00 o'clock. Where is it?'

'The Savoy is on the Strand, down a big alley. It's opposite...oh, you'd best take a cab. It will be worth it, I promise you.'

'Taxi?'

'Preferably driven by a loveable, over-opinionated Cockney who'll solve the Palestine Peace Question by the end of your journey.'

'Oh. Hmm.'

'Jolly good.'

'Jolly good, as you say.'

'Good. Great. OK. Marvellous – I'll see you there then. 6 o'clock tomorrow. I'm really looking forward to seeing you. Bye?'

'Bye.'

When the call ended William flung his mobile in the air, caught it and danced a little jig. Jayda, flat and listless, stared at the black railings of the garden square opposite. He clearly liked her a lot. She thought she might like him. As to why, she was a little puzzled. Whilst she was quite prepared for her behaviour to retreat to safety when tomorrow came, she suspected that he might cheer her up. She walked for five minutes to Kensington High Street, past the mostly closed shop fronts for another five and then turned back for the apartment. When she returned Jamil was locked in the bathroom, the smell of him everywhere else. The television was still on, rupturing the stale tension. She went straight to her room and closed the door as loudly as she could.

It seemed to Jayda that it always took minutes to have a chance with a London taxi. After the inevitable wait she hailed one to a halt outside the Gower Street bookshop where she often used up time. She had been free from 4.30 and the past hour had been spent looking for distractions amongst the books from thoughts of Jamil and William.

Unsuccessfully though. She thought about buying William a book and then realised that she had no idea as to his tastes and to buy him any sort of present would emit the wrong signal. She thought about Jamil and how she would have to speak to him before he left.

Then William again. The whole date was a distraction, borne mainly out of events nothing to do with him but tinged with flattered curiosity. At least she was unchaperoned. She tried to remember his appearance in detail: clean cut and decent rather than handsome but at least she had not decided whether or not he was attractive and her main hesitancy came from a sense of loyalty. Perhaps he was handsome in a western way but was she even meant, or allowed, to find a non-Arab, an infidel, attractive, even if he was a young English gentleman? And how gentlemanly was he? It annoyed and irritated her how he had suggested that he would collect her and then had made her take this taxi. London taxis were seemingly the world's most expensive but it was not the money that irritated. She knew that he had merely been thoughtless in this inconsistency and that made him, like so many other men, slightly disappointing.

It was whilst she was in this mood, wanting to be rescued from her disappointments but unable to define them, that the cab squealed its brakes and a top-hatted doorman welcomed open the door. Satisfaction at arriving nearly ten minutes late dissipated in the sudden fear that she might be underdressed. Jeans, jacket and blouse were smart for the lecture hall and would have to do now, without jewels or make-up. She asked a uniformed sentinel where to go and then trod slowly through to the bar, her eyes searching.

William was perched upon a bar stool, still in his

business suit and, drinkless, absorbed in his phone. A newspaper lay unopened beside him. The text upon the screen demanded: 'Why are you not returning my calls? Cosy'. He had recently been ignoring every call which he did not recognise, a coward's easy retreat from whatever emotional responsibility he might have created. When he saw Jayda he jumped down, erupted into a grin and met her as she approached. She started to blurt out her hello when he silenced and surprised her with his confidence in kissing her cheek using quick lingering pressure and inhaling her perfume. He slid an arm down to her elbow and edged her up to the neighbouring barstool.

'Here,' he announced, 'we shall drink martinis.' William had a crude but effective strategy: drink. Whether or not he felt any real affection for his target, his plan was much the same. Meet her at a bar near to where she started out from, home or office. Put at least half a bottle of champagne inside her on an empty stomach before moving on to a restaurant somewhere in the West End, carefully chosen according to whatever impression he was trying to make. There at the meal they would consume another shared bottle. After that it was usually getting late but his favourite tactic was then to suggest dessert at a second restaurant. Each location moved them closer to his Pimlico flat, where he could offer coffee or more champagne. He adhered to the old bachelor rule of always having a chilled half size bottle in the fridge. To further his options he was also a member of a late night jazz bar in Belgravia which bridged the worlds of a society nightclub and a seedy drinking den. It served many purposes, not least when occasionally, defeated by feminine deflections, he needed the solace of a final drink before turning in.

It was a stratagem of low cunning but one that had worked well for him. A huge part of him had debated against it for Jayda though. Purity of intent and approach to snare the best. For this occasion though, for the crucial beginning, he did not trust enough in his own talents and besides, he was so nervous he wanted to drink.

'There are only small differences between a vodka martini, a gin martini and a gimlet. Maybe we'll try all three,' he continued, certain of a confident beginning.

'Are they strong? I'm not used to too much alcohol, just wine.'

'It's not the strength you should be worried about but lack of quality and too much quantity. I shall be your guide on that and fill you full of food to soak it all up. You look lovely, by the way.'

'Thank you. I feel a little underdressed for this place.'

'Nonsense. And you smell yummy as well.'

The barman appeared in front of them with frosted glasses and began to wave bottles about as if in accordance with some sort of ritual. William had clearly pre-ordered, she realised and, with timid apprehension, a part of her wanted to be entrapped if it was all done with flattery and style. William stared into her eyes hopefully, smiled, and then gave his attention to the barman. Jayda regarded him quickly and tried to ascertain more. He wore a light grey business suit, light blue cuffed shirt and a heavy red silk tie, his hair was slicked back, the black shoes polished and, trumpeting loud as he crossed his legs, lime green socks.

'Do you always wear a suit and tie? In Jordan, men don't so often. It's far too hot.'

'Every working day I do. It's a uniform that speaks of my probity, trustworthiness and decent Englishness. Here. Yours is a vodka one, mine a gin. Cheers.'

She copied him warily, touched glasses and sipped. The chilled spirit burned down her throat. 'Goodness! That's strong.'

'Only the first half of your first one tastes strong. You must persevere. It's worth it. Take another sip and tell me more about your family.'

Jayda looked at him once again and saw a beaming smile emitting what she interpreted as happiness rather than any overt intent to seduce. So she surrendered and took another sip. She could feel it trickle into her belly, warming. The barman pushed forward a small plate of peanuts. They both picked without hunger.

'My parents are called Jad and Zena. Jamil is my elder brother. Fiesal and Fatima are the little ones.'

'Now, we have established that Jamil is not your favourite. Tell me about Fat, Fie, err, the two little ones.'

'Fatima and Fiesal. They are at school. I miss them.'

'Toddlers?' He nearly added, 'and you help with the nappies?' and immediately thanked himself for not making any such implications.

'Teenagers. Quiet, hard working, clever Jordanian kids.'

'Hmm, tell me about Jordan – after another sip. It mustn't lose the chill.'

Jayda sipped again, over halfway down, and began to enjoy the charm of being paid attention to. Whilst not unfamiliar to luxury she found the cocktail bar a rarefied experience. White-jacketed waiters glided amongst the tables, beside which the besuited and high-heeled sipped their drinks. In a room given over to relaxation she felt most conscious of the unfamiliarity of her being there. She counted to ten and forced herself to relax her shoulders. William was leaning forward. This was very different to the Abdoun cafes of home and the American chain coffee houses where she normally spent her socialising hours.

'Jordan is a waterless small triangle of desert, stuffed full of holy sites and antiquities and inhabited by the coolest, friendliest people ever. We don't have many resources, thanks to your Winston Churchill who made sure the map was drawn to give Iraq all the oil. If we'd had serious oil we'd be the leaders of the Arab world. Instead we have to settle for moral authority and being a bridge to the Middle East for the West.'

'Moral authority is easily ignored,' said William, wondering whether a serious tone would be to his advantage.

'Perhaps, but we have family, tribal and religious ties that you westerners just don't get. They go far across borders and can cut across ordinary patriotic concerns. The Arab race is a connected association, a huge bickering family but one that knows that it is naturally allied to itself against the rest of the world. I suppose everyone thinks themselves the most important but Jordan is at the centre of the web.'

'Hmm, is it a bit like we British still thinking ourselves influential in the world, reduced in power but culturally the barometer by which everyone else is measured?'

They paused and Jayda considered. William, noting her seriousness, gestured with a hand to make sure that the cocktails were finished. She found it strong still but, chilled, liked the strength.

'I don't think so. That's not an accurate comparison. Islam demands its own loyalty and just about all Arabs are, one way or another, Muslims. Whole countries are defined by it. Your Christianity is too weak to do that here in the West and your Britishness too diverse to mean much at all, from what I can tell. I don't think that many British consider themselves culturally number one, do they? Perhaps people from your background do.'

'I most certainly do. Gilberto, we need another

brace of these beauties here please: one gin, one vodka. So, tell me about Amman.'

'Amman is a big place, built on seven jebels, or hills, but small enough for everyone to know each other. Look, I'm not sure that I should have another one.'

'Oh, but you must. Martinis are like women's breasts, you know. One is too few but three is far too many. You, I can't fail to notice, have the perfect number of breasts and so you have to drink the same number of martinis.'

Jayda blinked but could not think what to say. No man had ever mentioned her breasts to her. What she could not decide was whether to be shocked or amused and so she blushed her eyes downward and noticed again the shine of his black shoes. Her father would approve of that, at least.

'Now then,' he continued, 'your turn to try the gin. Gin – infusions of juniper and other berries and things. The Taste of London. Cheers.'

Both glasses rose. Jayda's eyes were still wide with slight shock but fear of clamming up and seeming prudish made her pick up the frosted glass. She noticed that its first sip was easier to drink this time.

'Is Amman beautiful?'

'Yes, I think so. It's clean and spread out and they've got the scale of the buildings right. There isn't much high rise to ruin it.' Then she said without thinking, rather alarming her as soon as it was uttered because of the implications, 'You'll have to come and see it.'

'I'd love to.' He chuckled to himself and leant back.

Normally a woman who, however superficially, wanted to have a measure of control, Jayda had a sense of having lost it. She had mentioned his coming out partly from a sense of being obliged to, as a form of politeness, arising from the traditions of Arab hospitality drilled into her during childhood but now she suddenly felt stupid. To compensate for this and because he was grinning as if he had won an unexpected victory she decided to try and take control. Waving her hair with a shake she then looked at William, narrowed her eyes and tried to imagine what his naked torso was like.

'So William, how many girlfriends do you have?'

'I don't have any current girlfriend as such.'

'And how many have you had? How many liaisons have you been in that avoided marriage?'

'Marriage? Ah, well. If one doesn't count Practice Girlfriends but only serious relationships that could have or should have developed, then that would be a grand sum total of zero.'

'Practice Girlfriends? What are they?'

'Unimportant people who haven't captivated me.' His voice, half whimsical, half serious, made her pause. She could not decide whether he was a womaniser or a romantic. Uncertain again, she focused on the intricate patterns of his tie. With the martinis slowly promoting warm cheerfulness inside her, this was perhaps not the best time to decide anything.

'Now then, a good British expression meaning "finish your drink" is "Bottoms Up". I need to make good on my promise to give you dinner. So, "Bottoms Up" girl. In reply you are meant to say "Up Yours".'

Ten minutes later in a standstill taxi in Trafalgar Square, William was staring at her hand, resting on the seat between them, thinking how profoundly beautiful it was to him and whether he could hold it, or somehow contrive to touch it, when she turned to him and said,

'William, I don't think I should do dinner. I've drunk too much already. Please take me home.'

Without hesitation he agreed, asked her address, memorised it and, leaning forward, redirected the cabbie. Then, upon sinking back beside her but before she could react, he grasped her hand and asked how she was feeling. She replied, eyebrows slightly amused, 'I'll be OK. I'm just not used to strong alcohol and I think I'd better stop now and go back.' Only after a few seconds did she pretend to notice he was clutching her hand and therefore obliged herself to withdraw.

It was at moments like this that her long hair annoyed her. It was as if it knew how to embarrass her, the way it crowded her face like an unmanageable curtain. She felt a hot flush swell her face and scalp. She wanted to say that she was sorry, that she did want him to ask her for dinner again, but not now; it

was too soon and the drink had made her feel too out
of balance. No words came and she concentrated on
waving her hair back, to let her face cool. She closed
her eyes defensively, repelling his stares and muting
his conversation.

To her surprise, when the cab pulled up, he flung a
note to the cabbie and followed her out to the pavement.
She fumbled for keys. She was not going to let him
in. It was stupidly presumptuous of him to assume
anything, standing there beside her and grinning so
confidently as she delved in the rubble of her handbag.
She raised her head to tell him so, or least give a polite
but curt goodbye, but he announced,

'Now this is the part where, traditionally, the boy
kisses the girl.'

'Don't push your luck.'

He did. He moved in immediately, with his hand
to the small of her back and pulled her toward him.
He kissed and then withdrew only an inch. Stunned,
she did not move. He kissed again for longer, shifted
himself to front her and cupped her face in his hands.
She liked it but felt, in the pause of a second, that she
had a huge decision to make in that moment. There
was no time and the trajectory of her emotions shifted
by default. She did not make any conscious decision
as such but, tight there with warm breath upon her and
the smell of bergamot upon his skin, could not help
but kiss back and for a minute they continued. Her bag
slipped to the floor. It was beautiful to him, even if it

was inebriated courage that had allowed him to be so forward. He felt as if all his recent past had tapered into those soft, yielding moments and that all his future should blossom from them. She began to worry as to whether she should be giving in so soon and if she was responding well enough. Then she turned her head to his shoulder, held him as he rocked her gently and decided to be brave in another direction.

'I've remembered that my brother is upstairs. Perhaps I'll let you buy me pizza and coke around the corner, seeing as you've started something.'

CHAPTER VI

Jamil slumped into the armchair, flung his briefcase into its leather twin opposite by way of reserving it and waited for Jayda to arrive with their coffees. He concentrated intensely on her movements, partly impatient and yet fascinated by her. Spill stains and mug rings splattered over the low table and sticky floor but he knew not to be fussy. It was a busy, overheated place off the endless movements of Kensington High Street. She had been several minutes in the queue and he was dulled to stale testiness by the time she wobbled over with her hands full but he controlled himself with what he decided was admirable will power. Everything about him was composed but for his foot tapping furiously. Tall, thin and angular, his frame was not used to idling in deep seated furniture. When she placed their outsize cups and saucers on the table he reached, automatically, for his cigarettes and lit up.

'Jamil, you can't smoke here!' she hissed, embarrassed.

'Huh? What do you mean? This is a coffee shop.'

'When were you last in London? They banned smoking in public a long time ago and, what's more, they actually meant it.'

He stubbed out on his saucer and smiled weakly to

an incredulous, silent chorus of queuing shoppers, most of whom had turned to glare a wall of disapproving stares.

'Unbelievable. Just as well I'm leaving today.'

'Just as well.'

With that Jamil remembered his assumptions as to why they were there.

'So, why have you been avoiding me?'

'I've been working.'

'Not all the time you haven't.'

Jayda was avoiding his gaze, stirring her coffee. He knew that she did not take sugar.

'You've been avoiding me ever since you created that argument when I arrived. Why?'

Jayda did not reply and might have given an almost imperceptible shrug. Her being there was her peace offering. She did not want to explain herself, even though she was all unfocused coiled energy and keen for raised voices to find, eventually, an end to the tension between them. The words to explain herself though, even if she knew why, would be too difficult to find.

He grunted to punctuate her silence. Women confused Jamil, and his limited experience of them had not lured him to attempt to understand them more. Of those he knew well, his mother and sisters were the most prominent. He had a theory, not extensively researched, that all women were actually mad to some degree. Vague thoughts that it may be something to do with the lunar cycle, or the menstrual cycle, an imbalance of hormones, or all three, reassured him. It was a useful explanation for all feminine foibles, those he found malicious and those he merely misunderstood. Of those he liked best, the foremost was Jayda. He felt the pride of family acutely. Her beauty and fierce independence, living up to her name's meaning, reflected well, he imagined, upon the wider Talhoun name.

For Jamil, his family's strength and reputation was the purpose of his life. He felt its heritage more keenly, even, than his father. Their fortunes and prosperity had risen and fallen with the Kingdom's, often precarious though somehow having survived to stability and rising status. His great grandfather left the Hijaz with Fiesal for the Arab Revolt, killed at least three Turks from the back of his camel and rode as far as Damascus from where he returned with enough loot to settle in the unpromising village of Amman. He had built a house on a rocky slope near the dusty railway station and began to trade in spices and guns. His grandfather in turn served in the Arab Legion under Glubb Pasha, whom he loved, and then the traitor Maan abu Newar, whom he disliked and therefore soon left to formally incorporate the trading and do business building roads and schools. Years later, when an old man, during the Black September of 1970 he had dropped a brick onto the head of a solitary fedayeen gunman crouching in the street below his bedroom window, killing him outright. Immediately he left his family, leaving the dead gunman there amongst the stray dogs and burning cars, risking his life travelling across the city to the Al-Husseini mosque for afternoon prayers. He loved his king, he later explained, so he killed the Palestinian but he also loved Allah, so he was compelled to pray for forgiveness. His father was barely a teenage boy inside the house at the time and one of his strongest memories was that of looking out to see an expanding pool of crimson blood from the gunman's cracked skull as he twitched his last convulsions. Jad Talhoun, their father, grew up to see peace as an officer in the Royal Guard. He left his commission early, by royal permission when grandfather died, assuming his duties as patriarch of a growing conglomerate of family and businesses. Keeping what he inherited, he made it more efficient and built on it, expanding balance sheets, profits and power. Islam infused itself within the mixture as part of a balance. They were what they had achieved because God had willed it so and therefore He required charity. The Talhoun Foundation had grown its coffers with donations from corporate profit and thereby trickled out donations itself, to such local charities and causes deemed to be socially or politically expedient. In a small country they were not the largest of their kind but were growing, with a name to take pride in.

Jamil was, with most appearances, a confident and powerful personality but several streams of self doubt coursed through him. Doubt as to whether he had the abilities needed to live up to his fantasies, doubt whether he could carve a domain free of his father's dominance and, above all, fear as to whether he would find a wife to support him. Jayda was the one woman in whose company he had once truly relaxed. He thought of her as an honest friend and the little sister who used to run to him for advice and protection. She did not realise it but she filled the void that was his need to fixate affection upon. His mother was a small, quietly contained figure, almost aloof and remote in a domesticity that seemed otherworldly in its relevance. This despite the irony that, because unmarried, he lived under her roof.

His current worry was that Jayda, somehow infected by western liberalism far away from the *ummah* of Islamic life, was growing further away from him when he needed her more than she could realise, as an ally against their Baba and as a friend. Many times he had enjoyed comfortable silences with her but Jayda's unresponsiveness throughout his visit had been wilfully uncompanionable. He decided to provoke her.

'So, tell me again why I should let you join the Talhoun Group?'

It had its effect of breaking her silence. She exploded. Opposite his uncomfortable, ill-framed collapse she tilted forward, sat edged and alert whilst her hands gestured. As he expected she declaimed the insolence of his chauvinism and stupidity of his short-sightedness; the evidence of her own intelligence and the unjustified vanities of his. Corporate strategy had exercised her ambitions and she explained that, to differentiate them from other Jordanian conglomerates, they needed to internationalise their businesses, strengthening them from the variable winds of the localised Levantine economies. The ardour of her well-rehearsed argument triggered a rare dusky blush to her cheeks, making her big eyes gleam under their heavy, blinking lids. Jamil did not hear her actual words. He had heard them, or words like them, several times before. She spoke, muffled, as if through a cloud of indeterminate mass. The sense he attached to the vessel in front of him was not of speech but one of a lifeblood of passion. He loved and admired her, his little sister, for the energy she pulsed and an affectionate smile escaped from him as she spoke.

'Don't mock me with your grinning!' She edged on her seat, as if tempted to hit him. 'Answer me!'

'I'm not, habibi.' She would join the Group of course, if that was what she truly wanted. He had long realised that he could not bear it without her close by anyway. How his need for that could be accommodated in a corporate setting, he had no idea. It worried him, when he thought of it. Having not listened to her rant there was nothing precise to reply to so, with visible effort at having to surrender a concession but with some affection, he felt compelled to mumble, 'Maybe you are right.'

Jayda breathed perceptibly, nearly falling off her

chair in excitement.

'Say that again.'

'Maybe you are just a jumped-up little girl who can't get over that I used to pull her ponytails.'

Jayda did not feel very close to her elder brother, elder by a five years that seemed to delineate another generation. She felt that she understood him though, like she did her father, as a big man of simple principles, unreflective in his methods though tinged with piety. Boyfriends, husbands and fathers were all, she assumed, manipulable by one stratagem or another but over Jamil she felt less powerful. Her father was an Olympian figure, detached most of the time but alternatively volatile and sentimental when engaged. Jamil had been large in the knee-scraping tumbles of her childhood. Once, seated in one of the bright, modern cafes in the Mecca Mall on the edge of a gathering of half-friendly school acquaintances, sophisticated with their cappuccinos, she was teased for her railway track braces and some dull, clunky shoes her mother made her wear. Powerless and inarticulate, at a pinpoint of misery, she searched round and found her brother coming to collect her, striding tall, handsome and absorbing swooning looks from the girls. He collected her with the perfect balance of affection towards her and disdain towards them. Only then, it seemed, had she adored him for being himself. He still wanted that little girl adoration from her and she hated that.

She searched his face for confrontation and saw

humour. Exasperated, she expelled a disdainful puff and exploded her hand into a flower's bloom.

'Now I want a cigarette.'

'You know, sister, if you stopped fighting me we could be great allies. First though, you have to finish here and come back to Amman and find me a good wife. You know, a beautiful girl who is the exact character opposite of you.'

'Oh, I'm sure there are plenty of those back home and throughout the whole Middle East. You'll manage it before I get back.'

'I'm not so sure.' He shunted himself around in the chair, settling to a pretense of comfort. 'Women are not straightforward and I want to go straightforward and direct to marriage. Easier to have the thing arranged for me by mother or Baba.' He could tell by the way she drank her coffee, as if she did not realise she was doing so, that she was paying attention. 'Or by you.'

Being, at 29, an old bachelor from a good family had of course attracted attention. He could no more avoid this attention than deny his name. Meddling mothers rang his, mentioning their daughters. Brother officers from his old regiment invited him to their homes for drinks and then revealed their younger, mainly plain, sisters. His mother would moan social suggestions to his father, who then rolled his eyes in resigned consent. A round of parentally-induced socialising often followed; always some shy young girl placed at dinner beside him or somehow brought to his indifferent attention. The duty of it dulled him and, no doubt, many of the reluctant candidates. Many he knew, or knew of, already. The unspoken convention was that the event itself spoke of both families' tacit approval so, if he and the girl wanted to, they could meet again and, if they repeatedly did so, the pitch and frequency of maternal communication would intensify; all hesitations concluding, no doubt swifter than was perhaps comfortable, in an engagement with Jamil at some dutiful moment trying to ask the question as endearingly as he could manage. The fathers and lawyers would meet with the betrothed couple to settle the contract long before the marriage day so that, when it seemed that half of Amman would be invited to a banquet in a hotel ballroom and both mothers reach the pinnacles of their domestic and social ambitions, the previously agreed grubby details of dowry and divorce could be veiled behind the opulent twin curtains of love and religious family duty.

'By me!'

'Yes, why not? You know the current set of Abdoun Rangers better than they do.'

'Jamil, you are being bizarre. Marriage lasts a lifetime and is the rock upon which you build for yourself and your children. *You* must make the choice. Nobody really arranges marriages anymore, not amongst our sort of people. They just line up suggestions. It is probably best if you went out and found your own suggestions.'

'Yes, sister, I could. I know that but I am too busy and I am too, too…' he looked to confirm the seriousness of her attention as he struggled to a confession. 'I am too awkward amongst the really pretty ones.'

Jayda erupted laughing. He leaned back, his pride recoiling. 'Don't laugh at me.'

'Oh Jamil, I'm sorry. It is probably difficult for you because you scare them. Scare them with your talk of tanks and guns and polo ponies. Not many Amman girls have an affinity for any of those things.'

'Hmm. Anyway, will you help me?'

'Help you? To find an unsuspecting, innocent victim?'

'To find a wife. This is really why I came to London, to speak to you about this. I could have sent Khalifa, our finance guy, to attend to the insurance matters.'

'Oh, Jamil.'

'Jayda, if you are going to join the businesses then I'll have you there as my partner. What I also need is a partner in my home, to arrange it, organise the servants, bless me with children and give me the strength to work well. It will be the most efficient way.'

'Doesn't love come into it?'

'I'm not a very sentimental man, sister. If I love my wife, all well and good. If I happen to fall in love with someone else later then I could always marry them as well. If the first one doesn't like it then I could divorce her.'

'That isn't particularly moral behaviour.'

'But perhaps it is. I'd be providing for two women instead of one. Providing for someone is always moral.'

'I think not, but OK, Jamil. I am very grateful for your change in attitude about my joining the Group. I was despairing even though I think that Baba would, in the end, accept it. And I'm flattered that you ask me to help you find a wife. Matchmaking would be good sport, I'm sure, but I'm over here. I have another year of study. And what if I stay over here?'

'Stay here?'

'Yes, what if I find Jordan too small, too illiberal and I want to have my corporate career in London? What if I fall in love with an Englishman and have him as my house-husband, looking after my children?'

Jamil, bewildered by this suggestion, glanced firstly at the crosscurrents of people and traffic in the street beyond the large sheet windows and then back to the self-assured, smiling woman opposite.

'Be realistic Jayda, I always try to be. Baba would not let you. Jordan is not illiberal. We even have women cabinet ministers and ambassadors now. Why would you want to stay here? Britain has a weak culture and is an ever-weakening power that does not know what it is, where it is going, what it wants or what it is for. The liberals weaken everything here with their constant change and constant policy fashions. And it rains. For over half the year, everything is covered dull by this dim light. And it seems very crowded too.'

'Yes, but it has charms too. Just because they are liberal does not mean they are weak. They allow fashions in everything because they are fair. They don't ban anything or dictate anything and so the artist and the musician and the unintelligent celebrity who captures the mood can flourish here. That's vibrant and healthy. The rain makes everything outside the towns lovely and green, by the way. At home we are all dust and only white, brown, yellow desert colours. And we are crowded as well. All those Palestinians needing welfare.'

'So sister, am I to tell Baba that you are not coming home and that you are going to marry an infidel Englishman?'

'No. Tell him that I am working very diligently and that, inshallah, one day he will be proud of me. And he could send me more money, so that I can have a maid.'

'You know, seriously, it may not be long before you will have to marry.' Jamil's tone was one of reasonable concern. Jayda wanted to explode but clenched her teeth and stared at her hands.

'Are you coming home for Eid?' he asked, quieter now.

'Oh yes. It coincides with the end of this term, near enough.'

Jayda's thoughts wandered to the night before. During the meal with William she had fallen quiet and unsure, as if the kisses he had stolen had frozen rather than broken her ice. He, however, had visibly relaxed and chatted freely, talking happy nonsense and laughing frequently. She had warmed to a smile or two and gazed with growing incredulity at first, and then fondness, as to the joy she seemed to be bringing him. She was unsure how it had come about and what it meant. Concerned overall not to surrender too much too early she ended the night as soon as she could, blaming the drink from earlier even though she had regained clarity. When he walked her home he clutched her hand but she instinctively withdrew it again. His shoulders drooped instantly and his pace slowed a step. She had every intention of escaping inside her building as quickly as she could, avoiding what he no doubt wanted. Once was enough. She needed more space to think it all through. When he deflated so, at the withdrawal of her hand, she could not help but feel as if she had wounded him unnecessarily and so, upon the steps, she found his eyes and held his sad, querying gaze until he moved, uncertainly, to kiss her again. And it had been, surprisingly, something she wanted.

In Amman to kiss a man like that was to either already be in, or accelerating towards a formal engagement for marriage. Jayda knew enough to realise that was not likely to apply here. She could tell that William was decent but sexually ambitious. It was a combination she could not cease thinking about. Whether it meant he wanted to marry her, whether that were even possible and what she felt about this were aspects too large and too close to gauge the outlines of. Thinking it through was not something she had had time for but, if nothing else, it had prompted the delicious suggestion to her suffocatingly conservative brother that she might marry an Englishman.

Jamil coughed toward the window pane. Their cups were empty and outside a thin drizzle was falling, giving everywhere an unrefreshing stain of wet irritation. Customers clanked and crowded inside the cafe, clumsy with coats, bags and umbrellas. With the perception that came easy to her, Jayda realised there was a deeper wrong.

'Why do you look so irritated Jamil? It's not because of me or your lack of a wife.'

Jamil, seemingly absorbed by the trivial messy scenes of traffic outside the window, made a great effort and without turning his vacant eyes said, 'I fought a man when I came here two days ago. He bumped into me, deliberately, in the street. I hit him to the ground. I was stronger than he was and I sensed that I could do it, so I did. Why did I do that sister? Why did I lose myself to anger like that?'

Jayda said nothing.

'Do you think if I had a wife that would calm me?' He was looking at her now, sadness in his eyes.

'Maybe Jamil, maybe. If you loved her.'

He was back to staring at the street and she was not sure whether he had heard her.

The phone by his chest in his coat pocket chirped annoyingly. He knew that it was Cosy ringing again and so William reached inside to press the button which deadened the pestering. At first he had felt that he should reply and even tried to, once. She had rung several times on the first Monday afterward so, with deep breath and fresh lies resolved upon his tongue, he returned a call. It went to answermachine and, reluctant at best, he hung up without a word, preferring now for an impenetrable silence to deliver the message. She did not give up though, ringing several times a day but having left just one message, delivered in a level voice, 'William. Cosy. Ring me please. I need to speak to you.'

Emotionally saturated with Jayda, William wished that he had never met Cosy. His sexual greed with her stained him. It dirtied the margins of his thoughts of Jayda and he could not scour it away. She was always ringing.

It was mid evening and the City had released its ants. He was seated on a pavement table bench outside the nondescript messy box of a quiet Pimlico pub. Buff, large, tieless in his suit with a bead of perspiration glowing on his brow, returned with two pints and sat opposite with a thirst for conversation on his smile. They were both slightly cold but neither would mention it.

'So, I hear that you are bonking the eccentric daughter of one of the country's richest earls and that she is deeply keen on you?'

'What? Nonsense.' William searched Buff's face to see if there were any clues. 'What? What has she been saying?'

'She, being Cosy Cheshire, has told Sam Fifoot, who has told me that you are adept at having it off in the bathroom and she, having experienced such delights, is now convinced you are charming and handsome and could be "The One".'

'Oh, no. No. Seriously?'

'Seriously.' Buff took a pull at his pint and gulped, satisfied. 'You've started something there.'

'Oh, no.' William had not touched his drink but stared at it. It looked thin and flat.

'You look troubled, my friend. In order for me to help you with wise advise I need to learn every detail of how you copulated with her. Was she noisy? Pray tell.'

'I didn't actually.'

'She says you did.'

'Well, I didn't. I lost the will. It was just a bit of groping, if you must.'

'Lost the will?'

'Yes. I was drunk and distracted and didn't want to follow through.'

'Doesn't sound like you. Doesn't sound like anybody.'

William now took a deep gulp. It disappointed, bitter without the bite. 'She's been ringing and texting me ever since but I haven't spoken to her.'

'Oh dear, I feared so, but if you didn't have a life-altering assignation of some sort or promise her anything with a romantic flourish, that may save you.'

'Save me?'

'From a sentence of frothing madness in a gilded cage.'

'Please cut to the point of what you are going on about. Give me the backdrop.'

'Now mate, I ought to tell you a couple of things. Cosy is a little…' Buff paused to allow his eyes to raise and pinpoint a precise word, 'unhinged. Sam's her best friend and I've known Sam for years and met Cosy plenty. She's fun alright but continually developing obsessions, usually about men. Shags quite a lot of them I understand. Probably a result of being deeply insecure and one of those girls who voms to stay thin. She's somewhat a wafer, you may have noticed, poor thing.'

'Yes. So? So are many other girls out there – unhinged in one way or another.'

'Not like she is. She's a career fruitcake with a rattling medicine cabinet full of pharma sweets. Apparently…' Buff made sure that he had William's gaze, 'apparently she is a devoted disciple of Hera, convinced that all her problems and fears have a silver bullet – a man to love. If she is targeting you then you have to be strong enough to take her on or be prepared for some histrionics.'

'Oh no. I don't need this. Buff, I'm keen on Jayda – that Arab girl, remember?'

'No doubt. After all, who there wasn't eyeing her? But William, you have bigger problems now than convincing the beautiful Arab girl that you're worthwhile. I really like Cosy but she takes the traditional feminine absence of proportion to extremes. If you don't handle it carefully you'll have her camping on your doorstep in a day or two, threatening suicide.'

'Look, you're exaggerating. She can't be that bad. She doesn't know where I live. If I just ignore her calls she'll just, just wither on the vine.'

'No. Be warned. She is altogether more energetic, resourceful and problematic than that. Believe me when I tell you that she turned into a stalker with her last great crush.'

William took another gulp of beer by way of response. Apprehension waved into him, the roots of which went back to the innocences of childhood amongst the sunlit certainties of repeated outcomes: a good boy was rewarded, a bad punished. If he had not met Jayda then maybe Cosy's tortured personality would have appealed to him, his romantic longing keeping him in the relationship long enough to save her from her own imbalances. But then, maybe not.

His bachelor life was a series of fleeting relationships that were experimented with beyond a core of real friends, each one a search for permanence amongst the perennial complications of lust, posturing and jaded sophistication. When whatever he was looking for found him, he assumed that he would know it because the ache to search would cease. That is what he yearned to find with Jayda.

Buff was continuing. 'My favourite story about her is how she got the nickname Lady Caligula. When she was a sheltered all-girls-school teenager she rode her pony into the local parish church one Sunday service and demanded that the priest marry her to the beast. He refused and demanded she leave and so she turned around, paused and let the horse drop a steaming turd in the nave. And then there's the one when she chased her married lover back to his wife in Australia where...'

'No! Stop! I don't want to know. I get the message. She's crackerjack.'

'Yes mate.'

'Why didn't you warn me about her at the party?'

'How was I to know what you were doing with her?'

'Look, the simplest thing is if I just ignore her.'

'Well, I hope that it's that easy for you.' Buff looked away, over William's shoulder, by way of emphasising through a pause.

William understood but made Buff deliver his message again, twice, talking it over for the next half hour, lubricated by two further pints which were flat to the taste and unenjoyable in their simple masculine ritual.

CHAPTER VII

It was only the second time they had been in the back of a black a cab together and William, sober but heady with the happiness of her being so close to him again, was too nervous to touch her hand. He could not stop staring at her though, nor cease talking and had been doing so since collecting her.

'Here used to be a brewery and over there a bedlam hospital.'

'Where? You're not even looking outside.'

'Yes I am. And there they invented the coach and horses combination.'

'Where? Really?'

'No.'

'Oh, you are joking? Oh. Look, stop smiling at me.'

'No. Can't help it.'

Jayda had thought she might want William to touch her, remembering how he had first done so in Trafalgar Square, maybe with an arm securing her but it was clear to her that he was being less of a man and more of a puppy, chaotic with excitement. He began again, 'I mean I...'

'Shh.' She put a finger to his lips, silencing him with the surprise of it. 'It will be fine, I promise.'

William blinked with further shock.

'It's supposed to be me reassuring you, in moments like this.'

'Well, where is the confident, sophisticated seducer who took me for cocktails at the Savoy?'

'I, err, I'm here.' But he was lying. 'I know it'll be fine. You'll be fine. I'll be...'

'I'm not unaware, you know. You seem to be very keen on me and it's obviously important to you, this meal with your sister and this other guy.'

'Buff. It's a nickname. Real name's Steve.'

The light had fallen during the stop-start journey and the spotted, dirty lights of the city began to flicker on and accelerate the dim. Perceived so accurately, William felt suddenly vulnerable and stupid. Before, he was all energy and tremors. It was as if he had been shamingly revealed in embarrassment, caught naked or cheating. If she could see his nerves so clearly that would mean she could read him with clarity, perhaps seeing through his intentions and the sham of his habitual bluster. That unnerved him. He gulped, stiffened to face the front and glanced his head to the street.

'I suppose you might be right.'

'I like it though,' she said, smiling unnoticed. Then she took his hand and briefly squeezed it.

The reassurance of her touch stunned him. That she might like whatever she saw his true personality to be; it was a raw exposure. Whatever he was, the combination of attitude, pride, failures and accidental background, was not something he had regarded for a long while. He was normally too busy or scared to analyse and then, inevitably, self-loathe. The possibility she might love him had been glimpsed, misaligning whatever composure he was carrying, turning his face away to the gloomy street-scenes scudding by, in fear of the impossible fragility that his happiness seemed to be built on.

Frances Clive flat-shared in a redbrick Victorian mansion in Queen's Club Gardens. It was an implausibly spacious apartment for what William imagined his sister might be paid and he suspected that she was not compelled to pay a market rent anyway. Frances was a secretary, so far as he could tell, at one of the major auction houses and her flatmate, who had inherited the property, was from the same department.

'Arab girl? What Arab girl?'

'The one I mentioned to you when I rang after that party in Chelsea.'

'I don't remember that.'

'Yes, I was asking you for...well, no matter.'

'What of it?'

'Frances, I'm rather keen on her.'

'Nice for you, I'm sure.'

'Look, I've a favour to ask,' He laboured the words. 'Could you, would you, you must please because it's really important to me and until now, you know, no-one has been important to me...'

Frances made an unenthusiastic noise.

'I'm not going to be a lemon on a date, falsely talking you up in some cheap, dingy basement restaurant.'

'Frances, no. You won't have to. Not much. I want you to meet Jayda and hopefully you'll both take to each other. It's a serious thing, she and I.'

There was a lengthy, sceptical silence from Frances, until, 'Normally I'd like you to plead with me a bit more.'

'I'm about to,' although William found it easy to keep his voice firm. 'This girl is the first one I actually care about. So I want her to meet the family, such as we are.'

'Family? Mother and Father and their lots? Cousins?'

'Well, you first.' He hoped that might seem a compliment. 'Could you give us dinner at your flat with a few friends? Lasagne, red wine, tiramusu – your usual?'

'Oh, so I'm paying am I?'

'I'll buy you lunch next Sunday.'

'You are anyway. It's your turn.'

'Would next Friday be any good?'

Frances sighed, 'I suppose you've never asked before, not in this way, so you might be genuine. What did you say she's called?'

About halfway through the lasagne William allowed

himself to believe that it was going well. Jayda was holding her own with composure and charm, although with understandable reserve. Frances and her flatmate, whose name he had never learnt, were chirping with relaxed if predictable conversation. Buff was concentrating on drinking more than his share of the wine and flirting with the flatmate, who was stonewalling him with frozen smiles and clichéd responses. His sister, though, was by now hosting with genuine warmth, which was what he had hoped for.

He had allowed Frances to meet some of his earlier girlfriends but in passing rather than by introduction for approval. His request had bemused her because he had asked with need and enthusiasm. There was of course the simple want to show Jayda off, to submit for blessing and jealousy of his happiness because his girlfriend was so beautiful, so rare and unknown. He was eating slowly, savouring the scene – a busy, clattering kitchen table in a high ceiling room, friends babbling rhythms of conversation and the unspoken focus on Jayda.

Jayda Talhoun, an heiress he had since learnt, and the object of his requited, infatuated, all meaningful impulses. She was sitting there, making every effort and even eating with what he perceived as almost bewildering elegance. It was not that she was from a sizeable business dynasty, although he had spent enough time at his office computer researching everything easily available online about the Talhouns, that was a huge incidental, it was that to love her made him want to improve himself. He now conducted himself with vague ideals of purity in mind, even when not around her, even when alone: more mannered, fewer cigarettes, less drinking, less masturbating, finer clothes, dulling down his diet for health, running and even praying. Just saying thank you to God, quickly and shallowly, but wanting to acknowledge the influence of the divine for the existence of this miracle of grace and blood, Jayda Talhoun.

'William? William?' It was Frances, forehead furrowed in arched, teasing enquiry.

He blustered, awake. 'Oh, of course, yes?' but he was so happy it did not matter if his sister was mocking him. 'I missed that.'

'William,' Jayda continued, smiling un-annoyed, 'I was asking Frances about your parents. I think she thought you were somewhere else.'

'I was. I was just…Frances?'

'Yes, William. William, as you can see, is an idiot but one I love to bits. The thing about our mother and father is that they divorced, when we were young but old enough to notice and care. It was all so very messy and we didn't understand. I don't suppose we ever will. We see them of course and there are step siblings on both sides. After it happened we grew up in boarding schools really. You might not have divorce in Arabia, do you?'

'Oh we do. But it is rare because it is so

embarrassing. Easy to do legally but hugely frowned on.'

'It was hell,' interjected William forcefully. Then, quieter, and not looking at anyone, 'Thing was, Frances and I only had ourselves then. We must have been not quite teenagers. We were close, if you remember sis. We may only be brother and sister now, living cramped districts apart, but I remember now we used to be close and that's why, that's why I wanted so much for you both to meet.'

The other two at the table stared at each other, respectfully silent.

'I used to be very close to my brother as well,' said Jayda, fully realising that she had steered the conversation on the family theme. 'Not so much now, but I'm still very fond of him. Maybe, because in Amman our whole family still lives in the same big house – children often stay at home till they marry – he irritates me a lot without meaning to.'

'Yes, fond as I am of my brother, I wouldn't want to live with him,' Frances nodded.

As Jayda noticed the cab return closer to Kensington High Street she turned to William and interrupted his analysis of his sister's wine and food, which she was not listening to.

'Will you come up for coffee?'

'Oh, well, yes I'd love to.' He searched her face with poignant interest.

'But it's just for coffee. I realise it's a code – 'Come up for Coffee' – but I'm not ready for that yet.'

'Oh,' and then, hastily, 'I'd still love to.' More than the prospect of sex at some future point which her last words had not ruled out, he was aware that her perceptive cool had unravelled him on the journey there. He did not want to appear frazzled again, or worse, frightened. Frightened, because the idea of a platonic relationship was one that would crush and demoralise him. He would not be able to accept or understand.

'I'll just tell you when to leave and you'll be gone?'

'Fine.'

It was one coffee and an hour later, perching opposite each other on the flanks of a lengthy sofa with William answering her questions of England and childhood and he returning with prompts and queries. These were generally about her predominant preoccupation, her future. 'I shall be a businesswoman and have a family, maybe even a large one.' Partly he had no choice but to let her talk, it was a well lubricated track of thought that she had to express, and he was aware enough that to listen attentively might endear him further to her. As she became increasingly animated and candid, he learnt all the more.

When she had exhausted herself, as he was nodding and wondering if he would remember all she had said, she yawned without opening her mouth.

He rose to his feet with a smile and stooped to kiss her, lingeringly, with his hands cupping her face. As soon as she ceased responding, long seconds later, he shunted backwards to the door, both of them grinning and whispering goodbyes.

As he burst through the heavy, spring loaded black door of her building, which slammed in a shudder behind him, he almost started to cry in shock at the frail happiness of it all. Was it love he was feeling or an intense infatuation? Whatever it was, it had imposed itself upon the inner core of who he was and who he would remain. The idea of even knowing an Arab woman, however affluent, westernised and beautiful, had been so unconsidered by his imagination as to be almost a social impossibility. Already a thin underlay of sadness began to strengthen because he was walking away from her. The wide spaces of time not with her had become grey, secondary voids of worried anticipation.

To fail with her would be agony, a torment looping endlessly in unrequited longing for years. It was not just desire, nor the need of her as a trophy. He had to feel that she loved him as he now loved her, irreversibly. The orange cyclops of a cab's light loomed closer. As William raised his arm he realised there were tears running on his face.

CHAPTER VIII

Julian Green was in a bored, listless and energetic mood as he perched the ample cloth of his suit's posterior on the edge of his new young secretary's desk. Being a backbench MP with pronounced areas of interest but no actual job meant that his working life was a series of stop-start leisure and intense, sometimes purposeful, activity. The morning had been empty so, in the absence of events or gossip to pick up as he had trawled Westminster's corridors, he had found himself behind his desk in Portcullis House, opening his own emails and sitting on the telephone to find someone conducive to lunch with. He had found no-one. He adjusted himself upon her desk to gain a better view of her and was about to speak, to attempt to shock her with some fresh avenue of lewd entertainment. Given that she had already learnt he was a notorious lech, whose wit had elements of unanswerable charm but mainly was of unembarrassed shamelessness, she was already ready with several stratagems to deflect. As soon as he intook breath and began an oleaginous smile, she interjected,

'A Caroline Cheshire called for you this morning.'

'Who's she?'

'She said, "A friend of Sam's".'

'Oh yes.' This was not, of itself, intriguing but

he had the reflexes of one who knew the conventions. 'I've met her a few times. Did she say what it was?' Maybe it was something he could ignore. That was his initial thought, which was then replaced by Sam's voice, its tone warmly affectionate for the eccentric Cosy. Irritating though it was, he had already learnt, with the compromises upon his natural selfishness that an expectant marriage flexed, not to ignore the surprisingly exacting trivia of his fiancé's friendships.

The secretary consulted a notepad, raising it to an unnatural height to block him from her view. 'Something about a William Clive.'

'Oh.' One of the emails that had occupied the past fifteen minutes was from his constituency agent, informing him, amongst other random organisational bleats, that Julian's latest recruit to the association had ignored reminders to collect his leaflet round from the office to pound the streets of the area's largest council estate. 'Get her on the line, will you Clemmie.'

He returned to his adjoining office to stand behind the desk, wait for the ring and frame his approach in charm.

'Hello Cosy, I'm delighted. But can't believe you rang me at work. Is it because of a newly discovered passion for politics?'

'Hello Julian. Goodness no. No, I'm ringing you to see if you know how I can get hold of him?'

She was being crisp and purposeful. The

assumption she made in not naming him demanded that she be taken seriously. It made him suspect that she feared the opposite.

'Oh, I see. I see. Don't you have his number?'

'Yes, but he is not returning my calls.' Her voice was unembarrassed and level.

'Well Cosy, my dear, doesn't that signify he may not want to, to, be in contact?'

'I knew you'd make that point. Mine is, so what if he doesn't? I deserve better and need to see him; even if it is just to make that point.'

'Cosy, I'm not sure if I feel that comfortable being involved.'

'Well you are involved. Sam suggested I give you a ring.'

'Oh. I see.' Actually he felt a little confused but was suddenly certain that he needed to appear helpful, if only to avoid domestic nagging.

'And I'd love to know if you know anything about him and this Muslim girl.'

'Cosy, I have got numbers for him but they are likely the same as the ones you have.'

'No doubt. Do you know where he lives?'

'Pimlico I think. But I've no address.'

'Where does he work?'

'I did have a business card but I gave it away, funnily enough.'

'Gave away? To who?'

'My constituency agent. I suppose I could find

out. No. Tell you what. Who. His sister, Frances. Sam is good chums with his sister. She'd know.'

'Yes, no doubt. Just spoken to Sam, who said that you'd met him recently because he'd rung you up asking about that Arab girl, the pretty one.'

'Yes. Yes, I know who, I know who. I know her father actually. Big conglomerate. He sells a lot of orange juice apparently. And cement mixers.'

'How interesting. Did you put him in contact with her?'

'No, they met at the party.'

'Yes, the same night as he met me.'

'Yes, I can see why you're upset but Cosy, these things happen. Doesn't life move on?'

'Men who are cads need confronting and to be taught a lesson.'

'You'll have your work cut out.'

'Pardon?'

'You'll…never mind. I agree with you.'

'Hmm.' She paused to think. There was a note in the tone of her mumble that suggested he had said something that derailed her. 'OK. So you don't know? OK.'

'You'll have to pester Sam again. She can speak to Frances Clive and find out for you.'

'Ok. Thanks Julian. Sorry to bother you.'

'No problem. Always fun to talk to you. Bye.'

Julian picked up the receiver again as soon as he had cradled it and dialled his fiancé's work number. He intended to berate her for setting the mad vixen on his scent and warn her of the return volley to come but her line was already engaged.

CHAPTER IX

Normally William would not have spent much time choosing clothes on a Saturday morning but he was up early, nervous, and had dressed and groomed with rare care. A fourth mirror-check prompted the ruffling of his hair. Polished brown shoes, white slacks, bespoke Savile Row blazer and Jermyn Street shirt, but without the cufflinks – the loose French cuffs a casual affectation. He breakfasted on a cigarette and then two apples, pacing between window and door. He drank tea and picked up a book, but only stared. The mirror beckoned again. He breathed on it, then sniffed, then breathed into his hand. It was difficult to judge but there was time to be safe so he mouthwashed and flossed until they ached. Eventually enough time had passed for him to run to his car.

He was a perfect five minutes early when he rang the bell of her flat. A few short moments kept him fidgeting before he had to ring a second time. There was then a long two minutes before his fingers frantically began to scroll down the list of numbers on his phone. The sight of her name and number reassured him but then her voice, soft from sleep and yet hoarse, rasped out from the intercom grill an abrupt, 'Hello?'

'Hi, it's me.' There was no recognition, it seemed, so he added, 'Are you ready?'

'Oh. No. I'm sure you're early.'

'May I come in?' He hated talking to a grilled box on a doorstep.

'No. I won't be long.' Jayda paused again as she readjusted her bathrobe. 'A long five minutes. Inshallah, as we say.'

Click. The phone was down. William shrugged to himself, exhaled out as if he had been holding his breath and then strode to his car and its parking meter, which now required feeding with a credit card to grasp a few expensive minutes' breathing space. Climbing in to his seat he stared at Jayda's door and drummed a variety of eager beats upon the wheel's brim until his fingers hurt. Women were always late and he must be patient, he told himself as a comforting generalisation, which he knew to be untrue. He just needed to calm himself.

Upstairs, she had turned from the entryphone by the door, a cow-heavy somnambulist, and padded down the short corridor to the bathroom. How could he be so preposterously early? Or even on time!

The glaringly-lit white tiled room had only one small window and so the shower's steam misted its space quickly, despite the subdued heavy clunking of a fan somewhere. The large nozzle sluiced through generous cascades, tickling, and then drenching her scalp and body. Jayda was not one for staring at her toes, even when groggy. She soaped herself, brushed and mouthwashed with speed, then repeatedly arched her hands across her temples and down her long hair. Once these ablutions were complete she turned up the heat so the water reddened her back and, folding her arms, rested her weight on one hip.

It was not merely annoying, this slavish, western obsession with punctuality, but surely impractical? They were slaves to their clocks! What if things were not conducive at the time, why bulldoze on anyway just because a time to do so had been mentioned? It was not conducive to rush today because it was a Saturday, a day of rest no matter what your culture, no matter what time had been suggested. She was certain she had said, 'in the morning, after 10.00' not, 'at 10.00.' She frowned and shifted her feet, the water running down her hips in waves and rivulets. This was a Saturday; to race time was therefore petty, stupid even.

She turned off the dial and the water vanished with a shudder through pipework. As she stepped out and began towelling her legs she thought of her father. How he would disapprove but how he would have probably done it himself, at William's age and with the opportunity. She turbaned her wet mane but did not actually dry it. As she walked around the apartment collecting clothes and toiletries for her bag the liberty of wearing only this headwear amused her. The feel of carpet between her toes, her small breasts slightly pendulous as she leant to pick up clothes, the freedom of air around her torso, cooling and drying and, above all, the feeling of damp hair all amused her. She shook her hair free and let the towel to the floor. A woman with damp hair in public is one who has just had sex, her mother would say. She laughed aloud. There was adventure in this. How long had she kept him waiting? Perhaps not long enough.

Thirty five minutes after he had returned to his car William had surrendered to the situation. The radio was on low with random dross and he was perusing a midweek broadsheet retrieved from the back seat, awkwardly spread out. Ten minutes before he was almost angry; pained that he had taken trouble to be keen whilst she dawdled. Was this meant to be an insult? Had she been out last night? They had spoken in the afternoon, confirming everything for today, but she had not mentioned going out. Was this some sort of deliberate distancing before anything more intimate began? He had to admit to himself, fingers drumming again frenetically, that he did not know. His worry, he managed to tell himself, was because he felt enormously excited and he knew enough from past clumsiness that too much of that can put the girl off.

The soft, much creased tan leather of his car helped to relax him only slightly with this self-knowledge. The car was his main indulgence and, as with many men, one which gave him huge inexpressible emotional comfort despite it merely being a machine, albeit a beautiful one. William spent the evening yesterday devoted to it, releasing it from under canvass in its Pimlico subterranean car park and driving it to a valeting garage, where ignorant immigrant hands had hoovered, washed, waxed and polished. It was a 1969 Bristol Blenheim: rare, old, to him uniquely sleek and he silently prayed that it would impress her.

The heavy black front door eventually clicked open and Jayda looked around until she saw him clumsily folding his paper. Her flat shoes then clipped upon the stone steps leading down from the stucco-fronted Georgian facade. She wore a friendly grin above a crisp blue blouse, her black hair wet and straight and her legs encased tightly in dark blue jeans, accentuating their length and the smile of her hips as she walked, an encapsulation of feminine confidence and vigour, towards him. A black handbag hung loose and long from a shoulder and this was balanced by the swinging of her opposite hand as it clutched a dark, blue suede holdall.

William's eyes were held, besotted, and she was almost to the car before he remembered to jump out and take her bag. He bumbled around her, opening her door. She liked that, his hasty awkwardness showed sincerity and meant that the issue of her timekeeping was irrelevant.

They settled into leather. He could not help but glance at his watch with a weak smile as he inserted the key.

'Nice car,' she muttered to the dashboard and William climaxed a small sense of emotional justice and a smile of relief escaped from him.

It was an inconsequential journey but Jayda could sense that she held more feminine power over him than before. She talked. He drove and sometimes contributed. He was not truly attentive to her words but her words were not attentive to any theme. Instead the words relaxed her as she observed his profile, liking the way his hair curled upon his collar and how the whiteness of his knuckles stressed his grip on the wheel and gearstick. He was tense. The day was his to conquer or fail with. As London at last released its tarmac into motorway she slipped off her shoes and placed her bare left foot upon the dashboard, occasionally rubbing its arch on the leather rim. He noticed this and at once felt excited and ashamed. The curve of her sole was a glimpse of the erotic and the natural tan of her skin forcefully occurred to him as he remembered his own fleshy whiteness.

She dozed a little during the motorway dullness, her hair obscuring her face as it had done before, in the taxi. He told himself that was a good thing, that she was relaxed enough with him to allow it.

He could feel apprehension suffuse within him as he rolled off the motorway a couple of hours later. His palms were clammy. They were nearing the destination and he realised that his attraction to her was fraying his nerves, increasing the likelihood of his making a stupid error. She had fallen silent and was regarding the grass landscape with its softly undulating fields, sheep, hedges and trees. He held his tongue but muttered a short prayer in his head. He often prayed a quick, trite, tri-theistic gabble of words under his breath for reassurance, often saying them aloud quietly to make them valid. 'Please help me Lord. Please strengthen me Lord. Please Lord, make this go well.' One thing that would not have escaped all five of them, William, Jayda and the Holy Trinity, was that he fervently desired her. It was that obviousness which made him nervous, he thought. As she sat beside him, her profile dreamily beautiful in a haze of rare late summer sun, he knew that he could love her, if not already did, but, given her impenetrable assuredness, any admission of that so soon would be a weakness too raw to expose.

He made a mistake, on his level, soon after but as with many perceived errors it did not matter. An incorrect turn as they drove into the city was not noticed since Jayda was immediately captivated by Bath. She knew two cities reasonably well: Amman and London. Her London was a vast mess of transport chaos, glass towers and white stucco fronts. Bath reminded her of Amman and also seemed unique. Sandstone-coloured buildings, modest in height, predominated and pleased the eye in both places. The day, though warm, began to be overcast with the pointless cloud that is prevalent throughout the English calendar and it occurred to her that the simple Georgian and Regency symmetries of this elegantly crowded place suited it in the same way that the flat roofs and clear lines of Amman's modern constructions suited its heat and flawless skies.

Jayda had spoken to him daily. She allowed him to eat dinner with her again, once Jamil had flown. She chose the café, met him there, drank smoothies, ate noodles and made sure that she paid whilst he visited the toilet to siphon away his beer. This had shocked him to a degree which amused her. 'No girl has ever paid for me before.' 'Well this one has and I am no ordinary woman!'

She liked him hugely, which surprised her. He filled her thoughts and had made concentration difficult, concentration on everything: lectures, research, revision, writing, shopping, conversation and sleep all becoming penetrated by thoughts of him. She could not sleep easily. What bothered her was the puzzle of what he wanted with her. Sex, obviously, but what else? If it were to be a relationship then he must assume that, she being Arab, Muslim and strong, would need to know there was a serious trajectory towards marriage. And marriage was a pool of unanswered complications. Perhaps, though, he did not assume any such thing. Perhaps he assumed a western style relationship: sex and friendship and maybe, eventually, marriage.

She was a long way from Amman, a place where her parents knew her every journey and every district held people who knew who she was. What she had was absolute freedom, for this window and for the first time, to make her own choice. She had not decided. William was, after all, so far apart from her likely future that there was a certain pointlessness to this. And he was a man, as clumsily thoughtless to a woman's irrational sensitivities as any other. He had already proved that he could easily inadvertently annoy her. She felt powerful enough for all of this, though, and quite prepared to do whatever she wanted, even if that meant not having sex with him.

His phone pulsated loud vibrations. He reached for it as quickly as he could, accidently answered it and then, fumbling, turned it off completely. Jayda did not seem to notice.

Slow traffic stopped and started beside offices, houses and shops; pedestrians ambled on cobbles and smokers crouched over their lit crutches, standing outside small grimy pubs. Small parks with busy mothers and crowded car showrooms clustered the route in. 'I like it,' she turned to announce. 'It is messy and charming at the same time.' She then returned her sight to her window, lapsing into comfortable silence. After enough time for her to begin to wonder how long this was to last, William, consulting scribbled directions as he quietly cursed the fact he had no sat-nav, turned the car into a long straight avenue flanked by ample villas. Slowing down to check the entrances, he turned into one, to the Abbey Hotel and raised his eyebrows in disappointment. Its facade was not imposing enough. He had originally wanted to try the grand hotel in the famous terrace but he could not remember its name and the credit card concierge had a room upgrade offer for here.

He gained a few points in his mind by taking control over the next few moments: the car door for her, passing keys and luggage to the porters, bearing himself tall, firm in voice and polite to the blonde, French receptionist, who might well have been pretty but for the fact his eyes were firmly attentive to Jayda.

Jayda noticed, of course, that the receptionist was attractive. Staff were never British in Britain, it seemed. She noticed the way William kept his gaze on her and how he stood aside for her to follow from the rear as the porter carried their bags upstairs and across corridors to their room. She watched, carefully not to be overt, to see how he handled the tip. The prattling Australian's eyes appreciated and his head bobbed in affirmative delight as William subtly shook his hand and slipped him a note. She liked that and could not help but smile warmly as the door closed. It boded well that her boyfriend knew how to tip.

It was suddenly there though, the bed. Fattened by a vast, plump, floral bedspread the wide, large bed dominated the room. It was actually a suite but the sitting room was unseen, beyond. It almost seemed comic, covered in cushions, hiding several pillows and with a headboard that climbed its imposing wooden plate one third of the way up the wall. She had half-wished for a four poster bed because she had not ever slept in one, but whatever type of bed this was, it represented the almost unavoidable unspoken coupling to take place, the base foundation of their visit there, of a journey seemingly composed half of sexual convention, half of curiosity. She stared at the bed, urging its floral chintz to melt away into desert clean linen, until she realised that her smile was hurting her.

William was regarding other aspects in a more decisive way, striding into the bathroom. 'Well, it is called the "Apple Down Suite", ' and out again, across and into the sitting room. 'Come here, Jay.' She did, noting that he had not shortened her name before. Like the first room, floral and pastel wallpaper predominated over cream carpet and dark furniture. The room had armchairs, television and a small dining table. It was, in all, an international hotelier's impression of an implausible English country house style. Given a couple of moments to appreciate its spaciousness Jayda decided that it was quite impressive after all. There was, though, the betraying nervousness in her face that William saw. He had thought this moment through in the car.

'Come on. We need lunch. And wine. I want to see what you think of this city.'

They were both a little nervous and hungry. A bistro pub, crowded but smokeless, with linen-topped tables and wood, helped with both. They ate. He talked, poured and gesticulated. She listened, sipped and sometimes smiled.

He was in danger of talking too much. The situation suddenly seemed artificial to him as if his own intentions might appear a sham. He was English and being male, pale, white and conventionally upper middle class, almost unavoidably too English. He felt clumsy and stupid and felt that there was nothing he could do to avoid this.

He had, of course, known other women. The point was that there had been too many of them. From the gracefully beautiful whilst selfish and sexless, to the overweight plain whilst kind and lustful, with all variations between; he had had them. He had even loved. Strong, inexpressibly frustrating unrequited desire that hardly seemed possible in a grown man had had a tidal force, unavoidable in its sweep and measurement, until the clichéd blandishments of a shocked woman who had wanted only friendship ebbed the force away. That desire had lingered, nurtured by obsession, for months until finally it settled upon a new fixation. This time the love had been returned and lasted through several seasons. The love then dissipated and the relationship continued for several weeks more. The woman had trusted him and he thought that he knew her. He told himself that he was self-aware enough to realise that this was not the love of his life but in fact, irritated by her gentle nagging and, essentially, bored, he ended it. It had been a messy ending. William was utterly taken by the pain he caused and surprised by the depths of pride and feeling he had roused in ending what seemed to him a dead-end relationship. On the same level that he pretended not to understand why she had felt so hurt, he knew also that he had behaved badly.

All of William's past girlfriends and most of the women he knew were English. In a somewhat thoughtless way he imagined that he wanted to settle down with someone of his background, a modern Sloane, but the truth was that they bored him. Even in workaday London with its crowded, unforgiving, money-orientated mix of nearly every race and class in the world, he assumed that the cultural gravity that defined him would keep him maritally within its bounds. Office, pub, club, church, urban village, restaurants of habit, parties of invitation, the annual sporting fixtures of a casually institutionalised social strata, all provided the pollen.

What confused and excited William was that Jayda did not come from this. She seemed westernised in a vaguely American way and, to his surprise, this did not annoy him. That, and the heady perfume of her overwhelmingly pulchritudinous grace. The sounds of her voice, the assured gaze of her eyes, the fluid poise and comfort with which she made even the smallest movements, all glided his senses into an uncritical transcendence of heightened dreamlike perception. This was, he suddenly realised as he poured second glasses of Condrieu for them both, completely daunting. Never before had he been hit so hard so swiftly by infatuation. This was dangerous. Even if she was lost to him, right now before it really began, he would be disturbed by memories of her for all his life. The thought paused him into silence and as the gap widened enough to disquiet him he hastened to continue with the first thing that came into his head.

'Why did you go out with that man?'

'Go out with? What man?'

'Julian Green. That conceited, bouncing, arrogant man.'

'Oh him. That wasn't much. What does conceited mean?'

'It means he's a wanker. Did you sleep with him?'

'Sleep with? Do you mean…'

'Fuck. I mean, did you fuck him?'

William, pleased with his daring, tried to find her eyes. She was looking at her plate.

'What's it to you?' Her head still bowed.

A waiter approached but William waved him away. He realised that he had gone too far and shocked her, spoken too quickly and ruptured her relaxed poise. But he did now need to know.

'I'm sorry.' It was mollifying but, through her silence, he was in control. 'How do you know him anyhow?'

She raised her fork and played with some fish. 'My father met him in Amman. He was part of some committee that came out to promote trade and my father met him and liked him, for some reason. I was going to London the next week and so Baba asked him to show me around Parliament. Big Ben and that. Well, I came here and not knowing many people I contacted him. He didn't show me Big Ben but he did show me the Commons and must have liked me because he wouldn't stop asking me out for dinner. I suppose I liked the attention. I did see him a lot when I first was here. He was fun, though preposterous. I even went to a church with him, to see how you Christians do it.'

She looked up and locked firmly onto his eyes.

'I did not fuck with him although he certainly wanted to. I am an old-fashioned girl from a conservative society. If I fuck together with someone I have to really like them.'

He nodded and looked away. She stared at him long enough to realise he had nothing more, then sighed and returned to her fish.

The streets were crowded with Saturday shoppers and browsing tourists as they meandered into the late afternoon. Whatever power the sun had had was diminished, revealing a premature autumnal chill, She used it to press close to him. With an eagerness to host but without knowing his way he was relaxed enough to indulge in an amateur street architectural lecture as they walked: abutments, dormers, fascias, fenestration, pediments and voussoirs. She was not fully attentive. She felt free to be happy and let him hold her hand when he reached out and grabbed it. Outside the Abbey she rested on his shoulder as he explained what a gargoyle was. He let a pause expand then quietly said, 'I'm really keen on you, you know.'

'I know.' She stared intently at the rooftops. 'I also

like the way you're jealous of Julian Green. Do you think his face should be up there, rainwater coming out of his mouth?'

'Of course,' he laughed.

'William, do you think you would come out to Amman to visit me and meet my family?'

'That's a certainty.'

When they returned to their suite Jayda, leaving William without word, immediately went to the bathroom and locked its door. The return cab ride had been silent and pensive for her but she had hidden her nerves behind closed eyes.

Staring at her mirrored image with half-inebriated honesty, she concluded that she was neither plain nor arrestingly attractive. She regarded her face vacantly, wondering if its appearance held any clues as to the knot in her stomach. Was now the time for this? Would another time be easier? At night she might feel too tired, or nervous. Why should she decide now? But no moment is worse than the moment realised that an opportunity has gone forever. What could shock this all too polite, too decent man and gain her an edge? Then it seemed natural to think of her father and to remember her honour. Not virtue, but honour in the sense of having pride, in determining the style of how confidently one went forward.

Suddenly she knew what to do and the certainty of a decision made clamped down on any rising nerves.

To be bold, surprising him, would allow her to control what was going to happen anyway into happening now.

He sat, shoeless and in shirtsleeves, bent forward upon the edge of the bed, its plumpness rising him without comfort as he waited for her, uncertain. When the door opened he gasped involuntarily in shock and with a little fear. Her skin was chestnut brown, smooth, warm and vibrant. Her breasts commanded attention, small, full, rounded, with nipples demandingly erect and the black pubic hair, wispy and unavoidable in its neat black triangle, competed. But her bare shoulders, as they commenced the sinuous lines that swept to her toes, gave her a vulnerability that belied the confidence in her face, her lips parted. Even as he wanted to move to her, he petrified.

She glided the few steps towards him, a curving loxodromic catwalk, yet naked, her hips unignorably at his crouched eye level.

'Well, kiss me before I change my mind.'

Half terrified in excitement, William, confused again, could only mutter, 'Are we going to?'

So rare, the moments in any life, when what is desired is there, offered but appearing too ethereal to grasp and too beautiful to despoil. At first he could only stare ahead of him to a warmth of thigh, enraptured. His breath was caught in an uncertain ache with the knowledge of all his hesitations, as if this rapture was concluding rapidly in a spiritual elevation of his senses. She reached out and stroked his cheek, a touch that raised his eyes to hers. His eyes spoke of amazement and admiration whilst, for the huge unforgettable expanse of seconds that they connected, hers glowed down, rich in confidence and hinting innocent trust. His hand somehow moved of itself slowly to gently cup her thigh, edging her toward him. He wanted to announce love but she leant down to his mouth with a crease of her belly and sink of her breasts that was fascinating to him in its perfect fluidity. She pushed him back, straddled him and kissed, continued kissing eagerly, randomly, on lips and eyes, cheek and neck, warm and ceaseless. His hesitations melted, one by one, into impulses.

Some few minutes later, enjoined, sweating, apprehensive and too alert to truly relax, he approached his climax to the point that he could not bear to delay it any more. He opened his eyes to check and memorise her. She was staring back, her eyes darkened to nearly black. Instinctively he blinked and blinked again but she was staring still and held her gaze, a spotlight searing into his soul demanding truth. Then, as her mouth escaped whimpers of ecstasy, he closed his eyes and exploded, deeply, with welcoming violence, until it was over.

They held each other silently for minutes. The cycle of male intimacy at first rapidly accelerated within William, instinctively urging him to retreat, to roll away, to walk around but some perception of the moment's uniqueness kept him there, their heat cocooned.

'I really like you, more than anyone' she whispered, as if it were a revelation. But that was too bland for her truth. She understood that she was now wounded by love for him so deep within her that she was branded by its imprint, not from his imposing but from her allowing it. Then she began to sob into his neck, confusing him as he realised she was crying and trying unsuccessfully to suppress the tears.

CHAPTER X

Cosy, unable to concentrate on stock-taking, abruptly chivvied her only browser out of the door and locked up early. She bicycled, helmetless, from her shop in Walton Street to the door of William's building in Eccleston Square, ringing his bell with a timid push of an outstretched finger. It was surprisingly loud but remained unanswered. As before, she rested on her bike opposite, by the square's garden railings, staying there some long minutes to catch her breath and stare comprehensively at all the windows, wondering which could be his. She had not actually expected him to answer, although she yearned for him to do so. At this uncertain crossover time of day he would most likely still be at work. The expedition was indulgent research.

Twenty minutes or so later she was home alone in a small, expensive white Georgian box in Chelsea's Limerston Street. Fear of theft made her keep the bicycle cluttering the narrow, scuffed hallway passage, behind three locks defending the door. She did not mind its angular intrusiveness because it felt virtuous to protect her bike as best she could as if it were a pet.

Dropping housekeys on the doormat underneath her feet she pottered, sighing, through the dimness of the hallway, past stairs and turning underneath them to descend into the deeper darkness of a basement kitchen. No part of the house was unfamiliar and with haphazard frugality she often neglected to turn on the lights. This time she did. The too-white light thrown out by recessed ceiling spotlights sagged her eyes with their brightness and yet left shadows in the corners. Moss green cupboard fittings over ochre black marble, spacious and largely unused, formed a design of hidden drawers and utility spaces, dark and heavily serious. It was a bachelor's kitchen, styled by the previous occupant, and her tidiest, least used room.

As she wavered timidly in the doorframe, her hand too hesitant to remove itself from the light switch, a wave of weakness caught her in a sudden radiance from the angry acids of her empty stomach. Having hardly eaten all day she needed to put some fuel in. Crossing the room in a self-pitying shuffle, she opened a large cupboard door to reveal the hidden white hum of an even larger fridge. There was not much inside, some cheese and chocolate. Once, soon after she had first moved in, she had done a large supermarket shop but it had been a strangely exhausting experience and most of the food had then been forgotten until its decomposition forced her to clear it out. Cosy had had a difficult relationship with food since her awkward teenage years, a self-inflicted torture that had nearly killed her. In a life embedded without fuss in comfort and privilege she had almost never been involved in the preparation of meals. At some point, at some unknown trigger, or perhaps as part of a slow sliding loss of confidence, normal enjoyment of food had dissolved from her. Life had become clouded with unclear, unarticulated suspicions and fears. Shadows were on the ceiling but only sensed, not seen. It was too far behind her now, whatever the beginning of it had been, for her to even try to recall or attempt to understand why, but over time eating became as dull and conformist an activity as any futile chore. As she had grown weaker her enjoyment of most other things were suspended but this was not depression. She was from far too much of a Jolly Hockey Sticks background for that, so life crept on as she flaked thinner, with no-one to save her from her thoughts. It had, perhaps, been fear of an unknown impending loss.

The Phase, as her family named it. Despite being an elfin slip of girlish charm Cosy had convinced herself, to justify this starvation, that losing weight would improve her stock of physical capital and some sort of beauty. She had dieted. Dieted with calorie-counting obsession. Restricting her intake was easy. She impressed herself in many ways with her self-control. When the weight flaked away she enjoyed the success of meeting measured goals and wanted to carry on. It was something, at last, she felt good at. As this inevitably brought unwanted criticism of her thinning appearance the pressure developed for her to eat. So she did. But she was very clever. She ate as she was nagged to do so by her parents and then puked it up later. The bile never got any easier to taste but she became adept at inducing the vomits. Head over loo, eyes tightly closed, fingers to the back of the throat and then wriggle them beyond what she could endure until her stomach lurched like a mechanical tidal wave.

She still found it easy not to eat. It was a familiar absence. The determination it needed used to be the defining characteristic she liked most, one she had decided to stick with since she suspected that to try and moderate her behaviour would be too difficult. But there had been a crisis of pain when, not two years earlier, she had fallen to less than seven stone, ending up chained to a hospital drip. Family had visited, awkwardly. Her parents, incongruous in tweed on an NHS ward, with tears and bafflement in their eyes and her brother, defensively haughty and embarrassed to silence, were as excruciating as the cardigan-tented, matronly counsellor who talked earnestly of protein drinks and wanted to know about her background. Cosy hated talking about her background. She disliked having to talk at all, much of the time. The memory of those accretions of embarrassment shocked her so much that nowadays, at least, she took care not to starve.

Soon after she had returned from hospital to the family home something else had clicked. While she had been away a full length mirror had been installed in her old room, most likely by her mother. It was one of those tall, thin antiques that tilted within its mahogany frame. Moving across the room one morning she caught sight of herself, dwarfed in favourite, now outsize pajamas. The image was hideous. How cruel of someone, she raged, to put a comic mirror there, to distort and warp her with the fairground imagery of a freak. But it was her, hollowed out like a concentration camp survivor. That was the first step, a realisation of the obvious, that she was killing herself and doing so in a manner so pathetic, so ugly and so absent of any style or romance that it horrified her. So she began to eat again or at least try to do so, joylessly and with the self-loathing that was still always present whenever she had to think about food.

To grow up in the corridors and crannies of a stately home, to roam its park and explore its woods, to spend entire summers in the stables or on horseback, to ride to hounds in its fields and live with a constant sense of being special, had all been numbed, slowly, over her childhood years as she realised she was not to inherit. She was not her younger brother: assured, chosen by birth, the viscount. Once she understood, it was a loss, not sudden but constant. Her irritation at not being a boy consumed her for a time, along with the sense of being condemned to a secondary role in her parents' eyes. She knew she was loved, in a distant English way, and felt it but she was not and could never be primus. It had just been her, before his arrival.

And when that empty harshness had receded its place was bubbled by other hopes, enquiries, careers and fancies; all shallow in the patience of execution, all frittered in impatience or abandoned for some fresh excitement. Cosy called herself a designer because it allowed her to zoom down new avenues of fancy; clothing, jewellery, furniture, curtains were all drawn, occasionally commissioned and sold. It was now all framed in a structure set up by her father, or rather his steward. She was a retailer. She had started out, to appease her father's wishes, as a hunt clothing outfitter, but with some of her handbags that had sold less well. Now she offered the full range of Sloane country clothing. There was just the one shop which she pottered about in, usually concentrating on anything but the task supposedly in hand. Not of the mind or patience to care much about the financials, or indeed the selling, she had great plans for a while to recruit a manager to ease the strain and have a stall at every countryside show worth an attendance but had not got round to it yet. Such management was beyond her.

She was not certain, really, how it all came together. Father had bought the lease on the shop but she presumed it was now hers. The house was hers but then she was not certain whether the money that had bought it was hers, father's or from some sort of trust, nor whether the money that supplemented her current account quarterly and seemed to increase every year was truly hers, whichever source it came from. All that sort of stuff was handled by the accountant in the estate office.

As she closed the fridge door Cosy realised she

needed to eat something to prevent herself from fainting but she was barely hungry. It seemed an eldritch evening, prematurely autumnal. Rain drizzled so lightly that its moisture seemed to suffuse from the ground, settling like a glistening slime blanket upon the pavement above her. If she did not eat, nausea would nag at her all night.

With little food in the kitchen she glanced at a rack holding a library of take-away menus but the effort of ringing up and then dealing with a delivery boy at her front door, well after these mild hunger pangs had passed, bored her to imprecise indecision. So, by default, it was corn flakes again. The main thing that she liked about meals now was her ability to control them. As she never ate breakfast but got whatever calories there are from coffee she congratulated herself for not being wasteful. Her mother had given her the cereal. Her mother, of course, always arrived with food and, with slight guilt, most of it was ignored.

It had been three weeks or so since she had last vomited. She had done that to dispel a bloated feeling upon returning from a dinner party. Chomping upon the cereal, she remembered something that she might actually want: a chocolate muffin, hidden in a cupboard five yards away. Whether she made herself puke tonight would depend on how she felt about herself if she indulged in that.

Cosy knew that she was warped but it did not bother her because she assumed that this enhanced her empathy and understanding of the world, especially its addictions. Not that she could change herself anyway. It seemed only luck that some greater addictive affliction had not lured her. Her childhood had been protective enough for her to associate drugs with a sense of working class squalor. She quite liked drink but drunkenness as a career vice seemed too close to her parents' habits to be offputting. Nicotine was only something for decadent parties, almost as a signal to herself that she was letting herself relax. Gambling appeared exciting but, if she was frank, she did not understand much of it and had always been embarrassed by money. Sex addiction was also something she had tried to think about objectively and decided, in a moment of strange clarity, that it was close to bulimia, with the same haunted, fatigued sense of being uncertain who you are supposed to be. There were the endless internal discomforts, too imprecise to be understood beyond the compelling desire to be accepted. Cosy certainly understood addictions but could not, despite such knowledge, help the way the wires connected her mind to her actions.

When she was too young to know how to use her beauty confidently she at least had it. Shyness had betrayed her though, as did not knowing, with any reassuring certainty, what she wanted from her youth. How was she meant to know? No relationship had lasted longer than a year. No boyfriend had proposed during the brief periods that she might, self-indulgently, have said yes. And now the anniversary of her fortieth year was on its belly, crawling toward her from the horizon whilst self-induced stress and the unavoidably destructive, petty habits of her lifestyle sapped her freshness.

Everything she consciously did was out of a need for recognition by the world; either that or for a search to find a man who accepted her and wanted to be with her. Unconsciously she kept herself frenetic, activity and physical tiredness pushing away any chance of introspection. The shop, her attention-seeking designs, her flinging herself at any man who looked as if he had enough patience to cope with her, were all part of the search. It was dawning on her that William was not interested. Nor was Harry, from the party the week before. Nor had the last man she had slept with, last month, whatever his name was. Actually, she did not have any special liking for sex. Whilst in the midst of it she lusted in its blissful otherness, insensate to everything else for its brief moments but she had no eagerness for it, of itself. She sought it because she felt compelled to use it, as part of her search.

She padded from the kitchen, muffin in hand, leaving the lights on behind her with the bowl unwashed in the sink and softly crept in the unlit gloom, as if in fear of disturbing someone, around each room of her house. The muffin crumbled in her mouth, unfresh. Her designer's creativity had exploded in an ill disciplined mess throughout the handful of rooms. Weak orange of street light haze outlined her way, gnawing upon the muffin as if it were an apple, its crumbs trailing. It was a comforting gloom. A cleaner came in for two full days a week but barely made an impact upon the cluttered comforts of a lifestyle given over completely to a searching self-expression: magazines, design sketches, unopened utility bills and suchlike, clothing, drapes, ribbons, sashes, colour charts and catalogues grew over her furniture. A home decorated by bombardments of energy and winds of absent mindedness.

Retrieving her handheld from the chaos inside her bag she scrolled to William's speeddial. Yet again it went to answerphone, as she expected it would. Although she did not have any words worked out, she knew the gist of what to say. She intended to be coquettish and playful, somehow maneuvering him into seeing her again. Once she had her audience in front of him she would challenge him. She would furrow her brow and say, 'Yes, I am a little unusual but I am different in brilliant ways. I am funny and endearing. I am pretty and like sex and I like you. I am a designer and have my own shop, purpose and focus. I have money enough and want a man brave enough to take me on. You?'

She sent him a text. 'C u for a drink 2morrow?'

She thought about checking his Facebook page again but knew it would reveal nothing new.

Kicking off her shoes somewhere downstairs, the carpet gave faint comfort to the aching arches of her soles as she rose upon the stairs, chin high to their familiar outlines, nested and shadowed beneath the orange grey stain of light that infused this central core. There were four rooms crowding around the landing: two bedrooms, a bathroom and a sort of cupboard-like mess that was the cleaner's domain.

She turned on the bathroom light and started drawing a bath, taking several moments to choose and pour in oils from a collection of small glass bottles perched behind the squeaking antique taps. She searched for and found a box of matches on her crowded medicine shelf and lit three perfumed candles. Her neighbouring bedroom's darkness was where she felt comfortable undressing, slumping clothes on the floor beside the unmade bed. William could be upon the bed looking up at her, his torso more chiseled, his manhood larger than was likely to be the reality. He might be leaning on an elbow, staring with tenderness and saying, 'I love you.'

'I love you too.'

'Now that you are naked, why don't you lie beside me?' said as a demand.

She moved closer, raised a knee to the linen but kept one foot on the ground.

'First you have to say how glad you are that I hunted you down in the beginning.'

'Again?'

'Every day for a long while. It's your punishment for ignoring me and the sensual bliss that I give you.'

'That was just a misunderstanding Cosy. I just didn't realise. You know that I couldn't be sorrier. Come now. I need you.'

She mounted the bed and straddled its centre. Leaning down she softly kissed William's forehead upon the pillow, withdrew to look into his reassuring eyes and then kissed him, passionately, on the lips. She whispered, 'Tell me you adore me.'

Her pelvis arched up and down, then ground into the mattress. She hugged the pillow and buried her face in its embracing cool softness, holding her breath as if to capture it, the reassuring, lustful, life-enhancing adoration. With a twist of her head to exhale and gasp intensely, the bath's cascading murmurs eventually penetrated the moment, ebbing it away, forcing her up and to their source.

She lay in the bath amongst the candles and their conflicting aromas and watched the cold whiteness of her skin quietly turn pink with the heat. Chin upon her chest she raised her forearms from the water to examine their fine cicatrices, first cut with decorative precision as criss-crossing diamonds with a razor months ago. She ran fingers along the slightly raised welts of each opposite arm; pale ridges above the rouge smoothness of her skin. Already they began to ache in anticipation. She reopened them, always with a clarifying gasp of pain, whenever she felt too numbed by life's rhythms to be properly alive, whenever she needed some sharpness to bring her back from the edge of whatever spiral she was peering into. Too often, but she had learnt not to cry. She had learnt to channel the empty disappointments that waved upon her, the sagging loneliness that eventually caught her attention, into something affirming and nicely strange, the cuts that focused and then relaxed her. She suspected that one day, when the ideas as to how to fight off the boredom that lay hidden behind everything had run out or when a culmination of failures eventually bludgeoned their way past the default cheerfulness of her upbringing, she would end it, sleepily, in this bath with her grandfather's old, cut-throat razor. But not now.

CHAPTER XI

Knowing that it was likely to be a lengthy lunch Jamil had tried to be productive that morning. Arriving on site before any workers or the construction manager, he made an inspection and was ready with questions as they turned up. It was no matter that he had not been there for two weeks, he told himself that his hour with the manager would be a spur to improved progress. Once done, he emailed the bank and insurer from his driver's seat that the development was on track, then telephoned the office accounts clerks as he drove in.

He liked to show himself around the departments. 'Management by Walking About' was one theory he had remembered reading about. Management books were usually the only sort he read, aware as he was that his father had no patience for business education. On occasion, he was deliberately seen wandering the office floors with such a book in hand, imagining that it presented him as a modernising force. The beginnings of this habit stemmed however from a lack of confidence. Not generally; he had been a captain in an elite tank unit and was a Talhoun, but he needed something to mix in the alloy to be able to face his father without being cowed by his bombast. It made him diligent, usually, even if he doubted his abilities.

Then there was coffee and a cigarette, emails and

the post. He noted with modest pride that his father had not even bothered to come in, staying at home to be with Jayda. She had arrived at the Queen Alia International Airport from London at midnight and Jamil made sure he was the one to collect her. It had been fine. Jayda did not seem to have any residual attitude from their London tension. She was talkative, given the hour.

Breakfast was at haphazard points in the mansion, if Jayda even bothered with it and with the demands of business, school and social life making a family dinner difficult, the tradition was that when a family member returned home there was a lunch gathering. Eid, the feast marking the end of Ramadan, had been the day before anyhow and they had been modest in celebration, waiting for Jayda.

Perhaps because Amman still felt itself to be on holiday the traffic's noon stiffening was worse than he had expected it to be. He was therefore later than intended, arriving home hungry and more in a rush to eat than making his entrance with any inflated sense of bustling importance.

It did not seem to matter. They had started the mezze without him. Jayda was answering a series of questions from her mother and the two youngest siblings, with their father silent but smiling at the head of the table. She was animated and happy.

'Now you are all here,' Jayda lowered her voice and with that tried to command everyone's attention with a break from the light rhythms of her talk.

'It's hardly my fault,' interjected Jamil, pouring himself water so as to be looking elsewhere rather than see what effect his interruption had. 'The traffic was appalling. I have been busy, keeping things together.'

'Thank you brother. Now, what I want to announce,' and she paused, partly nervous but also to ensure she had Jamil's attention. Her mother sat stiffly upright on the edge of her seat.

'And ask you something, by way of telling you that I have met someone. He's called William.'

'Oh,' said her mother. 'From the university?'

'No. From a drinks party.'

Jamil did not bother helping himself to any food. His father rumbled the obvious, 'William's name indicates that he's not Arabic.'

'He's an Englishman.' Without studying any reactions Jayda carried on, turning to her mother. 'He's lovely Umm. Handsome, intelligent, kind, funny.' Turning to her father, 'A gentleman. An English gentleman. You'll like him.'

'He sounds nice,' smiled her mother.

'Jayda has a boyfriend!' exclaimed Fiesel in a mocking sing-song.

'You mentioned something about asking?' Her father had uneaten meat on a fork.

'Well, yes. I'd like you all to meet him. Can I ask him to come out and stay? I think he could come next week.' She had calculated that if she asked quickly as a breezy announcement, during the first meal, then she would gain more ground than in any hand-wringing interview with either of her parents.

No-one replied to her so she continued, 'I've spoken about it to him of course. He very much wants to come and meet you all.' Determined to ignore their hesitations with cheerful excitement, she then beamed a smile.

Her mother spoke first, 'Jayda, you are serious, with this Englishman?'

'William. Yes Umm, that's why I want him to meet you.'

'Then of course he should come.' From a face of animated interest moments before Zena Talhoun had reduced to a visage of neutral concern.

'He would have to stay in a hotel,' her father muttered to his plate. 'It would not be seemly otherwise.'

'Of course, Baba.'

'How have you been doing your studies? I didn't send you to London for romance.'

'I didn't choose to go to London to look for that either Baba.' Jad looked up to regard her and she held his eye. 'And yes,' she continued, 'I have been very diligent.'

'Are you going to marry him?' asked Fiesel, innocent and curious.

Again Jayda felt the brief silence, heavy with their eyes.

'Well, Fiesel, I don't know. That's a very big thing.

Maybe though.'

Jamil scraped back his chair and made for the door, his lengthy strides reaching there before the meaning of it occurring to anyone.

'Jamil!' his father boomed. 'Where are you going?'

Jamil turned, his temper uncertain. 'I have a phone call to make.'

'Whatever it is, it can wait.' Jad gestured with an arm. 'Sit down. Your sister has returned. We eat together.'

Slowly Jamil returned to his place, unsure whether he had just been reprimanded and where the rising irritation he was trying to identify should be channelled. He became aware of conversation tentatively recommencing and its murmur simmering in a steady pattern. He was shocked of course, hesitant as to what his thoughts should be. It was not just Jayda's announcement of her boyfriend, that possibility had long been a fear of his and was therefore something he had imagined would happen, but his parents' reaction to it. His mother seemed to be cautiously approving and doing so without consulting his father, which was not how he thought their marriage should be structured or indeed how any marriage should be. Why was his father not raging? He had grumbled but seemed to be letting this pass in tacit approval, perhaps because, like him, he was stunned, although he suspected his father now weak, possibly confused, and indulging in a favouritism to Jayda that might countenance her escaping their influence into the sphere of some secular, poorer, London grime infected man.

'He's not Muslim?' Jamil found himself asking, not looking at anyone. Talk babbled on as before so he repeated himself, louder and raising his head to stare at his sister.

'Well, no, obviously not,' replied Jayda, having to do so once Jamil's question had punctured its own elliptical rupture, the silence it created ricocheting upon everyone's faces.

'You should not be playing around with him then, with anyone who is not Muslim. It is wrong. You must know that.' He kept his voice firm and level although he wanted to be shouting. He was thinking 'whore' and 'kafir' but knew that he must seem reasonable to get through to her.

'I can see anyone I like!' Jayda was riled. 'Your misogeny is absurd. Your religious views stupidly extreme. Grow up and live in the modern world Jamil. I'm not taking any instruction from you.'

'That's unnecessary Jayda!' Their father seemed suddenly alert, leaning on his elbows. 'Jamil has a point, my daughter. Have you fully considered what it might mean seeing, or even ending up marrying this Englishman?'

'I've considered it enough to realise that it's a serious thing. This is an important relationship. We're in love so, to some extent, we have no choice.' Jayda was addressing her father. Jamil thought this a snub to him. He interjected again. 'Think of your children. They should be born Muslim.'

Jayda waved her hand dismissively. 'I'm not marrying anyone yet. If I wanted to marry William then I would do so however the Islam thing was settled. Maybe he'd convert anyway. It's not something we've talked about.' She was acutely aware that they had not. They had not even declared love to each other but she knew it was there. Whatever she needed to say, she thought, to clear his way here.

'That seems sensible dear,' said Zena and with an instinctive default wish for harmony and gloss, she gestured for the maid to clear away the dishes and then asked Jamil how his building project was progressing.

CHAPTER XII

There was the usual autumnal gloom's drizzle, glistening in shallow pools. William minded his footwork between them from the Tube station into the grid of streets that make up Pimlico's smarter modern slums, the small Georgian houses converted into smaller, neighbour-noisy flats. She was gone now, returned home. Every idle thought for the past two weeks and now every waking moment was filled with Jayda. The sheer glow he burned when gloating over her beauty was most enjoyably time-consuming: her eyes, dark but fresh, her white smile, the waves of her hair and thin, vulnerable slenderness of her neck, her breasts, the oval flat warmth of her belly and curving miracles of her legs, moving her independently in this harsh uncaring city towards and alongside him. Behind his lustful and romantic wonderment was the predominant fascination that she had allowed him to penetrate the limitations of friendship so quickly and gloriously into romance and into the possibilities available to those who love.

He needed to tell her soon that he loved her. She had been ready to hear it in that hotel bedroom, lying naked and fringed with the uncertainties of a sad guilt from the imploded, overreaching confidence of their lovemaking, but his tongue had been frozen as soon as the wildness of their crescendo had ebbed away. Her weeping had surprised him, her tears dampening his neck as she quietly shuddered and clenched him tight, her nails digging in painfully. This had alarmed him but he held still. All women to him were, to some extent, incomprehensibly emotional. Moments earlier their purpose had been enjoined within a physical and emotional intensity that he had never before experienced. 'Have I hurt you?' he muttered to no reply. As the weeping diminished into an exhausted, close silence he realised that there had been no physical hurt but a wounding which witnessed him emotionally responsible.

He reached the porched steps of his building and, lost to these musings, keyed and slipped the big black door from his fingers behind him, its coiled slam shuddering an echo throughout the building. Turning into the corridor hallway, Cosy stood in front of him at the foot of the stairs. Bewildered, he stood still, his face revealing confusion, guilt and embarrassment. She smiled, fully observing his stunned, slack jawed silence.

It was, he thought within an instant, to his credit that he felt guilt. The miracle of Jayda had prompted a hopeful revision and shedding of many of his latent imperfections. He wanted to be a better person to be worthy of her and now, in front of an unexpected Cosy, he felt for a moment the awareness of some moral confusion. But the second thing he thought was, 'Oh

God, she's here. She must be a lunatic.'

Cosy bowed her head and took a step forward toward him, her eyes and crowsfeet smiling in the way she had rehearsed in the mirror. She was nervous but determined. She had not made herself think about the likely consequences of what she was doing with any rigour, its implementation most likely being the cathartic process she needed. Actually, that much she suspected, that this ambush was romantic suicide. Excitement had descended into disappointment when William ignored her calls, idle thoughts turned to fantasy and escalated into obsession and this had consumed her through to the moment when she was compelled to act. It was not just that her eating was erratic; it often was, but she was now waking in the early hours, unable to sleep or rest for longings of a life with William irritating her mind. Her work suffered. No creativity came to her blank foolscap sheets. Dust settled upon the shelves of her shop, except when disturbed by unengaged browsers. Most of all she knew she could not rest or meander onwards until she had settled her jilted pride and yearning emotions for William. It was a pattern she recognised, a head slamming into a boundary wall of unrequited longing until she could not charge anymore. It was a self-harming belief in the redeeming spirit of romanticism. If only she glowed enough passion, articulated the most poignant words or moulded herself into the best character then the quest would be resolved, her search over. Even though, when her man was captured, she had no thought as to how her foibles and flighty nature would engage in a relationship. The ensnarement was the goal. Her obsession was as much about the misery on her lonely journey as the unattained love itself. What prompted her to this new extreme with William, the lying in wait for his return, was her fear and expectation of failure because success would give her joy beyond her capacity to sustain or understand it and as a failed succubus she could literally lick her wounds, her bleeding forearms, and start again on someone else.

'Hello William,' she commenced in a low, soft voice.

He was too disconcerted to be able to reply immediately. An exasperated noise came out first and then, after an intake of air, 'Err, how did you get in here? I mean, how do you know where I live?'

'Yes, well, a "hello" would have been nice. Sam Fifoot told me you live here. She's good chums with your sister.'

'Oh.' He took another deep breath, determined to tackle this before a neighbour walked in on them. 'And so you're ambushing me?'

'Not really. I only popped by on the off chance. One of your neighbours came out and so I slipped in a moment ago. I was just about to write you a note.' This was not entirely true. She had been waiting for twenty minutes.

'Cosy, this isn't appropriate. I've been extremely busy of late and...'

'You had me and then you dumped me and you owe me an apology.' She did that well, in a good, firm voice with a low level sing-song intonation and a quizzical frown.

'Cosy,' but he then stopped, uncertain what to say. It was clear to both that he was hesitating out of guilt.

She let it pause and made sure that he found her eyes when they glanced back to her. 'You've been a naughty boy.' The lowered head again and half-step forward.

This was too much too quickly for William. From being lost in thoughts of Jayda, then this unwelcome ambush that seemed to alternate rapidly to what? A flirtation?

'Look Cosy, I'm sorry I haven't returned your calls but...' But what? There seemed nothing for it but to tell her about Jayda. He took an intake, his eyebrows raising, a precursor of sincerity.

Cosy spoke first. 'I think that you should take me upstairs, pour me some wine and tell me about it.'

'No!' That came out a little too forceful. He did not want to ignite an explosion so he continued rapidly and at a lower volume, 'It's just a bit freaky. I mean surprising. I mean I'm a bit surprised, by all this, by your waiting for me here.'

'Well, I believe that you owe me an apology and here,' she glanced around at the stairs and then the outside door, 'is not conducive to a sensible conversation.'

'Errm, no. Cosy, I don't feel comfortable with…'

'William, listen to me. I am here. Here for a reason. I have been ringing and texting you because I have something rather important to say to you.' This she stated at her most firm, loudest volume, a notch below a shout and yet with an exophthalmic stare which suddenly hinted a barely hidden, unhinged rage.

'Oh.' They stood apart, staring. William rapidly tried to assess where this would lead to but was confused by the sense of embarrassment from an unavoidable scene approaching. He knew that he had behaved badly toward her but was baffled to guess what it was she planned to announce. Cosy smiled, to reassure and because she felt that her last words had won her the first round.

'OK, OK. To the pub then,' he said heavily, his head nodding down and to his shoes. He turned abruptly and pounded to the door. She had envisaged the scene over a bottle of wine in his flat, or in the quiet corner of a plush hotel bar where a seemly quietude would assist her pleadings but the pub would have to do.

She pumped her legs to catch up with him to walk, astride but apart, to the end of the square and then across St. George's Road. A silence began which both noticed and, being uncomfortable, retreated into the typically English habit of small talk, inconsequential except for the fact that it took place.

'Grim weather, isn't it?' Cosy threw across as she skirted a puddle.

'But good for the roses,' he bounced back automatically and then wished he had ignored her.

As they entered a side street off the thoroughfare a group of lurking youngsters, bowed and hooded, appeared suddenly ahead of them from a mews archway. The moment of recognition that informed them this gang was constituted entirely of girls who moved, loudly and foul mouthed, saurian and yet permeably around them, also alerted them in confusion and shock. They seemed to be teenagers or younger and one tracksuited and bangled girl, barely thirteen, abruptly blocked their path aggressively.

'Got the time mister?'

William had to stop but he knew better than to glance at his watch. They were all so young that the situation seemed absurd. His first instinct was to hector them, to ask whether they should be doing homework back in their bedrooms but at the same time he could sense Cosy's fear, bristling beside him and it prevented him from speaking as he wondered how to reassure her.

'Got a nice watch to look at?'

'That bag looks pricey, lady.'

They were all around them. Someone's hand attempted to clutch at Cosy's handbag but she sprang it to her front and shunted herself to alongside William's shoulder. Immediate fear and instinct somehow forced him to act.

'Out of our way!'

The words came out as a croak. He snatched Cosy at her elbow and moved forward fast, smacking the obstructing girl's chest with the palm of his other hand and moving them through and on to the light of the pub, civilising the pavement a hundred yards ahead. Cackles of laughter trailed them. Once again he seemed to be retreating from unexpected street violence.

'Did ya see their faces? They was shit scared!'

'Yeah. We'll be waiting for yous when coming out!' rung after them as they shunted themselves inside, William first, and only just remembering to hold the swing door open for Cosy. She beamed gratefully and slid her arm beneath his, squeezing it against her as they hurried toward the bar. She began to gush, 'Oh, thank you. That was awful. They were, they were, so feral and you were so firm and I wouldn't have known what to…'

He extracted himself and turned his back on her to face the barmaid down the far end. Her words prattled on but despite noticing his discomfort at her praise she still felt the warm sensations of relief and attraction for William trickle through her, coupled with the need to stand as close to him as she could as protection from whoever may come in from the pavement and from the indifferent short looks clustering in from various corners of the half-filled saloon.

The next thing she realised was the barmaid

placing drinks on the dripmat upon the polished brass in front of them. William had ordered without her noticing and was now, without waiting for her, gulping his brown beer with chin raised and right eye slanted down toward her.

Her words trailed off and she wondered what it was that she had been saying. There was white wine in front of her and so she raised it to take a hesitant sip. Its thin acidity immediately coursed a waterfall's throw of bile into her unsettled stomach. She was a white wine girl normally but the scented plumpness of Premier Cru Classe was no preparation for pub Chardonnay.

'So Cosy, we are here now. What is it you want to say?'

Nothing about the incident outside nor about what she would have liked to drink. For a moment she wanted to chide him but then she remembered that she was the supplicant and this, possibly, was the crucial moment; yet she found herself starting to gabble as before.

'So, I mean, thank you. You're my hero.'

'Yes Cosy, whatever. Indeed. Now, what is it that you want to say?'

She calmed herself and shivered with the readjustment. Now was the moment for the second part.

'William, I want you.' She paused but he showed no expression. 'I want you because I know that you would be right for me. When a man makes love to a woman, whilst it may be easy for him to walk away, he changes her. She has emotional and chemical changes triggered within her and that means…'

'We didn't make love Cosy.'

Her face twitched with being set off course. 'Well, we did a bit. We kissed and you were really quite such a fantastic kisser that it had the same sort effect.'

William made a small involuntary noise from his throat that showed how unexpected this was. Sexual compliments to him were too few not to be noted without relish but his recollection of the reality of their rapid snogs, drunken and thoughtless, dissipated any fantasy.

'Anyway, I felt changed and I realised that you have been avoiding me and normally, of course, that would be that but throughout all of this, this…' she gestured with her hand, indicating the room but meaning everything in the world outside of it, 'I've not uncovered anyone who I truly wanted to attach with and be…'

'Cosy, you can't possibly…'

'Let me finish. I need to speak first. I know that this is unusual but, because I'm certain about you and I'm not a conventional girl anyhow, it is worth any amount of embarrassment and discomfort I may be feeling right now, tracking you down and placing myself here in front of you.'

She inhaled. She had been speaking rapidly. This allowed her to frame her face in exactly the way she had rehearsed to elicit sympathy for her troubled sincerity. William, instead of continuing to study his beer and the indentations in the brass bar top between them, now found her face to look at. Cosy noted his expressionless gaze with a glance but gave herself no time to study it further. She needed to unleash her crescendo.

'You are, I can tell, a gentleman and therefore someone who will behave with decency.'

William tried to imagine what it would be like to punch her on her curved little nose.

'You're handsome. I'm attracted to you and you have a patient, kind, intelligent face and that is exactly who and what I want in my life. I know that I could love you and I'm pretty sure that you could love me. I'm a catch. I'm one of the country's foremost, rising, eclectic designers, rooted in the countryside but based in London. I'm fun. I'm a bit flighty but that's why I need someone man enough to take me on and then I'll be the best friend, lover and, and...' she wanted to say 'mother'. It was the only word in her head but she knew that it was guaranteed to be offputting. 'You'll ever have.'

It took several seconds for William to reply and when he did he concentrated his sightline on her forehead, not her eyes. 'Cosy, that is very flattering for sure but also a bit scary. There being, you see, a disparity between our impressions.' He affected a smile, noticed her forehead's earnest frumpled lines and knew again that there was no happiness to be had for either of them from this conversation. She was about to speak but he intervened with, 'How do you know? How can you be so sure? You don't have any true idea of who or what I am. I could be a complete shit. You're only going on some infatuated, rose tinted first impression.'

'It only takes one sip to know if it's a good bottle of wine.'

'Yeah, I've heard that before but it doesn't hold true for relationships.'

'Are you saying that you have never felt overwhelmingly attracted to someone, on an emotional level, on first meeting them?'

'Well.' Even though her eyes were bulging again, as though she could hardly contain within her whatever intelligence she was hiding, William allowed himself his oft-repeated recollection of Jayda, of how she held herself as he had approached her with his first, clumsy words. Cosy sipped her drink, winced as she swallowed, and then waited for him. If she could not reach him with her words then to touch him might prove her yearning more poignantly than anything else she could think of. She placed her hand on this. He jumped as if shocked by a current.

'Don't!'

She looked as startled as he did, yet blinking and with a sudden reservoir of tears held back by a film of hope.

'Sorry,' he added. 'You jumped me.'

'Oh William, is there not any way for me to persuade you? You should take me for dinner a few times and make love to me a few times and see how it goes.'

'Cosy, stop it. There is someone else.' For the first time, within the slam of their own immediate silence, they heard murmurs of conversation from around the room. Someone came to the bar and ordered more drinks. She had advanced and retreated so much, so frequently, that, petrified by this bombshell of usurped rejection that she already knew about but dared to imagine might not exist, her feelings rose to anger. Silently she felt colour suffuse her face. William noted this as embarrassment so he tried to continue in a gentle manner.

'Someone who I met and was bowled over by, upon first meeting.'

She was about to erupt but wavered, still silent, uncertain how to start and he arrested her further by saying, 'Cosy, you should realise that, obviously, I am attracted to you. That is why what happened, happened. You are a very engaging and, and exciting person and if I had not met this other person then I would be falling for you.'

'When did you meet her, so soon after me?'

'Soon after.'

'You're a lying turd!'

'I'm sorry?' although he now understood that she knew.

'It's that Arab girl isn't it?'

He met her eye but did not reply, the moment's silence confirming.

'The pretty one I saw you talking to for half the night.'

He scrambled to assimilate her evident volatility and calculate whether a rebuttal would be plausibly deniable. Then he asked himself, why would he deny this? He had been on the verge of admitting it anyway but for her distress and an instinct to veil across some small muddying kindness, a white lie to ease her unhinged pain. He was undecided. She was reacting too rapidly.

'It doesn't matter whether it was her or anyone else. The fact is that there is someone else who's keen on me.'

'Who?'

'And who I'm keen on.'

'Who?'

'It doesn't matter who.'

'It matters to me. Hugely. Why are you denying that it's her?' Her voice had become very loud.

'Yes, it's her.'

Cosy exhaled and stared at him, not as if she had had her dream crushed but as if he were a despicable relation who had, nonetheless, to be forgiven.

'William, are you sure? You have to be very certain that she is worth it, over me. You're absolutely sure that you have a happy, viable long term future with this, this Muslim, Arab girl?' She paused long enough to punctuate but not to give him a reply. 'I'm being this forward because I have nothing to lose. I am confident in my own conviction that if you did choose me over her it would work. I am the girl for you William Clive. I'm loyal. I'm loving. I'm established in my own career and trajectory. And I have a huge gift — a vast untapped, swelling capacity for love and I could be giving it to you.'

'Cosy, I'm sorry. I'm truly very sorry that you feel this strongly but it wouldn't be right for me to see you whilst I'm in a relationship with Jayda.'

'Jayda? What a name! She sounds like a negro singer. Or something worthy and ethnic at any rate. Relationship? Are you sure? Has she told her people that she's "in a relationship" with you? Or would she be disappeared in an honour killing because of the shame of it? Do you honestly believe that they would allow her to have a future with you? They won't. Muslims don't function like that. Whatever level it's at, William, however much you are intoxicated by her beauty, different and exotic to you as she is, it won't last. It's doomed. She'll finish her studies and bugger off to be a housewife in Abu Dhabi or a doctor in Cairo or whatever. But the point is that she'll be engulfed by her culture and you, you liberal minded, young, professional, London Tory, won't be part of it.'

At this juncture William thought of the tiny advantage of doing what he did: raise his pint to his mouth and drink deeply, twice, to give him time to think and disengage from her diatribe. The essence was that he had those fears himself. His ignorance had led to improbable avenues of thought and, with other sexual and romantic possibilities crowding his priorities, he had failed so far to ascertain how far ahead he could love Jayda. She did not know herself, he suspected. All he desired was to continue loving her and if that meant, somehow, readjusting his life to do so in another country, with a different job, under a new religion even, then, he supposed, so be it. Those impulses were there but he had not had to think of them until now. He stared at the brass surface between them and felt the dull weight of having to reply, of having to be there at all, corrode his ability to fight back. He had to say something though.

'Well Cosy, I don't imagine that you are right about that. She comes from quite a western sort of Arab background.'

'Have you even thought about it?'

'Not specifically but...'

'Let me give you this thought. Maybe she's not as serious about you as you may want. Maybe you are her exciting western distraction – to be bade farewell to once her studies are over and she returns to the desert.'

'You are clearly a woman who speaks aloud what other people don't even think.' He said this as coldly as he could, even though, he wondered, whether she had a point. Maybe he was not yet instinctively familiar with all her characteristics and there was enough self doubt within him to fear whether he had truly penetrated Jayda. She may well prefer the adventure of a love affair with a besotted Englishman in London, which is what he had presented, rather than its essence, the quiddity of his personality as someone to love. He hardly loved himself, to do so would be a reflective narcissism alien to his unthinking masculinity, and therefore what elements he had that could be considered to be attractive to another were largely mysterious. The superficial was more concrete. Being superficial had, at least, allowed him to bed a few women in the past.

Cosy could not think what to say now. She had had her piece and a large part of her was convinced that she was unanswerably correct and yearned for some congratulation for her bravery, her forwardness, to compensate her for the regretful, sad, if only it were otherwise, rejection of her that she now expected to be confirmed by William. What she needed now was some hope, either that he would return to her to love her or that from this she could affirm that she was normal and capable of being loved by someone as a partner. She needed gentle words and understanding before she returned home to its comforting gloom and pain-deadening vodka. She made an exaggerated play of finishing her unpleasant drink. Without referring to her he turned away to say, 'Same again, please,' with a nod to the barmaid.

As he did so William cursed himself for the mistake

of prolonging the discourse by the reflex of another round. Whatever doubts she had stimulated he did not want to run through them with her. The drinks arrived. He could feel her eyes upon him as he paid and as she stood quietly next to him, slightly closer than before and more than was comfortable. Even though it was probably true that, had he not met Jayda, he would be attracted to the idea of being with Cosy. Like all bachelors he would devour whatever sex was freely offered to him from someone he found attractive and the idea of fraternising with aristocracy was an impulse in itself, but her earnestness was offputting. However forward, articulate and thought-provoking she was, however slim and lustful she appeared and however brave and aleatoric her approach in placing herself to appeal to him, far beyond the spirit of any reasonable woman, it did not need any more than this to confirm what Buff had warned him of: that she was tiresomely, exhaustingly, indulgently passionate. Something of this must have shown on his face as he turned to her. She was determined not to start the next rally but then, his face to her politely bored and demanding, needed a shock of some sort. So she snapped at him,

'Have you slept with her?'

'Now Cosy, I am most definitely not going to speak to you of that.'

'Have you?'

'Don't go there! It's not relevant. What is, is the fact that – very, very flattering as you have been and normally overwhelmingly tempting – I am in love with Jayda and therefore it is just not possible for me to…'

'In love? Don't be ridiculous. It's not plausible. You may have a crush on her but love is another thing. You're English and she's Arab. It's stupid. Stupid because it's not going to get anywhere.' It was a chemical reaction familiar to her. She could feel the loss now rapidly approaching, the falling into failure and the impacting defeat rising, eventually, to a despairing sense of aboulia, of pointlessness that made it all the harder to continue with the rhythms of life. To have to be stricken with it again, it was an involuntary choice from which she did not know how to turn away. She had a sense of losing control alongside the abyss, her heartbeat rising and a muddled anger frustrating the clarity she had composed with just moments before.

'You and this Arab must be too far apart. You must be lying. Lying! Telling me you love her so you have a get out.'

'Cosy, calm down.'

'It's just very convenient, isn't it? A hot flush of love that gives you the excuse to avoid me, someone you've had and bored of and want to avoid.'

'Not like that Cosy. You are losing proportion about all this. You and I met at a party and had a little snog. That's all. We didn't promise anything to each other. It was fun but was largely meaningless.'

She clutched the edge of the brass top, sticky to the

touch, with one hand whilst her other compressed the wine glass stem, rolling it so densely that she wished it would snap. A certain lightness in her head shifted and dislocated her as she began an emotional fall, an automatic pilot's descent into pain. She had one more plea.

'William, do you realise what you are giving up when you reject me? I'm the best prospect you'll probably ever have and, what's more, I'm genuine. I'm worth more than…'

'Oh God, I can't be bothered with this.' Descending his full pint firmly on the bar, he shuffled his hands to inside his overcoat and took the first footstep to the door.

'You're not leaving me here?'

'I didn't invite you into my life. I just kissed you for God's sake. Get over it.' He moved off.

'William!' as a shout, her bubble of vision just on him and the door beyond. He turned, morosely curious. She was tongue tied but had the overriding feminine instinct for the last word. She bounced the wine glass from her fingers to the cup of her hand and flung it. The wine splattered the chest of his overcoat and the glass bounced on the wooden floor, strangely intact. After a moment's silent sneering regard for her face, pink and contorted, William turned again and the cold, wet, outside darkness momentarily swallowed him from the swinging door.

The pub was silent, a dozen pairs of eyes staring. Cosy turned to William's beer and gulped half of it down without pause and then walked out, tears rivuleting down her face. She looked up and down the street but he was gone.

CHAPTER XIII

'Come on Jayda! I'm waiting.' Her brother's irritated voice rose from the stairwell as she changed her shoes for the second time. 'Let's go and pick up your boyfriend.' The last word Jamil mocked in a sing song tone. He could not decide whether he was to dislike or enjoy this chore, chaperoning his flustered sister again, her eagerness betraying the sort of needy vulnerability that he liked and deemed himself qualified to reassure. She had spent the last half hour buzzing around her room preparing herself whilst he had been meandering the downstairs rooms, car keys in hand.

Since she had returned home he had spent more time in the house, neglecting his tenant visits. He had declined accompanying his father to Kuwait yesterday so that he could be here for Jayda when her Englishman arrived. She served two purposes for him: she broke his solitude from feminine beauty and, again, made him reassess and confirm his yearning for a wife. His own efforts had been clumsy and lacked any redeeming element of embarrassed charm. Thankfully Jayda was now here to guide him and, he expected, find him someone appropriate from her own friends. Now though, her attentions were going to be diverted by her own romantic arrangements. In calm moments, trying to reason with himself, he still did not like it. A

Jordanian of her beauty should be reserved for a match with the very best, from an elite family, maybe even with one of the princes although all of the appropriate ones had already been captured. Her light should not be wasted and dimmed by a life in London with some Englishman who probably did not even revere his God, let alone be a Muslim. It was however, he could see, useless to state his prejudices to her. Yesterday, at coffee in The Blue Fig he had asked,

'Are you going to marry him?'

'I might do. It's not an impossibility.' She was stirring her cup again and looking away.

'There is no point in luring him here to taunt us all: me, mother, Fiesel, Fatima and especially Baba, who has to come to terms with his daughter being violated by a westerner, unless you are going to...' He could not bring himself to repeat it.

'Violated? You're being stupid.'

'I'm not really. This is a vast thing for us all to come to terms with.' He tried to catch her eye but she was distracted by something elsewhere, so he said it anyway. 'Have you slept with him?' That was it, the sense of a collective rape of them all and, perhaps, an especial insult upon him, mocking whatever residue there was of their previous childhood closeness. That and the subsidiary impact that the family, having failed to steer Jayda down avenues of acceptable choices, was losing her to her own strong willed adventurism.

'I might have. Or I might not and it is something

that I am never going to tell you.'

'You have then.'

'Why is it an important question for you?'

Jamil looked away. It was. Having been in Jordan all his life, at home and in barracks, he had had little opportunity. Suddenly prescient of this, confirming for her as it did the manifold instances of his tensions and social clumsiness, Jayda choose not to press the point. She supposed that, in Jordan, late virginity would not be uncommon but it was certainly not something she could discuss, or even acknowledge, with him.

He felt it too keenly. The absence of this experience grew an irritating void at the centre of his masculinity. To be a captain, a tank commander, to be adept with small arms and a fast driver, to own buildings and trading companies were all shadows on his ego because he had not, nearing 30, known sex. He was too pious to pay for it or even socialise with the purpose of it as an incidental possibility. But it was a rawness that returned to him every day, possibly every hour.

Jayda finally began to click her heels down the broad sweep of the stairs, the noise confident and slightly echoing upon the marble down into the hall but disguising her stomach's churn. She ignored his eye and busied to the door as her mother appeared from the kitchen. She wore a face of loving concern, tinged with the familiar regret of her own powerlessness. On this level her daughter did not need her. Jayda stopped, automatically glanced at the Koran on its shelf beside the door and adjusted the hitch of her jeans as if she stood before a mirror. Only Jamil spoke, mundane and irritated as always, 'You took too long painting yourself. Come on.'

The compound that housed the family's villa was high on an Abdoun hill and Jamil powered his saloon down through dark unnamed sidestreets to the main road below, shadowed by looming magnolia buildings which housed their neighbours' villas, offices and embassies. He drove energetically, fighting the wheel and gearstick to impose his will upon his chosen, familiar and largely empty route. It was a little past 11.00. The Heathrow flight came in at midnight. Once down the hill they crossed the angular modern bridge from one suburban heaped ridge to another and then on to the dual carriageway to the airport, flanked in urban orange light. Jayda, with habitual feminine pretence, affected an air of disapproval that Jamil had been impatient with her. This gave her the silence within which to relish her thoughts. The road swept into the continual progress of desert-colonising development on either side. Dim streetlamps overhung their grey-orange glow, a necklace of snaking dominance upon the land, blinding away the vast desert blackness beyond. As far as she could see though there were lights scattered across the land's interior. They faintly flickered like breathing campfires, revealing nothing from this distance but announcing their lonely pinpoints of progress where once, not long ago, there had been nothing but rock, shrubs and dust. To Jayda it had always seemed that they lived precipitously on the edge of civilisation, their brick and glass, oil and electric existence physically small against nature's immensities. Jordan, a small country within its boundaries, its people largely crowded within their urban huddles were thus seemingly vulnerable to the desert's vastness. There were isolated villages of course: their tribal loyalties fierce, but poor and always resentfully rooted now the nomadic ways had been recently lost to pre-history. And ancient it was, the history that had travelled, rootless, across those desert spaces. Sandaled armies of conquerors: Abyssinians, Egyptians, Canaanites, Greeks, Philistines, Nabateans, Romans, Crusaders, Turks and British. Ancient and modern refugees, holy men and merchants, their camel caravanserai trading food and water, silks and spices, slaves and finance throughout unrecorded history. This was a land which people travelled through, where oryx migrated to water holes, where rabbits and rats came out in the night's cool to search for grass and scraps largely free from predators and where the Hashemites had found some sort of settled destiny and made their home, exiled from the Hejaz and welcoming to all of the Levant's dispossessed. It was a land that had been traversed and conquered, argued over and exhausted, its water, deep and irreplaceable, being sapped away by the land's inhabitants faster than the drops of permeating rainfall, so little of it, replenish.

The car's headlamps and luminous dashboard made the outside a deeper dark but Jayda knew that, out there beyond its housing and irrigated fringes, the dirt sand, the rocks, shale and basalt, the fierce tufts of grass on copper-grey coloured sand, all rested in a lighter hue of cool blue light. Within the soul of every Jordanian, even within the core of those Palestinians who dream of returning to a homeland of dusty boxed villages and stony orchards, even amongst those urban children who lived in an air-conditioned, marble and concrete cocoon, the desert was the land that defined them because they were the ones who had chosen to make this land, a barren geo-political crossroads, their kingdom.

Jamil smoothed along the sparsely travelled route with his customary zeal. She had never, in this manner, done this journey before. Not at night, with a tightening welter of fear, happiness and yearning in her stomach, at the back of her throat and tingling nauseously at her extremities, preventing her from attempting speech. She realised that her brother, swollen sore with masculine pride, quietly disliking the task in hand of driving his sister to meet her foreign lover, would be wanting some kind of assurance from her that she was still rooted, emotionally, at home. She could not give it. She could not talk. This itself was unusual since she was typical of so many others in needing to cope with anxiety through repetitious chatter. The prospect of William's arrival was an emotional landmark too fragile to stain with thoughtless banter. It unnerved her.

She had already intrigued her mother earlier that day.

'He has lovely eyes, Umm. Green and yet kind. And he has a honeyed voice, rich like treacle. Those things and his smile make him handsome.'

'But are you sure?' she countered Jayda's too-overwhelming cheerfulness. 'An infatuated Englishman may be a pleasant thing but I think very different to what you are used to.'

'I have been four months in London.'

'And your life in Amman.'

But her mother was no matriarch. A home maker, mother and servant shuffler, she was no match for her daughter's will. And Jayda showed that she was happy and that silenced all misgivings, for now.

A mile or so out from the airport the carriageway became flanked by a palm tree avenue. A resting police car, its bored occupants smoking, was another signal of its approach. Dim grey arcs of light from concrete stalks avenued the immediate approach. They arrived, parked and ambled to the Arrivals Terminal, their silence now stretching. Jamil seemed to know where to go to and place himself so Jayda followed, a pace or two behind. It was a little past midnight, the darkness of the night heavy as a black velvet blanket touching the terminal's predominant glass, which flickered back the glow from low wattage strips, faintly iridescent from the mirrors behind them as they reflected the shuffling crowd beneath. A listings board cluttered its flaps to announce that the RJ flight from Heathrow had landed. A small crowd of relatives and waiting retainers ambled. Not long now.

She tried to imagine William as tired, excited, slightly dehydrated and apprehensively queuing, alone in a shuffling file of businessmen, untidy English tourists and bag-clutching Arab students. She imagined it all from above, viewed as if the terminal had lost its concrete dimpled roof and she was looking down. William, on the first floor and to the right of the entrance, now stating his purpose as a holiday and watching the stamp being slammed down. Herself and Jamil, down the stairs and escalators, through the carousels warehouse and brighter lights of the customs men and into the grey-green hall, where she sighed, rubbing her toes together in her flat shoes and trying to compose the rest of herself. Ten minutes passed, blunting her anticipation. Jamil began to pace and look about him, his extended neck rigidly oscillating upon a stiffened spine of parade ground seriousness.

William spilled out into the Arrivals Hall with the same sort of bewildered disorientation as if he had just come off a fairground ride; he saw her face shimmer from a tired vacuity into an explosive smile. They ran and when she reached him he dropped his suitcase, hugged his arms around her and span her around, planting as many kisses as he could wherever he could. The peals of her laughter and whiteness of smile paused only briefly her return kisses, quick and snapped. She put a palm to his chest and gently eased some space between them.

'We can't, shouldn't kiss,' she giggled. 'We're in public. My brother is here as well as, oh, there'll be somebody else here who knows my family.'

William then noticed Jamil, five yards behind and focused unblinkingly upon him. Since he looked alarming, with vertical lines furrowed above the eyes and cross lines dipping in concentrated intensity, William assumed that he was one of the sort of unhinged lingerers that meander into public spaces, so he began to look around him in an exaggerated manner but each one of the thinning crowd was greeting one other with comfortable purpose and strolling away. He was then conscious of Jayda introducing them, her voice clear and lilting and as he remembered it, and he turned again to face the Arab.

'You!' growled Jamil. He was angry.

'Err, hello. Have we?' William was computing as rapidly as he could but nothing surfaced.

Jayda gasped, confused. 'Have you two met before? Jamil?'

Had they? Jamil's nostrils were flared and he bubbled in an apoplectic silence. From kissing to confrontation within thirty minutes of landing, William's recollections were fogged by the improbable surprise of it all. Jamil looked as if he was about to fight, indeed his fists were clenched. From momentary excitement to doubt, Jayda's face began to puzzle.

Through teeth that seemed clamped shut Jamil replied to his sister, each word slowly stated and the wind around his eyeballs spiralling toward his sister's lover. 'Yes, we met near the antiques shops.' William glanced frantically from him to Jayda, trying to ascertain, his face blank with confusion. Jamil spelt it out. 'On that Sunday. In London.'

'Sunday,' muttered William as he looked at Jamil again and then remembered. He felt Jayda's wide bewilderment at his shoulder and sensed that he was at the edge of a dark hole of unknown depth. Happiness seemed so completely capricious and fragile.

Jamil was remembering most of all how he had felt that day, from the massively jarring shoulder pain and a thorax lump, adhesive at the back of his throat and then the walk past the insolent, mocking, silent crowd on the pub's small pavement. The crowd that had been sullenly stunned but judged he had been beaten, who he compelled himself to stroll past as slowly as he needed to do so to prove his composure and who had mocked him with their infidel sloth. And here he was, the English jerk who had, with typical western arrogance, expected him to move out of the way, standing by his little sister's shoulder as her lover. Both of them before him, as if they wanted his approval.

With the ease and friendliness that came natural to his character William decided that his best option was to gloss over this with bluster.

'Ah, yes. We bumped into each other.' He looked at Jayda to show his confidence. 'We accidently bumped shoulders in the street and,' he looked at Jamil who was stern but puzzled, his affected cheery tone having, he hoped, an effect, 'and, and, ahh, what was it?' He glanced the query at Jamil but gave him no chance to answer. 'Ah, yes, you asked me for directions to Sloane Square. So I told him. We spoke only for a few moments.'

The Englishman continued smiling his widest. 'Extraordinary. Amazing. That was the same weekend I met you Jayda. So, you're her brother?'

Jamil did not speak but had at least unclenched his fists. Jayda replied, 'He is.' She had been on the sideline of the last few seconds, usurped from the emotional centre of a night which she had assumed was entirely hers. 'You've met before? Wonderful,' she said with uncertain blankness. It might be good luck for them to have met before, perhaps might mollify Jamil's default prejudice against her involvement with an Englishman. Jamil looked at his sister's eager face and saw the worried, deluded freshness that he had many times crushed and many times calmed and assured. He fixed again upon William, 'Yes, it's true.' He raised a finger and stopped it, chest height, with a sudden judder. 'Just watch where you are going and don't bump me again.'

William tilted his head to the concrete canopy and burst out a laugh that seemed to reassure Jayda that it was alright to smile again.

'Jamil, take William's case. We'd best get on. It'll be nearly an hour's drive to the hotel.'

Jamil muttered something about his car and turned abruptly to pound his frame across the resonating tiles with his head dipped, leaving William to follow, bouncing the case upon his leg.

'Hotel?'

'We're not married. So, my love, it is more respectable, seeing as you are a westerner, that you stay in a hotel.'

William absorbed this for a couple of steps, long enough for Jayda to continue, 'But you'll see us every day and I'll try, I promise, to see you alone sometime.'

'I certainly hope so.'

'I know, I know, but please understand, habibi, that your being here at all is a big step.' She took his hand luggage and then held his hand as they strolled out, joined and balanced, but as soon as Jamil's car resonated its approach she let go. 'What was that tension with my brother William?'

'No idea. Seems strange doesn't it? I must be making a strong impression on your family.'

All three of them strolled into the hotel lobby through swing doors and then an airport-style security check. William still carried his bag. It was a spacious, tall, marble carpeted, five-star chain business hotel and William felt reassured from his apprehensions about his accommodation. Jayda stood beside him as he checked in, speeding the process along. Jamil paced in the background.

His surprise in London had been comprehensive when, walking together from a restaurant in search of a black cab, she had announced that she was returning to Amman that coming weekend. They had been three weeks in a loved-up bubble: phone calls, meals, making love, cinema, walks and the immense excitement of seemingly compatible closeness. At first he thought that she was leaving London for good and the shock of this frightened him, as if it all had been a vast joke on him for her amusement. He stumbled his next footstep and clutched on to her.

'Leaving for Amman? Leaving me? For how long?'

Even though he had not said it yet, Jayda knew from that moment's desperate concern in his face that he loved her and she, from then on, felt the same more powerfully than before. She thought she did before then but that was the instance when she could pinpoint her stomach rotate. So, not sure that she could survive a month without seeing him, she had asked him to visit.

A bellboy took his bag and ushered them obsequiously to a lift. Jamil strode in before the doors slid closed together and with only the muffled hum of the mechanism audible they elevated the floors. This lack of small talk seemed aggressive to William but his mind was still befuddled by the confusion imposed on him by Jamil. It was an improbability too unlikely to grasp with any clear sense of proportion, the appearance of the uncontrollably aggrieved and aggressive Arab man from the street as the brother of the woman he loved, the woman here in the lift who was smiling at him with happiness because he had flown through the night to see her, the first woman in his life who he had felt genuine and selfless love for. This man – what was his name? – was clearly wrestling with revulsion that he was here. How likely was it that he would tell Jayda his twisted version of their fight? They were close as siblings, perhaps, which is why he had driven her out to the airport or was that a compulsory chaperone thing? The only time that she had mentioned her brother was in London and with uncomplimentary irritation but whether she would take his side in their explanations of what happened was an uncertainty that dried his throat as the lift softly pinged to a halt. They followed the bellboy down a richly carpeted, bright, windowless corridor of dark wood doors to his room.

Once there he tipped and then all three were alone together. This was, for William, the strangest part yet. Jamil showed no eagerness to leave and was inarticulately frustrated, pacing the room around the bed. Jayda began to prattle about the next day's arrangements but William could hardly listen, his attention on Jamil. Whether she noticed this or whether she had it planned, she altered everything.

'OK Jamil, you can leave us for a while.'
'What?'

'Leave us to be alone. Go to the lobby, smoke a couple of cigarettes and play with your phone. I'll be down soon.'

'But Jayda, it's late. I should be taking you home.'

'Shoo!'

Jamil glared at both of them, awkwardly hesitant, and then left, leaving the door unclosed.

Jayda pressed her kisses upon him for a few moments. She broke off, trotted to close the door and then dived onto the bed in a smiling collapse. He kicked off his shoes and felt suddenly too tired to do more than crawl across beside her.

'Don't worry about my brother. I know that he's a bit intense but he's just a bit old-fashioned and wants to protect his little sister.'

'Jayda, I must tell you something.'

'OK.'

'It's a bit difficult for a man to say but I have to because my feelings leave me no choice. It's difficult enough to break through all the parameters that delineate us, between man and woman, brother and sister. Everyone, even between lovers.' He trailed off and she waited.

'I don't understand what you are talking about.'

'Neither do I. I'm sorry. There are just always barriers that have to be overcome at every stage and you have helped me overcome one of them.'

Where was he going with this? He could tell her about the street fight or he could declare love. She slid her hand down his arm and found his hand to hold and yet again he was reminded of the graceful fluidity of her movements. It settled something within him. There was no purpose in further hesitation although like many men, no matter how confident or articulate, it was an uncomfortable admission, like a weakness. Even now the culturally genetic emotional timidity of the English made him flummox any vestiges of polish.

'Jayda, I'm trying to say that I love you more than anything or anyone else and I won't love anything in my life as much as I love you now. I feel giddy and lost and vulnerable and yet I'm certain that if I love you like this that we can surmount anything together. I love you Jayda el Talhoun.' He lightly tapped a kiss on her forehead and felt tears squeeze into the edges of his closed eyes.

'William, William, so do I.'

CHAPTER XIV

The Chairman and Chief Executive of the Talhoun Group sat fiddling with his desk furniture, waiting alone in his bright, cool, spacious marble-floored office. The desk surface was largely free of paper, which was as he liked it. Paper was for middle managers and secretaries. He demanded documents and handed them back. A clutter-free desk showed a clearer mind, he told himself. Not that he read much paperwork at his desk, preferring the lengthy meeting table beyond the leather sofas at the far end of the room. To sit behind his desk was to telephone, whether to use his mobile or the landline, or to pass the time in thought, as he was doing now.

For a man who told himself that he had total self confidence, Jad Talhoun felt a little nervous although was too proud to recognise it as such. Jayda was possibly his favourite. The blotting pad needed realigning. She was certainly the prettiest. He put on his suit jacket and twitched the knot of his tie. Did she truly love this man? Was he to become his son by marriage? In Islam? He did not always wear a tie but this was not a moment to present oneself too casually. He stood up abruptly and went to the wall of glass that afforded him an eagle's gaze of the traffic and muffled but continual noises of Amman's fluid, messy, Third Circle. At least the boy was not American, but being British was not much better. We send our children to Washington and London, he mused, to learn politics, finance and a western cultural sheen but that does not mean we want them to become children of the west. What did he want from Jayda? Like any Jordanian, indeed any Arab, overall he wanted family, stability, prosperity and Allah. Those things and something useful for his business or social standing. But from Jayda he could not think that he wanted anything except he was certain that did not want to lose her; not so much to lose her to another man but to be placed beyond her cultural roots, away from her upbringing. As father observing daughter, surprised that the girl evolved into a woman, he knew some other man would eventually tarnish her beyond his influence. He would prefer her to choose an intelligent boy from a good West Amman family. Maybe things would come around that way in the end. Pedestrians and vehicles ambled far below in the prickling brightness. Car horns, muffled by glass, and the towers of rising heat came from somewhere unascertainable. His office was flooded with light, glaring off all glass and polish, its warmth neutered by the overwhelming chill purring out continually from the air conditioning. The achromatic brightness was so universal that, combined with the perspectives bought by the office's height, it radiated an overwhelming Olympian sheen that seemed to confront his paternal fears without affording any shadow for doubt or hesitation. His throat ached for coffee and a cigarette but he knew that they would be with him soon.

Does it last? This uncharitable mix of jealousy and resentment towards Jayda's first serious boyfriend. Serious enough to be lured here for his approval after days of her fretting and pining. How is a father meant to feel? He could remember the rage and disgust he had felt at that Syrian a year back but he knew how to behave. He was the quintessential modern Arab. He would be affable and try to make the boy feel uncomfortable through the words and deeds of excessive hospitality. This was his duty. Although he had only one line of thought his mind was messed with worries. He closed his eyes, felt the brightness of the sky intrude, and tried to readjust. He tried to make his worries become lines of enquiries but, as noise from the streets below and the quiet, rhythmic pumping of the air conditioning crowded his attempts at clarity he gave up and simply frowned. What now? To sit behind the desk or be pacing the marble? He stood beside his desk, uncertain, and then remained still, staring at its green leather surface. The past week had, so far, been busy and he had had no time to reflect. He enjoyed the fact that he had been away, until flying in from Abu Dhabi that morning. Zena, Jayda and even, in his ruminating way, Jamil, would have been nervous and incomplete because he had not been around when this British Boy arrived last night. Landing early, his driver had picked him up for home where he had spoken to

Zena, nodded at Jayda as she smiled and wrung her hands together, showered and then been driven here. Jamil was now bringing the suitor to him for his analysis.

A secretary padded in quietly, interrupting his thoughts. 'They are here,' she said softly from beneath her hood.

He jolted and instantly felt foolish for doing so. As if to compensate for having been surprised he barked to her, 'OK. Show them in. Bring coffee, water and cigarettes. Yella.' The girl went out and Jad Talhoun's eyes followed her to the door, resting his gaze there until it widened quickly as his boy, Jamil, dressed completely in black, walked through with a serious expression upon his face. Following him was the British Boy. There was a smile underneath a floppy fringe of hair, a striped blue shirt and white trousers.

'Marhaban! Welcome!' boomed Jad.

'Shalom al ekam,' replied William, clearly but hesitantly and outstretching his hand.

'Shalom, 'said Jad, chuckling to himself. 'Yes. Yes. Shalom indeed. Well done. Sit. Sit here.'

Jad went behind his partners' desk and the two young men reverberated the leather upon the tub chairs opposite as they sat.

'Your flight was good?'

'Yes, thank you. Thank you for asking.'

'Royal Jordanian are very comfortable, are they not? The hotel is to your standard?'

'Oh yes, very much so. Although I was woken by the sounds of prayer being broadcast outside.'

'Good. Prayer does a man good anyway. Well, welcome to Amman. The most elegant and cultured city in the Levant. Beirut has too many ugly buildings. Damascus is a troubled mess with, I admit, one or two fine buildings remaining and Cairo is sheer chaos. But Amman! Amman is clean, safe and beautiful.'

'And what about Jerusalem?' asked William cheerfully in an innocent tone. He had been enjoying these preliminaries but then immediately realised with his last words that he had somehow overreached himself. Jad dropped his beaming smile and growled slightly. Jamil's eyes bore upon him in silent incredulity. Arabs liked Jerusalem, didn't they? thought William.

'I don't know. I haven't been to East Jerusalem since 1967,' said Jad in a clear, slow, less effusive delivery. That moment taught all three of them William was ignorant. Ignorant in a way that stemmed from naivety rather than insensibility. To be British was supposed to mean knowledge of the region and, somehow, culpability for its history. William felt a couple of seconds pass in embarrassment and then in irritation at how this could be used against him. If he knew of something appropriate to say he had the confidence to say it but he did not want to apologise. It was too soon to sound weak and was this a test of some sort? He had been there only a few moments. Another second passed and William, with the reflex of every Englishman, was about to say 'sorry', along with something else that he had not thought of yet.

'Do you know what happened in 1967?' asked Jamil in a tone of voice that could be interpreted as either neutral or menacing above the creasing of leather from his jacket and armchair. Jamil had been mainly silent for most of the past hour. William had been in the lobby at the appointed time, breakfasted and alert. He was at first attentive to the throng, then bored, then mildly interested in the Jordan Times before Jamil had ambled in, minutes late, to perch on a lobby sofa and order coffee. For twenty minutes Jamil and William had sat opposite each other, making the barest of small talk. Jamil smoking and always looking away from him at the ever changing scene of passing people. He had expected at some appropriate junction when they were sitting there for Jamil to raise the matter of their bizarre street altercation, to settle it and defuse the rapidly multiplying grains of tension. However, the longer it continued without comment the more William felt that he could not initiate the subject, wary that he might be considered impolite or unsophisticated for doing so. It was a strange, prolonged encounter. Jamil had asked, 'How is your room?' and 'Did you sleep well?' without interest, but little else. William found that for the most part Jamil was intent on studying his face, languorously and with an undisguised veneer of contempt. They had driven here in silence.

'Well, err,' William glanced at their faces but,

flustered, could not read them in any way. What could he say when he suspected that the tide had suddenly ebbed him almost to the rocks?

'There was a war?'

'Yes there was but never mind! Do not worry!' exclaimed Jad with momentarily outstretched arms, suddenly regaining his original character. 'Here you will find that in Amman we are very modern – half western but fully Arab!' At that another secretary, a hijab-like black top hiding all of her but the most impassive of bare faces, pattered in with a gilt gold coloured tray upon which there were small coffee cups and tall glasses of water. There was also a carton of full strength Marlboro reds, which Jad stretched across for. The secretary placed the cups, tiny but steaming. Father and son lit up and leant back. William waited until the others reached forward and then sipped cautiously, tasting the extraordinarily strong yet sweet thick blackness trickle down inside him. Surprised at its strength he then gulped his water down and realised as he set the near empty glass down that he had no more to complement the rest of the coffee. The two Arabs observed him without comment, each making drifts of smoke to the ceiling where the air conditioning dispelled.

'So my young British friend,' spoke Jad as the nicotine soothed him, 'how long have you known my Jayda?'

William knew from its delivery that, although he

had to answer the question, his interrogator was more interested in the future than the past.

'About seven weeks, sir,' replied William. He could tell now that Jad was big hearted, open minded and yet would be quick to condemn and disapprove should cause be given. Jamil was smouldering barely-concealed menace opposite. Ahead of him was a verbal trail with potential chasms of mistakes on either side.

'And you met Jamil in London, but not with Jayda?' Jad fixed William with bright eyes under a quizzical forehead but William knew that he had to gain some face at this moment so he met his stare, not replying immediately. He surmised quickly that the father knew nothing, that Jamil had told neither him nor Jayda anything of their first meeting. He had been through this moment several times since last night. Was it a trap? As he declined the cigarette that Jad proffered he broke from the gaze and turned to Jamil, who was rolling a black cylindrical lighter between his fingers.

'Yes, I didn't remember at first but seeing you again last night,' he nodded to Jamil, who stared back unblinkingly, 'made me remember that we'd met in the street.'

'In a street?'

'Yes, yes,' hesitated William.

'I asked him for directions to Sloane Square. I remembered your face as soon as I saw it again,' muttered Jamil, his voice coming from the front of his mouth but sounding flat, slow and coiled. He was looking at his father.

Jad made a guttural noise that seemed vaguely approving. 'Still, what a coincidence! But a good coincidence, I think. It must be good for the future that the two of you have met before?'

Jad's eyebrows arched again as his eyes darted between them. Jamil nodded slowly and silently. William for the first time felt a small flush of bemused gratitude towards him. He decided to wear an expression of wry amusement, so as to cover various interpretations to whatever Jad Talhoun could mean. Some sort of mixture between a father's optimism and suspicion, along with a superstitious backdrop, was there, he assumed, in the old man's personality. Was he a blustering romantic? He could like that. In contrast his son seemed cruelly unemotional with, at a minimum, the intent to unsettle.

'Ah, anyway you arrived in Amman to meet all of us. What is it that you do William?'

'I am an insurance broker.'

'I also own an insurance broker business. It makes a little money at the moment. What is it you insure?'

'Well, I mainly specialise in marine and offshore structures. I don't do the policies. I place business for my clients in the Lloyds market in the City of London.'

'Hmm. Offshore structures?'

'Oil rigs and the like.'

'Ah. In Jordan we don't have many ships and we don't have any oil to speak of.'

In other words, thought William, you are assessing that I won't be much use to you in that area as a son-in-law.

'I will take you to that business before you leave.' Jad drew deeply upon his cigarette. 'I have several trading companies. I will tell you about all of them one day, maybe. In the family we have several buildings and developing prospects. Jamil looks after that side of things. He tells me that he is very good at making sure the tenants pay their rent. I say to him you don't have to be a business genius to collect rent. The work is getting the tenants in!' It was as if with every sentence Jad had to raise it to an exclamatory pitch. 'Now then,' he continued, his volume rebased down, 'do you shoot?'

'Err, yes. We have a little farm shoot at home.'

'What is it you shoot? Foxes?'

'Oh no!'

Jad erupted into a bubble of chuckles, clearly pleased with his joke. 'It would be more efficient, no? And less silly. If you shot the foxes instead of riding around in red tailcoats!'

'We lay down a few partridges and shoot those along with any stray pheasants that are around.'

'We have a place in the farmlands. Off the King's Highway. We grow fruits. It is a little place but I have been investing in it as my bolt hole retreat. I like to grow things, inshallah. It is not easy since we have such little water here. Anyway, we have a dam with a small pool there with some duck. Wild duck. I spend a fortune on feed for my manager to leave out for them. So, I like to shoot things as well! It is like your partridge shooting, I think?'

'A little.'

'We have some rabbits from the desert as well, which make good eating.'

Jamil muttered a phrase in Arabic. He sounded harsh and guttural. Jad nodded and continued,

'The army does some boar shooting on the north border. A couple of the princes. Jamil is invited to go there soon. Well…' Jad now spoke in Arabic to his son and sounded as if he were ordering someone's execution but looked, with beaming smile, all avuncular happiness.

'Jamil will take you to Umm Qwat and show you the ducks and farm. You can eat some of my oranges. He has shotguns and other guns that you can play with as well. Anyway, tonight you are to dine in my house.'

'Shukran. I look forward to it.'

'Yes, of course, but before then I would like to ask something of you.' Jad Talhoun had come to his point. He was seated, rigid, with his arms extended to rest upon closed fists atop the empty green leather. As the two pairs of Talhoun eyes bore into him, William noticed and felt somewhat alarmed by Jad's overnight stubble above his collar and tie. There were different conventions here to what he was used to.

'Yes sir?'

'So, I ask you, as man to man and as the father of

my daughter, what are your intentions towards Jayda?'

William could tell that the enquiry was coming from a few moments out but that had not made it any easier in knowing how to reply. By his own moral measurements he had behaved well towards Jayda, because he loved her and from that he knew that he could continue, with a purity of intent to try and keep her loved and happy wherever the journey travelled. Guilt rose in the rear of his throat though, stalling his answer. Cosy's lust, Cosy's madness, Cosy's breasts, all jumped down on his tongue.

'I, well sir, I don't know. Well, errm, I mean I do know but I don't know how to adequately put into words at this moment. I, err, want to reassure you that...'

But what did he want to reassure? This stumbling was the most ridiculously embarrassing thing. He felt his cheeks reddening. Was he meant to mention marriage? Would that be what was being searched for or would mention of it be an incendiary? He did not want to appear presumptuous of marriage, love or sex or seem too casual or sound as stupid as he was no doubt coming across. He found some words, earnest that they should work.

'I'd like to reassure you, Mr. Talhoun, of my...' He tried to put his face into an expression of sincerity, 'honesty and responsibility.' Whatever cultural differences there were, those two attributes would surely meet with approval. 'I have the most honourable intentions towards your daughter, sir.'

William felt that he had grasped the moment with that and turned it round. The fact that he actually meant it half surprised him, equal to the overall purity he felt towards Jayda.

Jad Talhoun narrowed his eyes and the let the tension rise a little with his silence as he stubbed out his cigarette until, with less of a smile than would have been truly hospitable, he muttered, 'Good,' and then, as if a joke that only he understood had been played out, erupted into a belly laugh. 'Honourable! Honourable is good. I shall keep you to that. Honesty and responsibility! I like that. Jayda said that I would like you because you are a "Jolly Decent Chap"!'

'I didn't realise that you'd like me because I was so amusing.' Being a caricature did not fit in with William's self-image, although it was actually somewhat similar, but being a cavalier gentleman in the environs of SW1 amongst his peers was in his eyes perceptibly different to being regarded as a Bertie Wooster by a bombastic Arabic paterfamilias. This, in a small way, he felt, tilted the advantage to him. He suffused an expectation of credit for even being there but whether from Jayda or her father he was not sure.

'Oh. No, no. I didn't mean it as that. Just that... anyway, Jayda was certain I would like you.' Jad picked up a biro and repeatedly clicked the nib back and forth. That was enough for now. He stood up, indicating the interview was over. 'Jamil is now to take you to Jayda for lunch and you will be seeing some of Amman this afternoon. You will enjoy it, I am sure.'

An hour and a bit after they had left Jad had fielded three telephone calls, browsed some share prices and currencies and summoned, interrogated and then dismissed an accounts clerk. Quiet at last, he found a spare moment to reflect again. He could not pinpoint why but he did not like the British Boy, even though he had seemed polite and earnest enough. It was not a racialist prejudice; a fresh-faced young English gentleman from Britain, seemingly steeped in manners and with a certain open sincerity, had much to commend him, but rather he did not like the idea of anyone loosening his daughter away from his influence. She was how old? 22 or 23 and old enough to marry – he had confronted this thought before, when the Syrian boyfriend had been sniffing around her. In an uneasy reconciliation with his love for her he had concluded that it was inevitable at some point she would no longer fill his hallways with the music of her laughing, lilting voice. The precious gifts of her beauty and confidence would grace another man's home. He loved his other womenfolk of course: Zena his wife and Fatima with her gauche, shy, schoolgirl innocence. But as the marriage years had disappeared behind him, thirty of them now, and all romance with Zena had dripped into the steady familiarity of domestic partnership, it was Jayda who had absorbed his admiration and indulgences. The arrival of all his children had seemed like miracles to him. Firstly Jamil, a honeymoon pregnancy, so soon after the nuptials as to be Allah's immediate blessing upon their union. Then Zena had had problems. Exhaustion had provided two year's reluctance to have more children and then, for reasons unknown, difficulties in conception and eventually, anxiously, two miscarriages. When Jayda came all the blessings of their life had seemed complete. A further eight years on the twins arrived at a time in Zena's life, in her 40s, when Jad would not have deemed it possible although he had always preferred to remain ignorant as to the possibilities of gynaecological medicine. The twins had been a double miracle, a surprise, yet all his children had fallen from heaven, it seemed, almost randomly, to grant him the ability to continue his line and his commercial empire.

Jayda wanted a role in that empire and the thought of that made him proud but hesitant. Even with all the distractions of childhood it would have been difficult for an offspring of his not to have imbued at least something of his commercial obsessions and a sense of family destiny. She was cleverer than Jamil, he knew that, and had more of the skills that were appropriate to the role of an owner-manager gifted to her by Allah than her brother. Were she a man she would be formidable but she was not and Jad needed the family line perpetuating. Whilst Jad would marry eventually and breed, inshallah, Jayda, with her beauty and intelligence, would certainly produce fine children if she married a man with the right name and background. But they would not carry his name. And Jad Talhoun instinctively knew that he did not want the husband to be this Englishman, from a godless country thousands of miles away. As soon as they had left the office he had picked up the telephone and left a message for an ally to return his call. Car horns blared again from far below, the distance blunting their earnestness but then his desk telephone suddenly jumped its stridency.

'Chairman? I have Mr. Julian Green for you.'

'Good. Put him through.'

'Jad? How are you chum?'

'Oh I'm good. It's just everyone else is the problem.'

'Ha, ha! Excellent, Jad. Now then, you rang earlier?'

'Yes, I wonder if you could help me. Recommend someone. I need to find a lawyer or an investigator or someone who can undertake some due diligence for me in London. Not on a company but an individual.'

'Hmm.'

'Jayda, whom you know, has returned home for Eid and has now presented an English boyfriend to me for my approval. He arrived last night. I want to confirm who and what he is without his realising.'

'Very wise Jad, though I must apologise for not keeping an eye on her to the extent that I even knew about a boyfriend to report about.'

'You must be busy, don't worry. Are you a minister yet?'

'Not quite. I'm now what they call a whip. It's a kind of parliamentary enforcement officer. So, who is Jayda's very lucky man?'

'A man called William Clive, an insurance broker.'

'Oh.'

'You know him?' Jad's worries would have multiplied beyond satiable concern had he been able to see or sense Julian Green's huge smile broaden wider still as the MP savoured the prospect of a delicious morsel of imminent intrigue and self-satisfying revenge.

'Yes. I think that I can save you some money, Jad. He's not good news I'm afraid. I know him in passing; shared friends and suchlike. Reputation for being a bit of a womaniser. Must say, I thought he was in a relationship with a friend of mine called Cosy Cheshire but I'm sorry to have to say that it wouldn't surprise me to learn he'd been cheating on her with your Jayda.'

Jad growled involuntarily and shifted the leather of his chair.

'Or cheated on Jayda with this Caroline, or someone else. Also, he's not a particularly reliable character. Says he'll do something and then doesn't follow through if it isn't convenient for him.'

'Hmm. He has just been in my office. He seemed sincere.'

'I'll give you a quick example. Not long ago he

volunteered to do some local political work for me in my constituency. Probably offered to do so to impress me. Anyway, he didn't turn up to do it and has given no explanation why. It may not seem very important and perhaps isn't but he has let several people down.'

'I see.'

'She's better off shot of him. Tell her to drop him and I'll find her some decent Englishman to meet when she's back here.'

'Well, thank you. Actually I think Zena and I will find someone for Jayda from now on. Mistakes are what happen to young people when they make their own choices.'

'Does she love him?' Julian tried to sound offhand. Jad paused, his rumblings properly considering her feelings for the first time. 'I suppose that she might, otherwise why would she bother bringing him to me? But then she is a woman, and a headstrong one, so I've no idea what she thinks it is she believes.'

'Do you imagine that she will give him up easily?'

'No, no she won't,' Jad sighed. He could visualise the tantrums. He could also write the script that his wife would use as she came to him, late at night, as a supplicant but nonetheless seeking to soften whatever stance he took. His wife, if convinced of Jayda's sincerity and innocence, would be irritatingly idealistic. 'But ultimately she needs my approval, especially if she wants to marry a foreigner and live in London.'

'You know Jad,' said Julian, enthused but serious

in tone and enjoying himself to a rare degree, 'marriage may well be on Jayda's mind but I guarantee you that it hasn't occurred to William Clive. He'll be more concerned with baser achievements at this stage.'

Jad felt dryness sore his throat like ineffective adhesive but whether this was from his last, unsatisfactory cigarette or the involuntary image shunted into his mind of Jayda and William together in ecstasy, he knew not and it rapidly irritated him that he was assessing that image. The embarrassment of the thought heated his face and with a panic of vulnerability he wondered, for a moment, whether he could ask Julian if he thought it possible, or likely, that they would have had sex. He opened his mouth to speak but there was nothing and he was, then, relieved at his hesitancy.

'And another thing to consider my friend, is that a man like he is will have had many women and therefore may well be a carrier of some nasty STDs.'

Jad was worldly enough to guess what an STD was and grunted, but the enthusiasm that had escaped from Julian's voice suddenly triggered an awareness that the MP might, somehow, dislike this British Boy beyond objective advice.

'So,' continued Julian, 'and I'm no expert, but those sort of infections can make pregnancies difficult, which is not something Jayda ought to risk.' He let a pause develop but, realising that Jad was now deliciously hesitant from the effects of his advice he could not resist a further indulgence. 'You know, we have a word for it. Miscengenation. It means "an inter-racial marriage". I'm no racist pal, you know that, but put it this way: I think that, regarding Jayda and William Clive, the "mis" would stand for "mistake".'

Jad's natural decisiveness could not choose what now to do or think regarding his daughter's relationship. The embarrassment of a conversation having gone too far pulsed through him. He had no immediate certainty of opinion and the strangeness of that confused him. There was no instantaneous assessment of one's own mood that can come with a heightened sense of drama. He was impatient to ruminate as to why.

'You might be right, Julian. Thank you for your time,' turning the handset and abruptly pressing the red button as quickly as his thick fingers would allow.

CHAPTER XV

It was dark but William could tell that the house was of mansion size, white, low level and yet stately in its roadside imposition. Its outside walled door, large, heavy, wooden and indented with metal studs swung inwards lightly, its heaviness creating an oiled gust, opening to an intimate outside courtyard rimmed by an open cloister. A small running fountain brimmed water over a low stone basin. Various greenery, lush even in the dim light, spilled over from tubs and pots too numerous to count and made any route through the courtyard's centre impossible. He could hear Jamil driving his car somewhere to the rear and Jayda paused at his shoulder to grasp and squeeze his hand but instead of meeting his eye as he turned to her she gazed skywards, to the roofline, with a look of sincerity on her face as if she were in prayer. Then she tugged him around by the right to the second door, opposite the first, smaller in size but still dark wood and framed by blue and white tiling with Arabic calligraphy swirling its concepts around the frame. She turned the latch and yellow light flooded them. He felt a sense of entering the examination hall. Releasing his hand she bounced ahead eagerly and he followed through into a large marble hallway, the stairwell gaping down into the space opposite them, its marble curves hugging the bare, clean wall. This space was largely empty, apart from a huge crystal chandelier but Jayda did not give him time to glance around because as soon as she acknowledged him close the door behind them she tapped her heels through to another hall off to the left.

This, an architectural surprise, seemed to be the centre of the house. Its octagonal or hexagonal shape, he did not have time to work out, rising tall and whitewashed to a small lattice-capped atrium. A centre table, rosewood and inlaid with Damascus pearl, held silverware and trinkets and the walls were plumped with cushions and divans from which, seemingly at once and from different sides, figures rose to meet them.

Jayda was kissing her father. Jamil was already present, rigid in a doorframe. The mother approached him, her appearance almost alarming but for his determination, sweaty in the palm of his hands, to make a good impression. She wore a white hijab, its clothed fringe covering all her forehead and seeming to flow down into her cotton blouse of the same colour, the arms thinly hugging to its delineation.

'Marhaban William. I'm Zeina Talhoun.'

'Tasharrafnaa Mrs Talhoun.' It raised a smile. She had enormous eyelashes, it seemed, underneath the headrobe.

'Very good! Kayf haalak?'

'Errm?'

'Never mind. Come. These are Fatima and Fiesel.'

'Hi.' He shook hands with them, both adolescent but curious. William could see questions in their eyes but had no reassurance or answers beyond the firmness of his handshake and even then, when they had separated and he stood before them, in the short moments that followed when they all wondered what next to say, he feared that his greeting and its enthusiasm had been too mockably American in style.

Jad, who had been whispering with Jayda, now came over to boom his welcome. He was dressed as before but now tieless, the whispers of his last cigarette trailing into the atrium from its half-stub in an ashtray behind him.

'So, William, marhaban. What's your poison?'

'Oh, thank you Mr. Talhoun. Err, what do you have?'

'I have everything.'

'A gin and ginger?'

Jad Talhoun's grin sank into annoyance. 'Gin I have. Ginger? Root of ginger?'

'Err no.' He had not meant to be awkward. 'Ginger ale.'

'No.' Then, not to appear flustered by the young stranger to whom he was obliged to be hospitable, 'I will get you gin and tonic.' This was as a statement, not a question. He turned away to a corner drinks tray.

'So William,' said Mrs Talhoun now seated, hands expectantly clasped upon her knees, 'where did Jamil and Jayda take you today?'

'We lunched with some of their friends in a restaurant, the name of which I don't remember but it was very nice and then Jamil took me to see the amphitheatre and its museum.'

The afternoon had been unusual for William but, with his optimism and inquisitiveness, not too uncomfortable. There had been a crowd for lunch in a restaurant on the top floor of a hotel that looked like a steel and glass office block. The women all had long dark hair, blouses, drainpipe jeans and flat shoes. The men, with short hair or cropped heads all had some sort of facial hair or stubble and looked slightly sinister, like hitmen or, at least, men capable of sudden violence. He had been introduced as 'the boyfriend'. Everyone was very friendly to him. Most of them smoked. The conversations had been of local gossip and trivia but he could sense that all were assessing him and, alongside, observing Jayda. He could not remember any of their names.

At some signal which William did not notice it was apparent that dinner was to be served and he followed through a doorway. The dining room was dominated by its table, seemingly antique European with late-empire curved chairs and elegant silver candelabra. He was ushered by Mrs. Talhoun to a seat to her left and facing Jayda. Jad collapsed himself into the throne-like chair at the opposite end facing the door and launched immediately into his favourite dining room anecdote. Opposite him, above the door through which they had entered, was an enormous swordfish, improbably blue and silver, a taxidermist's showpiece.

'Yes, William, see that fish? I was vacationing in Florida. It took me 38 minutes to reel that beast in and was a monumental tug of war. Better than Hemingway because it was real life.' Jad's voice trailed into a continuing background whilst the cook, hijab-covered like Mrs Talhoun, appeared to serve a starter dish which William could not identify, seemingly of pasta, mince and yoghurt. Jayda and her mother listened to Jad with bored attention. Jamil played with his email handset and the other two, with respectfully low voices, conducted their own conversation in Arabic, with amused glances at William. He noticed this and, between smiling at Jad, the rest of the room. It was impressively prosperous, painted a yellow which contrasted with the Damascus pearl-inlaid sideboards. Oil paintings in heavy gold gilt frames, probably by romanticising 19th century Europeans, of desert Arabs praying on mats at dawn or dusk, of a trading caravan of camels and people stretched in front of a mountainous background and of charging, wild, white-robed bedouin cavalry, all leaned heavily over the table.

'I had deep blood from the cuts on my hands which stung like hell from the salt water. It took weeks for my fingers to heal. They continually re-opened,' finished Jad, flourishing his hands ahead of him.

'Do you like fishing sir?' prompted William, perhaps a little too obviously to seem sincere.

'Yes,' snapped Jad and then shifted into a crouched silence. William had not meant his tone and scrambled for a conversation change. He wished there was more drink to hand but all the table offered was a water jug. He took a last gulp of his gin and tonic, upending it.

'So, Mrs Talhoun,' he announced his new tact brightly, 'tell me what Jayda was like as a little girl.'

'She was a most dutiful daughter. We are waiting to see how she will turn out,' replied her mother glancing at Jayda, and then, without missing a beat, 'William, what family do you have?'

From her words and manner he understood what was needed from him. He launched, smiled throughout and kept his voice lively, as if amused, though varied its modulation when appropriate. He started with home and childhood, parents and sister, boarding schools, sports, hobbies, university and then how he had stumbled into his present job and unplanned career. He spoke quickly when he had to mention his parent's divorce and subsequent second marriages. Zena listened and, between eyeing her two youngest who mumbled amongst themselves, asked attentive questions. Jayda knew most of the story already and watched her brooding father and still silent brother as they listened.

The starter was cleared and the cook and a maid brought in a dozen or so small dishes of meats, vegetables, breads, olives, hummus and various other mezze. His monologue over, William was able to relax a little as the family's outstretched arms descended from their respectful listening and into a free-for-all banquet. It was stilted though. At the core of the moment the family were reserved or hesitant because of the presence of their foreign guest.

After a few minutes of this, as such talk as there was subsided, Jayda prodded the conversation along, prompting William with questions that he could answer well. What do you think of Amman? The weather is rather different here to London, is it not? After two or three stale and obvious question and answers from the double act trying to impress their audience, Jad lost patience.

'Do you know Julian Green, William?' He used the Christian name frequently, as if to continually remind himself of his guest's name.

'Yes sir, I do.'

'What do you think of him?'

'Well, he's clever and charming but he's a politician. So one has to be wary of everything that he says and question the true motivation of every action he takes. Like any politician I suppose.'

'Julian Green is a good friend of mine.'

'Oh. You no doubt know him better than I do, so I apologise if I'm out of turn but I haven't seen a truly sincere side to him yet.'

'Hmm.'

'Baba, he's creepy,' interjected Jayda, eager to make a point. 'I realise that you asked him to look out for me when I first got to London but he has wandering hands.'

'He wonders about what?' frowned Jad, the tempo of his demeanour arrested.

'Wandering hands. He's loud and smarmy and he touched me inappropriately.' Her chin was raised defiantly to her father and the rest of the table suspended its eating. 'He was an inappropriate guardian Baba, considering that he is living with and supposed to be marrying his girlfriend.'

Jad did not reply. He had half-intended to, somehow, raise or allude to Julian Green's reservations about William but this new information made him pause. There was the sound of cutlery upon plates.

Jamil spoke for the first time, 'How did you both meet?'

'Julian Green,' said Jayda flatly but her eyes were alive to the irony of it. 'He introduced us at a party he held, so at least I can thank him for something. I don't understand why you like him Baba. He's so boisterous, unpleasant and over-opinionated.'

Jad kept his thoughts within him but they included the awareness that being outgoing and confident was what he had liked about Green. The possibility that he had entrusted his daughter to a philanderer though, stunned him into uncertainty. He wanted to ask for details but felt it embarrassingly impossible. William could not help but remember Cosy and the unprotected, unspecified and most likely unresolved danger that perhaps she was still. Jamil smarted at the slight by his sister in that, although she answered his only contribution thus far to the discourse, her reply was directed to their father.

Jamil was feeling susceptible to any slight. Whilst he had quite enjoyed how the morning had gone, taking some pride in William's wide eyes as he wove in and out of the traffic across Amman, which he interpreted as silent admiration or approval for the bustling urban backdrop and he certainly enjoyed watching William's various inadvertent discomforts throughout the day, especially as the submissive suitor in front of his father, mostly though he had been irritated. He had felt out of place at the lunch. Everyone's attention had been on the two lovers. Whilst the other men had nodded acknowledgement of his natural seniority as they arrived he was annoyed with Jayda, bubbled in her love, for not introducing him with sufficient attention to her girlfriends. They had seemed not to notice him and he, as a result, barely said a word to any of them. Another opportunity to forward his own future had therefore been lost. He was hardly in a better mood when he took William away from Jayda, afterwards, to the Roman amphitheatre. Taciturn, smoking, smouldering, hating the way the Englishman's absurdly white face and neck flushed in the heat, he had left him to his own inquisitiveness and an old, toothless, money-desperate guide. He removed himself to halfway up on one of the worn stone benches, stared at the washing lines of the small perpendicular block houses on the opposite hillside and wondered at how powerless he felt.

William caught Zena's eye at around this point and asked if he could wash his hands. The matriarch blinked her eyes as if he had said something obscene. He rephrased, asking for the loo. She smiled and pressed a button on a handset beside her. The maid appeared from the kitchen and, after some brief Arabic instruction, gestured him up and to follow by withdrawing the back of his chair and flowing her arm in an impatient wave.

It was off the first hallway. Once alone he stood astride the ceramic and noticed his urine was mustard yellow. The heat had dehydrated him but he had more of a yearning for liquor than water. He then stood in front of the wash basin and clutched the rim of its sides watching water cascade down from the taps and pooling. He was still nervous and unsteady. This was, just possibly, one of the most important days of his life and it was unresolved. The girl loved him and would say yes. Whether he had the courage to ask it partly depended on whether the family would tolerate him and whether he could tolerate them. He felt jittery. For an absurd moment he considered masturbating. Was it Talleyrand who recommended to his clerks that they did so before they came to work, so as to relax and clear their minds? A small headache leadened his forehead, its appearance shaming that impulse away.

He squeaked the taps closed and bent to splatter

his face, the water noisy between his fingers. Slowly he raised his face to the mirror and, despite apprehension to the contrary, was reassured by what he saw. His skin had pinked lightly in the sun, camouflaging the eye bags of weary sin and jet lag, and his visage still gave out an impression of boyish honesty and trust. He smiled at himself to confirm this, shameless in his vanity, but then a darkness in his psyche shifted and self lubricated, stirring itself from exile. He shivered. It was something, passing, within his eyes and behind him. Whether this was from within him or a malevolent presence headaching the backdrop fleetingly he could not tell but he felt, suddenly, faintly nauseous. Then it left. An invisible darkness had floated by like the shadow of a bird of prey, observing, its movement signalling a code he could not understand, waiting patiently to strike.

He took some deep breaths, grinned unconvincingly at himself and walked out. The maid was there waiting for him, as expressionless as a sentinel. Back in the dining room he took his seat with an affected smile, accepted a plate of small, honeyed pastries and listened patiently as his host related a story, told to impress his foreign guest, about when and why he had last met the king.

When the family eventually rose from the table Jad gestured Jayda toward him at the far end of the room. He took her by the elbow and whispered into her ear with a fluid bob of his head as they followed the others out, 'I am sorry. I had no idea.' She tried to turn to meet his eyes, to reassure him, but he kept his head bouncing above his feet and accelerated away from her. She wanted to say that she was quite capable of looking after herself now but this admission from her father, short, unexpected and vulnerable, clammed her.

They took coffee in the atrium hallway. William thought about requesting tea but then feared to be a nuisance, so he sipped another small cup of the thick, dark, sweet liquid, so strong that the base of the cup held a mud base of sludge. The caffeine seemed to animate the family into a general discourse, more relaxed than earlier, of trivia and teasing. William placed himself, at last, next to Jayda. He made sure their knees touched but that was as far as he dared mark his territory. Lost to distraction amongst the knowing gossip that he could not contribute to, he maintained a polite smile to the room and raised his knee, slowly rubbing it against hers. He adjusted and managed to rub the top of his foot against the back of her ankle. A few moments of this covert intimacy electrified her. She stood up suddenly, interrupting a rare relaxed story from Jamil and grasped William's hand, tugging him to his feet.

'I shall take William to his hotel now. Baba, can I take the Mercedes?'

'I will drive you.' Jamil was also on his feet, his story forgotten.

'No need. I'm sure I can find my way home safely.'

'But it is more appropriate that I take you.'

'No Jamil!' The slam of silence that billowed open forced them to meet each other's eyes. Her exclamation was too loud for polite harmony. It had been much louder than she had intended. There was nothing to save her except to be brazen and quick. She decided to laugh, glancing away. 'You'll have plenty of time to see William tomorrow.' With that she firmed her grasp of William's hand and led him out of the room as he mumbled some hasty thanks for dinner over his shoulder to the seated, silent parents.

Jamil turned and stared at his father, silently and expectantly appealing to him, but Jad sipped coffee and said nothing. He did not feel that he could.

The crumpled white sheets had a moonlit sheen in the warm gloom of the hotel bedroom, despite the only light that seemed to penetrate was the blended night fog of metropolitan miasma. Jayda smoothed hair away from her face and placed it upon William's bare chest. Their clothes were strewn. Their heartbeats subsiding.

'You did well with my mother. Do you think Baba liked you?' she said, her voice happy.

William was confused and she could sense his frown and interpreted it, adding, 'My father. Do you think he liked you today?'

'Jayda, I just don't know. He's tough to crack. He'll take some convincing but if he does eventually approve of me then my guess is that he'll be my biggest fan.'

'Yes! That's true.' She stroked his chest with a finger, making playful circles. 'But he will come round to you if I choose you. He'll have to. He usually does.'

She had her doubts though. Much as she sensed that he enjoyed indulging her she understood that her father was a proud ego and sensitively conventional in observing the traditional boundaries of Arab masculinity. Marrying an Englishman and, presumably, a Christian, proposing to leave Jordan and live, at least for a time, in London was going to be problematic for her in convincing him. It had been done before though. No less than one of the princesses had married a London financier and was now growing her family there, but she was not royal, with all the implicit internationalism which went with that status and, for now, she lived off her allowance. Not just for the money did this prompt hesitation because Jayda, for all the independence that she shone, still craved her father's approval.

Although she was wise enough to realise that the first few weeks of love with William were scanty experience to ascertain whether he was compatible for a lifetime, it was heady; a realisable happiness with the vista unveiling of a home life in London, the crowded, wet capital of financial possibilities and freedom. Anyway, if not William, whom she loved, then who? Someone selected by her mother or, worse, brother? There would be the dignity of a veto over their suggestions but the reality remained that, even if she chose the supposed stability and tranquillity of a local match and even if that was for love, she was not likely to know or understand her fiancé to any greater depth than she knew William now.

She had made her ambitions known to him in weeks past. That she wanted to run her own businesses, have at least three children, ski every year, own her own island and, more than anything else, prove to her father, Jamil and herself that she was as good as any man in anything she chose to do was clear, or at least had been nakedly implied, to William.

'Abda, I've been doing a lot of reading and research, questions about marriage, since I returned.'

'Oh yes.'

'Islam and Christianity are very, very similar. We all know that.'

William was sleepy; the physical crescendo drained from him, but slowly sensed he should now be at his most alert. He made himself blink and then found she was too close to focus on and her smell, of warm vanilla, almonds and the aftermath of sex, was an overwhelming, immediate sensation.

'Whilst it is forbidden for a man to convert to Islam for the sole purpose of marrying a woman as a quick fix, you can convert quite quickly.'

William froze, holding his breathing. This was unexpected.

'And if anyone goes through sufficient instruction and says the Shahadah, the words saying you convert and accept Allah Almighty and all that, then it is accepted even if your intentions might be impure, as they have to accept you based on what you show them. You're then a Muslim. The thing being that Allah will sort you out on Judgement Day if you've been hiding your real intentions.'

'Oh. Hmm. I'm sure.'

'William?' She was staring at him, head raised.

'Just seems a bit intense and sudden, that's all.'

'Intense?'

'You wouldn't convert to Christianity would you? I mean, if He is the same God and...'

'What? That's thinking stupidly, William. My father would go ballistic if that were presented to him and mother would be very distressed and Jamil would see me as a traitor.'

He had said the wrong thing. Her fingernails tensely crouched, her voice became harsher. 'You know you should, ought to, have to, consider this. I should be part of you and you part of me. If you loved me and you've said you love me then you have to think this through.' She let this sink in for a moment. He knew that she had more to come but allowed himself to exhale since he was now reaching the limit of comfort in his breath-held tension. At the moment he had finished exhaling he realised that it must have seemed as if he were petulantly bored by the subject.

'I'm no exotic plaything, you know. I'm a serious prospect. You English may have your manners and your charm and, yes, your hypocrisy but we Arabs are proud and we have our honour. You dishonour me by not, by not marrying me. I have been dishonoured before. I've been...' Her voice, from angry and firm, faltered and she scratched her nails downward and across his chest, 'I've been hurt before.'

Wincing from the scratch, William gasped, stalling the words or gesture of reassurance that was rapidly becoming overdue from him.

She started to weep. The tears dampened her eyes and interspersed her breathing in short, hurried bursts but, as a sudden slide of natural energy, she sat up over him and was flooded by the anger that her fear generated.

'Do you realise what it is like here to be considered cheap? You don't. It's a battle against everyone to exert yourself as an independent woman here and if, if they think that you're a slut then it's doubly hard.'

'Jayda? I never thought any such thing. I've only just arrived here.'

'Not you! Unless you do consider me cheap?' Two tears coursed down each cheek, which she paused to wipe with a sashay of her head upon one hand, the other still poised upon his chest. Not knowing what to say he made an urgent noise signifying incomprehension.

'So you must not dishonour me. If you truly love me you will not cheapen me as if I were one of your English casual sex girlfriends. You have to marry me or, because you have come here and met my family and my friends, if you do not you will disgrace me again.

I cannot have that again. You will convert and we will marry and we will live in London for a few years. We will be married and have children and you will have to be prepared to look after them if I need to work.'

It became too much. She needed something to hold onto and placed her hands over her face, letting the noisy, wet frustration convulse between nostril snorting intakes of air, arresting in rhythmic breaks the waves of tears that became, eventually, tearless shudders, then calming slowly as William, staring enraptured, began to stroke her arm.

Casual sex girlfriends. That had certainly been accurate and William had always avoided the moral guilt that burst from his actions. The lies and false reassurances, the casual cruelty, telephones unanswered, calls not made, messages unreturned, letters discarded and, once or twice, the awkward conversations, or confrontations, when the girl demanded some sort of emotional closure. Despite this he had still considered himself a gentleman. It was precisely because he did not consider these girlfriends important that he had managed to blind himself. They had largely been entertainment to meet his physical needs. For the past year, since the break-up of his last relationship, his targets had been from amongst those that he was unlikely to settle with: waitresses, secretaries, shop assistants and the like. This was to increase the likelihood of casual success and so that he could maintain suitable distance afterwards. The exceptions to this stratum were, of course, Cosy and Jayda, both born of the same night.

Cosy was the last of her kind though, he told himself; an embarrassing flush before a sudden conversion to become a better person in front of Jayda's quality. That he loved Jayda was beyond his doubt, which was, however, within the practicalities of developing such a thing. As he lay there beside her, impressed by her passion and amazed with himself for not being repelled by it, as he would have been with any other past woman, it occurred to him that whatever difficulties there were to come, be it converting to Islam without fraudulence or submersing himself in Amman's style of Arabic culture, be it controlled on his terms or an aleatoric submission to Jayda's family, he should do so, wherever the course that his love for her would naturally flow and, perhaps, as some sort of punishment for all his former sin.

He reached up and eased her down beside him again but hesitated in speaking. That bit about his looking after children for her might have been deliberately provocative. If he promised marriage to reassure her she might take it as a proposal and he had imaginings of some carefully staged romantic event for that, not amongst tears in gloom in the early hours. He opened his mouth at last to say something but she sat up again abruptly and shifted herself from the bed.

'Jayda…'

She moved quickly around the room, gathering

her clothes and dressing in moments.

'Jayda, don't go yet.' That clearly did not work. 'Don't over-react, woman.' Neither did that. 'Jayda, I love you and we will be together.'

She did not reply and, without looking at him, gathered her bag and strode from the room.

At the same time, three miles away across the subdued but still endlessly circulating cars of the now orange-illuminated and shadow-pooled city, Jad and his wife Zena lay quietly awake in bed. He stared at the dark blankness of the ceiling waiting for the sounds of his daughter's return, his imaginings restless, fearful and accurate. She was on her side and into her pillow, drifting into sleep with thoughts on a broader theme of the excitements of love. Across the landing in their rooms Fiesel and Fatima shifted within the cycles of their sleep, secure in their separate worlds. Only Jamil was clothed and awake in the foreground of the night's slumber, sitting in an armchair in his annex in the mansion, a cigarette burning unsmoked in an ashtray beside him, a concentrated vacuity on his face taking him to visions of violence and compulsions of warped duty.

CHAPTER XVI

William was just climbing out of his shower when the telephone's electronic burr jarred the solitude of the room.

'It's me. I'm in the lobby,' said Jayda. This was a little alarming, the earnestness of her being there, unannounced as a surprise. He could not tell from her voice what sort of mood she was in, so he tried lightheartedness.

'You've not been there all night?'

'No, I'm here for breakfast. Come down as quick as you can. I'm hungry.' She seemed friendly.

For her it had been a night of fitful turns, the moon through her window bathing the world in a restless bright greyness, her agitation glowing enough energy to rise her relatively unaffected by lack of sleep. Had she gone too far last night? Had the descents of emotional indulgence been, yet again, too easily drawn from her? She loved him so much and wanted a joint future so poignantly that, she sensed, she could be starting to seed some doubt into the kernel of his masculine reservation. Presumably being a man he was emotionally reserved in romantic sensibilities – Arab men generally were – and being an Englishman must mean that he was culturally preconditioned to be hesitant. So, even though the connection between them had barely seen two months she considered herself on the cusp of a lifelong relationship. She had placed herself at that choice without fully expressing her feelings to William before now, for fear of being off-putting. It had been a slightly deceiving silence. Though she would have thought it wrong to act falsely for him, the natural instincts of the huntress had tried to suppress any presentational blemishes: gawkish eagerness from being so innocently happy, illogical fears that she might lose him and the natural inflexibilities of prejudice that came with being a strong character. This was a world where she needed to fight just to be herself. Now, at home presenting William to her circles of Amman and wanting approval from her family, the plateau at the top of the climb seemed within reach. Last night the emotion had bubbled over.

When he approached her from the lobby lifts she could see instantly some puzzlement and a residue of annoyance in the lines of his brow, confirming her suspicion that he would not consider last night's disharmony to be his fault. Once he was bound to her in marriage she would not of course, with any future ripples of ambiguous blame, admit any responsibility. That would be the powerful wife's prerogative. For now though, he needed reassurance.

'Morning handsome.' A kiss on the lips.

'Morning,' replied with a happy, slightly baffled expression.

He led the way to the dining room, avoiding

familiarity by a pace ahead. Once a waiter's attention had been achieved he ordered Eggs Benedict. She ordered the same, for symmetry, even though she had never had it before. He replied warmly enough to her conversational fillers, even with a smile once, but settled in to examine the English language Jordan Times. This was her punishment, a newspaper barrier to let her know that all was not forgotten from the night before. From being merely amenable she launched into being likeably solicitous, her voice poised in a softer husk than was usual.

'I think last night's dinner went well, habibi. Everyone liked you.'

'Hmm.'

'Fatima thinks you're funny.'

'Oh yes.' He was still looking at printed text. She knew with certainty that he could hardly be interested in whatever local story it was.

'Funny in a good way. She meant she approves of you.'

'Your younger sister approves of me because I am funny.'

'Yes. And mother likes you. You were very good talking to her.'

'Uh.'

'I haven't spoken to Baba or Jamil yet but Fatima was up early and in my room.'

'Good for you.'

'And I still like you.'

'Do you?' The paper was folded and dropped to the floor with exaggerated emphasis. His eyes, which had been elsewhere since the kiss, were warm.

'I'm sorry.' She whispered it.

'Yes, well. You erupted rather unnecessarily.'

'Sorry. It was a long day. Anyway today you and I can spend together. I have you to myself and I'm going to show you all my favourite places. Tonight there's a group of us going out to dinner. You'll see a bit of modern Arabic cafe culture.'

'Won't Jamil disapprove of you being left alone with me for so long?'

'I haven't asked him.'

'Good.'

'You don't think he likes you?'

'I don't believe that he has warmed to me yet. What do you think?'

'Well, you are to spend most of tomorrow with him. Baba wants him to take you to the farm to shoot guns.'

'I'll try and be appropriately macho.'

Beyond wanting him to herself all day, Jayda had not planned how to fill it but an idea came to her, or at least how to provide an interest of his for the morning.

'You have one thing in common with Jamil. Cars. You both love stylish broom brooms. And me. You both love me.'

He nodded and took a large mouthful; golden yellow yoke trickled down his chin. Smiling, he wiped and chewed, clearly enjoying himself and intrigued as to where she was navigating the conversation.

'I think that this morning,' she announced, 'I shall take you to the Royal Automobile Museum.'

She did. It was somewhere on the city's outskirts, its Bauhaus architecture crouched on a slope beneath a huge blue sky. The last king loved cars so much that his son, the current king, constructed a modernist stable for them and called it a museum, complete with photographic displays of the young country's history as told through his cars. King Hussein had an especial love of Mercedes sports cars, silver and green, along with more predictable plush limousines and as William ambled around, holding Jayda's hand in the windowless gloom, regarding perfections of polished bodywork and chrome, wondering whether he could pull her into a dark corner and steal a kiss, he decided that he admired the style of it all as well. It was there that he glimpsed a sense of Jordanian national pride and liked it. The museum was somehow declaring the country's élan with fast cars.

She drove him there and afterwards around Amman. She had only ever driven at home and it had been some months since she had last done so. It was exhilarating, shifting through gears, commanding purpose, speed and schedule, relaxing into the fluent narrative of a guide, pointing out buildings, explaining districts and trying to impart some of the city's casual energy to her guest. William also enjoyed it, giving himself over to a tourist's unthinking submissions and relaxing to an extent that would have been impossible had she been driving him in London. He was content to stare out of the window with the fascination and mild surprise that afflicts every tourist.

Amman surprised him. It was wider, brighter and altogether more spacious than he had expected. The brightness of the light delineated everything clearer than he imagined it could or should be, as if it were a high-definition moving portrait of a fluid urban landscape, yet too clichéd to seem authentic. He had sunglasses but did not like to wear them, feeling that to do so, since Jayda did not wear any, would be too contrived or seem American. As a result the continual glare gave decompositions of colour that his eyes were unused to, the light breaking down into unnatural veils. The sun hazed everything gold yellow, sandy and sepia. Through this he saw wide roads and junctions, bridges and underpasses, modest towers of glass and stone, villas of grilled windowed reticulations, dusty family saloon cars, sleek black limos and fume-belching ancients on four wheels. Avenue upon avenue of concrete, rectangular parades: showroom or office above, shop or warehouse below. The achromatic purity of the brightness dazzled him, clarifying the bustle, the reds and rust, the sand and kicked-up noise from car horns and shouting, as if Jordanians could only express themselves with exclamation marks and gesticulating hands. In between all this, constant in all but the smallest, most affluent blocks, were the toothless gaps. Level or on a slope, the city was riddled with empty plots of land, abandoned or fenced off, awaiting eventual development upon their sparse shrubs and skeletal building foundations.

There did not seem to be any parks, indeed there was not much greenery at all but there were other fascinations: neon signs and minarets, domes and rectangles, roadsigns in Arabic and English, four by fours on the freeways and goats grazing on the building plots, shepherded by thin boys in t-shirts. Public buildings, of which there were many, had soldiers or grey uniformed gendarmerie guarding and each whitewashed frontage carried a portrait of royalist propaganda draping the side, usually of the king in an enormous photograph, smiling confidently in open shirt or ceremonial braiding. One could be in no doubt this place was ruled by a monarchy that considered itself benevolent. Men wore long tunics and sandals or long sleeved, tieless shirts above dark trousers. The women were occasionally covered in hijab or niqab, clustered in dark drapery or clicked their heels below tight jeans with free flowing hair of confident sun-shined beauty. Mainly they were dressed in a combination of these and the sight of them reminded William of the need to turn his head to pay attention to the constantly babbling woman beside him.

He was, as usual, only half paying attention to her talk, the white noise of feminine prattle, but admiring the gentle firmness of her voice and exotic lilt with which she spoke her English. Suddenly, isolated and clear, he heard her announce,

'I want a house for us here, as well as in London. London is no place to raise children – it has no decent lengths of sunshine or space.'

She said it for a reply so he found himself nodding and answering, to be equivocal, 'I wonder.' She smiled triumphantly and he realised that he had not been vague enough but the heat and other worldliness of it all allowed him to think it wise to be looking out of the window when she then said,

'I shall drive us around the smarter residential areas, so you can see.'

At around the time that they both felt mildly hungry they were near the Talhoun mansion. She had planned it so. Outside the vehicle's air conditioning the sun was at full power, thickening the air to an invisible quilt that baked everything, and inside it made the house a variance of pools of light and sharp-edged shades. Only her mother and a maid were inside, occupying themselves with unknown domesticities until they were disrupted by their entrance. Outside in the garden Abdul slowly watered and clipped, undisturbed.

William then had the task of being charming again to Zeina Talhoun, which he did without fault over a lunch of potato salad, water and coffee. Jayda beamed and prompted little conversational pieces by way of encouragement. He would have clammed up or been too stilted and polite had he thought of Zeina as his future mother in law; instead he imagined that she was an aunt who he was fond of and from whom he needed a favour.

As the maid cleared away Jayda exclaimed, as if it had just occurred to her, 'Let's jump in the pool! You and I.'

'Oh, errm, my trunks are back at the hotel.'

'I'll find you some of Jamil's.'

'Oh.'

Why she wanted her mother to see William's torso, she would not have been sure but there was certainly a subliminal element of showing off what was hers.

There was a small, white tiled pool house in the garden. The pool itself was light blue tiled, rectangular and sunk in harsh, greenish, permanently sprinkler-fed grass. William changed quickly. Embarrassment of the glaring whiteness of his skin made sure that he did not linger out of the water. He dived in and did a couple of laps of noisy front crawl, a suitably masculine way of exercising, he imagined, for when his love arrived. She took much longer than he expected though and by the time she emerged he was wallowing, admiring sunlight on the water's ripples. She was in and beside him before he had time to observe her, planting a couple of kisses on his lips and cooling the redness of his neck with a glistening arm. Up till then he had been nervous of her declaration of need for a family house in Amman and her drive-by tour of Abdoun and Sweifiya villas. How could he pay for it, how could his career and lifestyle commute between two worlds, how could expectations of family and the constraints of culture and religion make any possibility of this seem feasible? The eager yielding of herself to him though, in body and in trust, dissipated practical reasoning in a moment, as in so many moments with her, into a stunned, half-disbelieving love and sudden, unignorable, primordial lust, raising priapic greed. The flank of her thigh rubbed against his but she twisted away as swiftly as she came because, with a heightened perception missed by him she sensed her mother's approach. Zeina Talhoun appeared around the corner carrying a tray of glasses and juice.

Jayda lifted herself out of the water and William, desire reducing him to a gulping silence, watched the water flow off her back, lissomly cascading over the arcuated penumbra of her buttocks.

Mrs Talhoun spoke invitingly and poured juice but William could only see the olive smoothness of Jayda's legs standing beside her so, aware that he was ignoring whatever was just asked of him, he turned, glided himself underwater and then thrashed out several more lengths until nature's demands eventually subsided and it was safe for him to join them, his heartbeat pounding, his chest wheezing.

Mother and daughter observed him in a pause from chatter as he lifted himself at the same place that she had dripped herself out but then he had to walk away a few yards to recover a towel. Both had different thoughts along the same theme. Mrs Talhoun noted how poignantly pale William was and thus how impoverished of sun the English world must be. Jayda saw only his face, pinked healthy, framed in a continuing effort to be pleasing to her mother and felt another silent swoon of luck. She realised that she had, of course, created and left unresolved last night's argument. Self-aware enough to understand her emotions demanded regular histrionic release without admission of any responsibility for them, he had passed some sort of test which she had not realised she had been setting. It was now a question of when she tested its limits again.

By not proceeding the discussion with linear logic, by avoiding it at breakfast for the sake of harmony, either through manners or cowardice, he was confirming, again, that he was man enough for all her long term foibles. Beautiful though she was and aware of her beauty with a stylist's eye for detail, she was also nonetheless rawly conscious of her impenetrable imperfections. 'Strawberry juice?'

'That sounds delicious Mrs T.'

'It will cool you. Do you holiday much in hot countries William?'

'Well, I, err. Well, I suppose like most London bachelors when I realise that it is August and there is no one else in London and it is too horribly hot, I find out where a friend has rented a villa and go out and visit them.'

'That sounds very bachelor like, William.' Then, with a daring that surprised her although the thought had been within her for days, Zeina added, 'How many children do you think you will have when you have a family?'

At first William thought he might have misheard so he mumbled an affirmative noise as a reflex but as he did so the unavoidable enormity of what he had been asked was confirmed by Zeina's gaze holding on him. The answer had not occurred to him before and, between the pincers of four eyes, had to shortly.

'I suppose that will be up to my wife, as and when.' As he spoke he shifted along a rattan sun lounger, excusing himself into shade as a way of deflecting the moment and the eclipse before his unadjusted sight prevented him from noticing their reactions. Zeina and her daughter held identical, weak smiles, their hopes tangible but unspoken.

He was in a good mood as he descended in the hotel lift at the agreed time for collection, happy and hungry and not minding the idealised photo adverts of other parts of the hotel. They were framed unignorably at eye level on the mirrored walls of the elevator and normally annoyed him. He was expecting to place himself, seated, within view of the entrance so that she could walk into his arms when she arrived to take him on to dinner. She had dropped him off two hours earlier and, to his impatience, had laughingly found excuses not to come up to his room and be jumped on. Now, washed, groomed and perfumed, he was ready to try again to goad her upstairs.

When the mirrored doors shunted their imperfect glide open, William's expectations jolted. Jamil was in front of him, as if waiting for an elevator to lift him to the room he had just left. The Arab looked unfriendly as he nodded, said a flat hello and then fell in by William's shoulder so as to march him outside.

'I am joining you for dinner tonight.'

'Oh. Very good.'

'I think that there will be several people there.'

'Really?'

'So, to give Jayda time to prepare herself, I told her that I would come for you.'

'Oh yes.'

'She usually spends a long time grooming herself.'

He expected that Jamil would drive directly to the dinner, hoping that Jayda would want to retain independence of movement with her own car, but they returned to the Talhoun mansion. They did not have to get out because Jayda came through the kitchen door as soon as Jamil rolled into the rear yard. She said a bright hi to them both as she got in to the rear seats but then remained taciturn; a pointed message that it had not been her choice to be usurped.

At dark, Amman seemed a little sinister to

William. Its pools of hazed orange and the dim white eyes of several thousand uncurtained rooms seemed to enclose the wide vistas of confident buildings that had stumped underneath the vast blue sky of day. They drove amongst narrow sidestreets as their destination neared, cushioned by parked cars and flanked by grilled metal fencing, woven with greenery, on top of the pavements' boundary walls. Everywhere, to his untutored imagination, seemed an apt place for an ambush. Who would ambush only his imagination could formulate: religious fundamentalists, lurking criminals or indigenous racists hostile to his trespass? Perhaps, he tried to reason, this was his reaction to Jamil's driving. Sitting in the front passenger seat, he was acutely aware each time Jamil's right hand forced its way through the gears, close by his left thigh, which was angled away as far as he could place it.

Even the way Jamil parked was aggressive. A reversed shunt from a fluid turn of the wheel ended in a sudden, bounced stop as the former tank commander looked out of the rear window beyond his sister's meaningful blanking stare. After dismounting, Jayda hurried to link arms with her boyfriend and stride him on ahead, her brother following quietly behind, his eyes upon them.

Jayda's friends seemed to occupy the entire restaurant. Several tables full of drinking, smoking, eating and laughing Jordanian twenty and thirty-somethings, all armed with handhelds, lighters or handbags, talked across at each other. Most of those from lunch the previous day were there, along with others. All were dressed in casual western styles but predominently in dark colours. All came up to William at some point, to say hello and silently note his unavoidable otherness. They came also to verify what they already knew. He was there being paraded by Jayda Talhoun as the London boyfriend that proved her sophistication and the redemption she needed since her Damascene lover had abandoned her the summer before. Everyone greeted them with that knowledge behind their smiles but Jayda did not mind. How opinions of her would twist when she was away again was beyond her care. She was happy.

Jamil broke away and joined a friend with another, separate circle of diners. He smoked quietly and stared at the girls and wondered how he should start to talk to them.

After an hour or so a man came over from Jamil's group and introduced himself as Rami, leaned across to William. He had described himself as a government lawyer. Everyone in the country, it seemed to William, was either a lawyer, engineer, a doctor, an architect or owned a trading conglomerate.

'Do you want to smoke hubbily-bubbily?' asked Rami with an animated exclamation of his hands.

'Is that legal here?'

'Of course!'

'Really? I mean, aren't you rather strict on drugs?'

'Drugs!' The immediate four or five around him burst into laughter. Jayda tried to find William's forearm to rest her hand on it, to start to explain, but missed it as William dropped his arms to his lap.

'Yes of course,' said Rami, his face joyous with laughter.

'Really? Then why smoke them?' William, naively confused, was hurriedly trying to work out how to deflect what might be mockery without seeming more stupid than he already felt.

'There are no drugs in the nargeela. Well, no illegal ones.' Rami clicked his fingers and spoke to a black African waiter, himself dressed all in black. Moments later a glass and gold braided water pipe smoker was placed on the floor between them and William was initiated into the gentle art of smoking a shisha pipe.

Apprehensive that he would cough and splutter, he did not. It was surprisingly smooth and aesthetically pleasing, with the bowl's gentle bubbles rising to a cooling mouthful of fruit flavoured smoke. Rami gesticulated to share and, when William handed it over, he removed the plastic mouthpiece and covered the end with his own.

'So, Englishman, how do you find Amman?' The nargeela was the frontispiece but excuse for conversation.

'Well, it is more modern and cleaner than I was expecting.'

'Modern? Cleaner? What did you expect – camels

and tents?'

'I, err, I wasn't sure what it would be like actually. Never been to an Arab country before.' He was aware of an eagerness to take offence, or at least combatively engage, in Rami's tone so he added, 'But I like it here. Everyone's very friendly.'

'Ah yes, we Arabs have great traditions of hospitality. So, you are Jayda Talhoun's boyfriend?'

Jayda, only noticing peripherally before, casually paid attention.

'Yes. I am very lucky.'

'Do you think that you'll convert to Islam if you marry her?'

'Or she might want to convert to Christianity. Neither is such a leap of faith.' William rather enjoyed how quickly he had countered with that.

'She won't do that. I don't even have to ask her to know that she won't, can't, do that.'

'Hmm. Well, I, hmm. Can I have another tug on that?'

Rami passed the pipe back and William, quite conscious of the hanging question in this exchange, added his retained plastic mouthpiece, drew up mouthfuls of smoke and hoped something would occur to him. Enough moments passed for him to realise that Rami was waiting and not going to end the pause.

'Extraordinary, isn't it?' Smoke trickled out with William's words. 'I mean, given the cultural differences. Which aren't that huge anyway, actually.' A puff or two more and Rami's face was framed neutrally but hostile nonetheless and Jayda was silently purring warmth and concern by his shoulder. 'Extraordinary that something attracted her to me in the first place. Wonder what it was?'

Jayda was about to speak but Rami interjected, 'Might have been because you seemed exotic and different to her.'

'Must have been,' clipped William, staring at the mess of glasses, dishes and ashtrays on the table top. 'Ah, well, seeing that it is, He is, the same god for the three big religions around here...'

'The Abrahamic faiths,' said Rami.

'Yes, those. And seeing that the other two religions, the Asian ones, seem just plain stupid; well, I don't see any huge thing preventing me from converting to Islam so long as the girl carries on loving me enough.'

He paused to notice Rami remain expressionless and then glanced to his side to see Jayda broaden a smile. She leant forward, swept back her hair and pecked a lingering puckered kiss on his cheek, a display noted by most of the room in a small ripple of silence, which she adored as a territory-marking victory.

'I see that you are gripped by the best of convictions,' muttered his inquisitor. 'And your children – would they be Muslim?'

'Oh, I'm sure they would make their own minds up, when the time comes.'

The night's socialising took a long while coming to its close. Long after the meal had finished the conversing groups continued. Jamil was enjoyably aware that the two lovers were impatient to leave and reliant on him for their departure. Only when the woman he liked most decided to leave, not long after he had managed to introduce himself, did he feel that they had no further gain in lingering. The awkwardness of his shyness slammed into him more irritatingly than usual, the relaxed completeness of Jayda and William rubbing him like raw, salted skin.

He was pacing the hotel lobby and waiting for Jayda to descend from William's room, having loudly declared that he was going to leave without her after ten minutes, when a text bleated onto his handheld. It was Rami.

'You're right. He's a jerk. And stupid. You can't allow your sister to marry him.'

CHAPTER XVII

It was not his habit to be early to the office but Jamil had not slept well and woke early. He knew that this day with the Englishman was an unavoidable chore so, to emphasise the inconvenience to himself more and grab some time to be productive he avoided the rush hour's horns and got to the office before the secretaries arrived. There was no in-tray as such but a large pile of documents, files and unanswered correspondence on the left side of his desk. He stared at it for a moment and then fired up his computer to distract himself with emails.

He had agreed to collect William at 9.00am, so that was the time he decided to have a last coffee before setting out to do so. He remembered to ring Mohammed, the farm manager at Umm Quat, to remind him to have some lunch prepared for them and then left, dulled by the prospect and saurian in his demeanour as he angled his thin body forward towards the office elevator in jerking strides, eager to get it over with.

His sister had looked at him, he thought, strangely last night; a mixture of pleading and defiance as she gave her final words to him before they parted for their rooms on the unlit landing. 'Try and be pleasant tomorrow. You might as well get to know him. He might be around for a while,' had not elicited more than a reluctant grunt from him at the time.

Defiance of Jayda's flowing course of action pumped through him though. It was not inevitable that she married him, nor that the Englishman would be around in his life beyond this week.

He had relayed the fight again and again in his mind, so often that the actual images were worn and of imperfect accuracy but the emotional memories were still taut. He remembered the sudden burst of sunlight from behind a cloud that had made him lower his head as he approached the Englishman rolling toward him and the repulsive feeling of indignity colliding him like a wall as he realised that he was expected to step aside. He remembered the underlying anger with Jayda that morning and how the shock and pain felt as he had hit the ground. Everything else was overthought and overanalysed to be recalled with anything but the positional familiarity that rebooted his hatred of William.

Allah was testing him. Testing as to how he would react to the dishonour, the personal dishonour to Jamil of having the jerk Englishman, the man who beat him to the ground in a grubby street altercation, become his brother-in-law. Even if no-one ever knew of that beyond the two of them he would have the irritating shame of it forever staining the hope of any acceptance of him. The Englishman was clearly, in relation to Jayda, an adventuring chancer who had used her feminine vulnerability to gain her. He must have isolated her socially somehow and snaked his way into her affections, wanting her beauty as his possession, to marry her so that Talhoun money could pay for his life in London, far away from the natural influences of her family. He was her brother. Their father would probably have his own interpretations of the dangers of losing Jayda to the jerk but only he had the insights, from the fight, from his love of Jayda and from his pious observances, to be able to save and redirect her. It was his certainty that the Englishman was corrupting, drawing her away from Allah and her home, seducing her to the base life of a western city where even her children would be lost to Islam and her family. William would take her beyond the reach of God; a kafir debasing her purity. At the very least Jamil had no inclination to offer him anything but the most neutral of hospitality and it did not take long being in William's presence with Jayda for him to struggle with the barest veneer of politeness. William took each opportunity to mark what he considered his by constant tactile connections: stroking her, clutching her arm as they walked, holding hands like children. It was abhorrent. It raised bile to his throat, the taste of which lingered continually.

This time Jamil waited for him in his car outside the hotel, ringing up and telling him so curtly. For the first few minutes as they drove out of Amman William remained attentive to the passing street scenes and made several attempts to open conversation but each time the Jordanian clamped it shut with replies as brief as he could make them. William realised that he would have to raise the subjects of fight, Jayda and religion to begin to clear matters and understood that Jayda hoped for her two men to understand one another better after today. However, rebuffed on the weather, cars and itinerary, William sensed that this was not the moment and felt too tired to bother further. The night had been late, the day was hot, the rhythm of the car's progress bobbed his eyes closed and he dozed for a few minutes. When he awoke the bright openness of the land surprised him. They were along the King's Highway with flat dust and shale to the horizons on either side and, with Jamil glaring ahead, knuckles atop the steering wheel, it was easier to maintain the silence.

As they arrived Jamil became talkative, for him. William had been awake some minutes and maintained his tourist's observations in silence but a few miles after they had turned off the highway onto a minor road, they forked off again down an untarmacked gravel track which threw back billowing dust from the rear of the car.

'My father bought the farm, 470 donuns of it, in the early '80s. He gave over the farmhouse to the farm manager and built a new house, higher up, overlooking the Jordan Valley towards Israel.' Jamil delivered this as flatly as he could and still looking ahead, which anyway as a road required more attention than the state-maintained highway.

'Does he farm the land?' William was willing, although he had been comfortable enough with the silence.

'Fruits. We planted orchards of orange trees. Some lemons. It thirsts for a lot of irrigation, some 40 donuns of it. As for the rest, it is for landscape or goat grazing.' For Jamil, that was a speech and, as William now saw there were buildings ahead on a hill's crest and realising that they were on the driveway approach, he made an appreciative grunt.

As the crest came closer, with an undulating stony slope to the right, William could see that the property was fenced. By the gateway there was a small bungalow of whitewashed concrete, the original farmhouse. Inside the large compounded area the road surface changed to black tarmac and the right side slope held a large orchard that dipped and rose again, stretching to the horizon and rimmed by a bowl of low hills, their dust seeming white in the sunglare.

Atop the crest, with no visible backdrop of land, stood a cluster of low sandstone buildings which, as the car slowed to its halt, revealed that they were connected and of a higher elevation than first appeared. It was a modern leisure pavilion of comforting architectural lines: large, squat, smooth, its thickness hinting at the refuge of a cool interior. William blinked a circumference, dazzled by the sun and, yet again, was surprised by the thick, hot quilted air outside of the car's continual chill. Jamil, having no inclination to narrate the introduction any further, clunked his driver's door shut and bounded up a flight of wide brick steps, his gait angular in advance, and went through the unlocked main wooden door. William followed after a moment of hearing the engine's cooling ticks and then noting how the fat silence emphasised the short snuffle of his leather soles on the upward steps.

Inside, his eyes took a few seconds to adjust but the main room was ahead of him underneath a brick and windowed atrium, more dome than cupola and bathing light upon a large, curved space whose corner focus was a fireplace. Ash mounted in the grate. The walls leant upon a mass of cushions and lolling diwans. Rooms span off to his immediate right and left and from that side he saw the back of a woman carrying plates to a table in the kitchen. Jamil was elsewhere so he edged forward into the main room. Carpeted with rugs and kilims of varying sizes, he crept forward, assimilating all he saw. The stack of board games in a corner, the low coffee tables, the outmoded stereo system, the bookcase full of sun-bleached, creased paperbacks all spoke of a much-used holiday retreat. He turned the corner of the L shape and saw a glass wall of sliding doors, with Jamil on a balcony beyond, looking out with his back to him. The door was closed.

William joined him after awkward shifting of the

sliding barriers and saw he was smoking. Interpreting the closed door as maybe something to do with the air conditioning, rather than another snub to him, he closed it behind him feeling grateful for an opportunity to try and improve things between them. He thought he would open with, for him, a rarely used ploy.

'May I pinch one of your gaspers, Jamil?'

Jamil turned to him slowly but with surprise.

'You smoke cigarettes?'

'Very occasionally. Now's a good time.'

Jamil still wanted to take every chance to be distant and considered saying no, along with a lie that he had run out but, as he knew that he would want to smoke again that afternoon, he realised that that may be difficult to sustain. Hesitantly he drew out a soft pack of Marlboro Lights and looked away as he gave fire from his lighter to William's bowed head.

From his first drag William felt lightheaded and he then noticed the drop from the balcony was deep and craggy. The view was breathtaking, literally, since the height gave a faint breeze. Ahead of them was a deep gorge of rock and dust rising on the far side. Beyond the first rise were a series of higher hills, each rocky, the view of each distorted by heat over their distances.

'That's Israel?' asked the tourist.

'Yes.'

'I can see why your father chose the spot.'

'Hmm.'

'Did it take him long to build this house here, at

this elevation?'

'I don't know. He used his own construction company but I expect it cost more than was planned.'

Jamil spoke hastily and then turned inside, sliding the glass door to close behind him and leaving William to the large scale harsh majesty of the view. He finished the cigarette anyway.

A couple of minutes later the large woman from the kitchen knocked on the glass and wordlessly beckoned him inside and to follow her to lunch. Jamil had already started. Water and a bowl of salad, predominately of black olives, tomatoes and crumbly cheese, none of which William particularly liked. He sat down and poured and scooped nonetheless. The farmer's wife, if that who she was, then disappeared. He tried again.

'So, you were in the army?'

'Yes.'

'And you were in tanks? What was that like?'

Jamil was jolted again for a moment. He had been asked a question that he actually wanted to answer. Most people like to talk of themselves but Jamil often thought that it was pious to be modest in this regard and this close proximity to the Englishman, an itching gnaw of irritation to him because of his look, his mannerisms, his smell and his abundant relaxed self-satisfaction, constantly reminded him of his need to be distant.

'Yes, I was. I commanded men and several tanks. What you would call a Sabre Squadron in your army.'

'What was it like?'

Again, Jamil felt surprise with the rejoinder. It seemed the sort of simple question a child might ask. He found himself lowering his voice an octave, not because he wanted to attract but there was the compulsive need to seem impressive that Jamil craved.

'Well, it was...They were usually very hot. And noisy.' The gloom inside the mobile oven of the tank, the cramped closeness of the other four men, the smell of diesel and taste of dust and cordite, the wheezed, distorted cackle of the radio, the sweat on his hair and sticky ache on his back, the leaked stink of oil on the floor; all from a past when responsibilities and direction were simple, orders and hierarchy unquestionably valid. And on long exercises the claustrophobia and grime, the reeking body odour, the grinding churns of the gun turret, ponderous and dense for even the swiftest movements. He missed it. If he had not had the inexorable magnet of the family business to join, he would still be there.

'Did you get out much to play with them or was it all in barracks polishing the gun turrets? Most soldiers spend a lot of time in barracks, don't they?'

Jamil could not tell whether William was teasing him or asking with disarming simplicity.

'Even in our small country we have plenty of space to go out on manoeuvres.'

'What sort of tanks were they?' William was eating but mostly playing with his salad leaves.

'Challengers.'

'Wasn't that a British tank?'

'Yes.'

William smiled inadvertently with the pleasure of remembering this trivia from somewhere within him and with the sense of making some progress. Jamil detected the sickly smiling arrogance of one who was attempting to score a point from him and who, he suspected, may have steered the conversation to that moment.

Lunch was abandoned to its following silence. The two men soon rose and Jamil invited his guest to admire the garden; as William made his way to it he realised that his host had no intent of accompanying him. He walked on harsh, brightly green grass, wet from sprinklers' sprays and looked at dense flowered borders. There was a swimming pool, bathed in shadow. He waited, bored.

Jamil had retreated to the armoury. It was a small converted garage underneath the house which he had Yousef open for him. Most of his own and his father's guns were kept there in a masculine den which was a tribute to Jordanian father-son bonding. In the centre was a table and chairs, on a corner table there was a surface of glasses and spirit bottles. A large ashtray, empty and clean, was the centrepoint of the room. The walls, however, held the cabinets and these dominated. They were mostly closed metal boxes but a glass fronted wooden display case held a rack of shotguns and several handguns, pinioned upon a backdrop of green velvet.

He had instructed Yousef to set up a firing range in the flat base of the orchard, which was reported as done, so Jamil directed that a trestle table be lugged there through the heat, to be able to rest the firearms and ammunition on. Yousef moved off slowly, with the expenditure of the barest amount of necessary energy, each step a grudge. Jamil glared at his back with exasperation and yelled for him to take the remainder of the day off. Turning to the cabinets he opened doors and drawers and made his selection. Rows of rifles with cartons of ammunition stacked below, the sight of them steadily soothing Jamil, the metal barrels' dull lustre and the darkened patina of their wood relaxing him with their familiarity. He took out an old M1 carbine, its shape pleasing him as he rolled it in his hands, placed the butt into his shoulder and admired its balance.

Next, the handguns. These were kept in drawers, mainly in cases where green or deep red velvet offset their guests of metal power. He and his father had a preference for 9mm ammunition handguns but there was an assortment of types from years of collecting: several Brownings and Berettas, a Spanish Star Model A, a Czech CZ83, which was one of his favourites being small, punchy and with a 15 shot magazine, an old Webley Mk 6, which might even have come down from the Arab Revolt, a modern, clunky Heckler

& Koch P7 and his habitual handgun of choice, the Glock. He handled several of these, a sheen of transported distraction over his eyes, but selected only a couple. Inserting them into his belt, grabbing several ammunition cartons and slinging the rifle's strap over his shoulder with a fresh resolve to make up time, he called for William as he marched out into the overwhelming brightness and heat toward the large orchard.

Jamil felt slightly unnerved. It was a situation that he should be dominating. He was the host and the experienced alpha male introducing this affected peacock of an Englishman to the affirming power of firearms and, thus, he expected a little deference but instead all he received was a pose of wry amusement, as if William was deliberately goading him without explaining the joke.

They shot the carbine rifle first. The makeshift firing range was one that had often been employed before. The orchard's slope levelled out to a base of sixty or so metres before gently rising again. At the far end of the level before the land rose again an old makeshift, lengthy, wooden, table-like structure stretched along an otherwise hidden vehicle track that broke across the avenues of fruit trees. On it were nailed paper targets, the standard Nato running infantryman and, resting on top, a row of aluminium cans and two empty coke bottles.

Jamil had run through safety rules and noticed William grinning rather than listening with the intensity which he would have preferred. 'I wasn't even in the corps at school,' he stated at one point, as if proud of the deficiency.

'The magazine clips in here. Like so.'

'Yeah.'

'And you put it to your shoulder like this.'

'Of course.'

'Putting your cheek on the butt and aiming your eye down the barrel.'

'Like a shotgun.'

'This is a 9mm Glock 17,' announced Jamil in a clipped, nasally tone. He grasped it quickly and brought it up to his eyeline. 'Simple. Largely plastic. Beautiful. Tough. Little kick to it. Here.'

William took it from Jamil's extended hand and bounced it in his palm. 'It's light,' he remarked and searched for something more to say. He could feel his shirt sticking to the small of his back. The handgun was clearly something serious. Black, slightly granulated but smooth on the handle, it felt, however, oddly like a toy to William with all its plastic.

'A little over 1.5 lb. I have the magazine. Here. To me.' William gave it back and Jamil grasped it and, with a single fluid movement, snapped in a short, angular magazine. He crouched, raised his aim and, with an almost theatrical intensity, fired off two rounds, disintegrating one of the coke bottles in a satisfying glass explosion. William's eyes involuntarily winced. The two barks of noise sharply slammed themselves and then lengthened into a single echo. Jamil straightened his knees, lowered his arms, exhaled as if he had exerted himself and then turned to face William.

'Army and gendarmerie issue.'

William picked up a clean paper target from a stack on the trestle table, rolled it and began to amble down towards the splintered wooden target stand. The sun. The mind-altering heat. An invisible thick wrapper atrophying thought and reason. Jamil stared at the slumping gait of the Englishman's back and sensed pure hate swell within him, distilled through enough observation to know it with certainty. He grasped the Glock in his right hand, appreciated its balance and loudly clicked in a fresh magazine. The sun pricked his forehead, sweat beading. Heat and death. Decomposing and regenerating. The scorching sun turning grass to sand, withering life. The Sun as a god in his destructive domain. No reasoning God can forgive hot death. No tripartite, thritheistic God of the Book. Not Allah or Yahweh. But no unmerciful God needs to forgive justice. Yahweh had killed Baal using fire.

The nipple of the Glock's short barrel was poised between his eye and the back of William's head. Apophis the Destroyer, God of Evil, an old God of the Nile. Astarte, the mother Goddess of the Levant, give impetus and witness. Witness this Englishman:

foreigner, gentile, infidel. A despoiler of virtue with his pale, unjustified superiority. The death of an impotent Europe. The falsehoods of Pax Americana. Bland, populist idiocies. Jamil raised his left hand to steady the aim of his right. The handgun, the modern scimitar; metal moulded into a death-giving weapon. The sword is more honest than the pen. The might of action justifying the deed. Astarte, witness this murder.

The anger was there, still there, still freshly steaming in the heat. His aim shuddered slightly with the passing seconds so Jamil blinked, realigned his feet and forced his mind to clamp down, into a neutral space to fire from. Mottled patches of sunlight through the trees seemed to freeze as his hands and gun bathed in a spotlight. The silent heat. The erotic power of the gun. His finger filmed in sweat across the trigger's metallic curve.

William's feet slowly crunched the gravelled and dry soil to the target. He bent to the hammer, prised out nails and then banged up an innocent paper soldier. He was aware of being watched intensely by Jamil and of the unsettling silence, abrupt after the plangent, uncoiled barks of gunfire. Walking along the deserted range beyond the orchard's edge, the crunch of his steps resonating as if he were boxed in, he picked up and placed the cans and tins, not once looking back to the bench where Jamil stood. This not looking was a way of protecting himself, of re-establishing a better distance from Jamil's artificial masculine bonding of bullets, cars and simmering machismo. Then there was a moment when all sound was silent. Both men felt and knew, beyond explanation, beyond eyesight and within instinctive fear, a sudden, vast, malevolent energy suspended in the physical space between them. The kinetic propelling heat, flared by the whole parabola of blue-drenched sun, towered from the ground then succedaneously collapsed on itself, as if exhausted, in a watery haze. A click. A loud clear echoing click of metal upon metal. William, sudden white, jerked his head around and jolted his frame behind it, angled forward. Jamil stood, legs apart, arms by his sides with the Glock in his right hand, its magazine in his left. He was breathing heavily, nostrils flaring and his eyes upon William's. He formed a smile. A smile was weakly returned. Astarte the Deceiver, an inconsistent goddess.

Jamil looked at the sudden fear still held on William's face and liked it. He slowly moved his left hand across, reinstating the magazine with a metallic snap and then rested his arms by his sides, the Glock pointing to the soil. His eyes never left William's.

'Stay there,' said Jamil in a voice of fresh harshness.

William, petrified anyway, was more in shock than fear at the thought of murder for the instants that the prospect held him, with Jamil's eyes drilling into his, hate and mania emitting from them. He cast his eyes away, to the side through the dappled rows of fruit trees. The possibility he was in danger slipped away as a stupid and improbable thought. He shook his head to clear the moment away and took a step forward.

'Stay there I said!' Jamil recoiled a pace and raised the Glock to aim at William.

'Jamil?' William stopped. 'What are you doing?'

The heat pulsated silently.

'Jamil, I know we got off to the most monumentally bad start imaginable. You want an apology. I know, I know. I can see that.'

Jamil blinked several times. The thickness of the air was smarting his vision. His extended right arm began to ache earlier than it should. He felt dizzy and dehydrated and he needed to be strong.

'I'm sorry. I apologise about our street fight, Jamil. I should have...' he searched for a sign that his words were having an effect, 'should have avoided what happened.'

Astarte and Apophis failed. Allah was stronger and the Englishman was beyond the reach of God: an infidel, a kafir. There are moments for justice.

'Jamil, I realise that you're annoyed, upset, angry that I'm in a relationship with Jayda. I mean, I wish it could be different but, truly, I can't help being in love with your sister. I need your help Jamil, your advice.'

Since that had come off the cuff from William he had lost his concentration on Jamil's eyes and, impressed by what he imagined to be his own eloquence and persuasive tone, he began forward again.

'Stop! Stay there!' Jamil was still aiming for a headshot.

The air between them magnified and eliminated its distance, giving a tunnelled sense of intimacy; the heat cloying unmercifully, demanding a moment to ebb away from. William sensed that Jamil had not been listening. He splayed his hands outwards, desperately.

'Put your gun down Jamil and talk to me. Jamil? Jamil! Jamil, put it down. Jamil, please. I haven't, I haven't done anything wrong. I don't know why…I shouldn't be…Jamil, please. Please.'

CHAPTER XVIII

Jayda was at home and wondering how to fill her daytime until the men returned to Amman. Their night's occupation, another dinner with friends, had been adumbrated with only the loosest confirmations of intent, most likely to be finalised in the casual relaxed manner of Jordanian socialising, nearer or even after the appointed time. Her handheld then rang. It was her father. He forgot his usual introductory affections.

'There's been a message left for you in the past hour.' Terse, his tone suggested something more than mere urgency. 'Someone calling herself Lady Caroline Cheshire rang the office from London and said that she wanted to talk to you about William.'

'Oh. Who? I've never heard of her.'

'I didn't speak to her directly but the secretary who took the message said that she seemed very earnest.' He spelt out the name and number as she scrambled for a pen. 'You'd better ring her and find out what it is about,' he growled.

'Do you know anything about her?' asked Jayda, confused, but he had hung up, eager to minimise the length of his message. Something from that told her she would have to report back to him later.

The shop was never very busy in the early part of each

midweek morning, indeed it usually only received its first customers as lunchtime approached, so when Cosy had called the Talhoun Group head office it was at least in part another ploy to distract herself from mundane chores, listless thoughts and begin to shape some purpose to her day. Less than an hour had passed since then and when the call came she just knew that the ring, indistinguishable to all others, was stridently emanating from abroad. She ran to the door and locked it, flipped the sign and skipped to the phone in the back room that she cluttered as her office.

'Hello?'

'Is that Lady Caroline Cheshire?'

'Ya.' She did not habitually say 'ya' or usually use her title but they were easy armour to wear, even if she considered both to be at least a decade out of fashion. 'Is that Jayda?'

'Yes. You rang for me.'

'I did. Is William in Jordan with you?'

'He is. Yes. Why do you ask?'

'It's important, believe me. Is he with you now?'

'He is visiting us in Amman but he is with my brother at the moment. How do you know me?'

'So, are you going out with him?'

The expression was not familiar to Jayda and the tiny pause she gave herself to consider it made her realise more fully the wholly alien nature of this hasty but un-ignorable conversation. She had rung back out of curiosity and fear and because there was something in the tone of her father's voice that made her give impetus to action. For a moment then she had been willing to ride the current of words because, given the early bright earnestness of the Englishwoman's voice, this could have been some sort of emergency but it seemed, now, to be something perceptively more emotional. If there was something regarding William that needed to be learnt, to be done, an obstacle to be cleared, an argument to be shouted, a drama to be confronted, then she wanted it now. She had dialled the London number without pause once her father had hung up. If the suspicion she harboured within her half-formulated thoughts was true, that the intensity and romance of her happiness was too perfect to be real and perhaps too fragile to be sustained, then the longer it survived the greater, she feared, her emotional collapse would be. It was an amorphous anguish, whispered only beyond the margins of her emotions, suppressed unformed before any clarifying moment could blossom to catch up with her. She steeled herself and made her voice harsher.

'Going out with? What do you mean?'

Cosy began an intake of breath but Jayda, feeling foolish since the first word and now impatient for control, talked on. 'Stop. Hold on. I don't mean to be rude but you ignored an earlier question of how you know me. Who are you, why are you ringing me and why are you asking me these questions?'

'I'm Cosy. That's my usual name. I know what

you look like. You're the Arab girl who was at the Sam Fifoot-Julian Green drinks a few weeks ago. I know that because William Clive spent a long time talking to you.'

'Yes. And?'

'William Clive, you see, I think you should be warned.'

'Huh.'

'Or at least you should be aware that…that he was with me that night.'

'Oh.'

'By which I mean that, if he was declaring his love for you that night he was also declaring it to me.'

This time Jayda did not make a noise.

The shock that impacted her was not so much from horror at the message but a baffled repugnance toward the messenger. She was not certain whether to be curt, angry or solicitous so continued holding her breath, apprehensively receptive for whatever was next.

'I don't know what you think of that?' asked Cosy, half sympathetic in tone, by way of demanding a response.

'I don't know what to think but I am thinking – why do you want to tell me this?'

'Don't you see? He was two-timing both of us. He's a rat. He promised me and he hurt me because of you and I wonder that if you realise what he is, whether you can believe in whatever he's promised you, because of me.'

'Hang on; you're saying that while he has been in a relationship with me he has been in a relationship with you?'

Cosy glanced upwards to smile at the grey gloom of daylight, madefied with light drizzle, outside the thin cold pane of her small office window. This was her achievement, to arrive at a point where the tiny tremors of doubt in the Arab girl's voice, even though she was replying more forcefully then she had expected, were clear to her ear, where the power to destroy or grant clemency upon love was hers. She could still control what she had unleashed and there had been no small height of hesitation to overcome before she made that first call. She had spent days running imagined conversations in her head, rehearsing this revenge.

'I don't know. I don't know the details of your affair but, I think, for a period at the start, probably yes.' Cosy felt impressed at how easy that was to say. She had not yet rolled that premise around enough in her head for it to harden as her perceived truth but saying it aloud seemed to make it so. She listened to Jayda thinking and felt the lightness of a particular happiness swell within her. She had sprinkled darkening obfuscation and the scents of victory were faintly weaving to her through the telephone.

'I don't see it clearly. I don't understand how that could be,' said Jayda.

'You should be thanking me.'

'Thanking you – I'm not sure why.'

'Well, things aren't that likely to last with him anyway, are they? I mean, it must be difficult enough what with him being English and you being an Arab and everything. You rooted over there and him coming from rural Shropshire or wherever it was he blurted from. And now that you've found out that he's a love rat...'

'And why do you want me to know this? Whatever it is that you have lost, why have you gone to such efforts to find me and tell me?'

'Because you ought to know.'

'Yes, perhaps, but everyone has a past and everything and, and, maybe I don't want to know. Why did you want to track me down and tell me?'

'It was the...' Why was the Arab girl suddenly so aggressive in tone? 'Right thing to do.'

'Are you jealous?'

'Sorry?'

'Jealous. Are you trying to hurt me because you want or wanted him for yourself? I mean, why find out from someone that I'm a Talhoun and ring my father's office from London and tell me all of this? Why?'

'Well, Jayda,' struggled Cosy. 'It's important to keep things in proportion.'

'Proportion! Were you in love with him? Are you?'

Jayda bristled with words and wanted to cry aloud, to groan out a noise and then flood out many more words but she had asked some questions and remembered some advice of her father's, about the power of remaining silent when the other person could end the pause.

'I'm not sure what being a Talhoun, or whoever you are, means as such but I felt compelled to ring and tell you this as a matter of…', she struggled. She could hardly say the truth when at the forefront of her mind was that she had rung as a matter of sport and revenge. 'As a matter of truth, of sisterhood decency.'

'That's not what I was asking. Were you in love with William?'

'Well, of course. In part.'

'Are you jealous of me?'

'Oh no, no. Not jealous.'

'OK. So exactly what did he promise you and exactly what sort of relationship did you have with him?'

'Well,' Cosy could not think. Despite having benefited from a glance at her at the party, before she had imagined a timid girl cowering beneath a dark burka, pretty but easily dominated. 'Well, he gave me the impression…'

Jayda waited. Cosy knew that she could lie and indeed, within her shifting core, understood that this conversation was a lie but one that had been justifiable for her own catharsis. The knowledge of what was the clear truth and what was the kneaded, emphasised, much brooded upon, filtered and embellished enhancement of the same was not something she felt, at that or any other moment, able to discern. Such niceties had always been smothered by the blanket of her immediate emotional impulses and she felt a heat flush prickle her face, pinned down by this back blast of interrogation.

'He gave me the impression,' Cosy repeated, slowly and uncertainly, 'that I was the woman he wanted.' She added, rapidly, 'Wanted to be with, I mean.'

Jayda's discomfort, sudden and confused, did not allow for the patience necessary to negotiate anything more. 'Actually, I've heard enough. I'll be talking to him now and not to you again. He's mine and whether or not he remains mine will be my choice. Goodbye.'

Snapping her phone shut with a turn of her whole body, as if she needed to move quickly to another place, Jayda then stopped, convulsing a shudder that started upon her shoulders and tremored down her back. This delineated the end of the moment. She concentrated her thoughts. The morning sun was approaching its highest point and her room was harshly bright, making her wince and understand that there was no rest for her there or anywhere until she resolved this. Scrambling through her memories there was no instance she recalled, no reservation created, that had doubted his sincerity but this strange, unknown woman had now called, motivated by pain or perhaps something incomprehensible, with the intent to explode her happiness. She flicked the phone open again, pressed for William on speed dial and began to pace the room.

CHAPTER IXX

'Jamil, where have you been? Why did you take so long? Where's William?'

'He's back at the hotel.'

'Why is he not answering his phone?'

'I don't know.'

'Why haven't you been answering yours?'

Jamil breathed out an exhausted sigh. He hated it when anyone control-freaked him and he had known she was going to.

She repeated herself, louder.

'Ran out of juice.'

'Has William run out of power as well?'

'Don't know.'

'Why is your hair wet?'

'I've had a shower. It's a hot day.'

'Why are you not looking at me? Don't turn away Jamil. Have some bloody manners when I am talking to you. Now, it has been a long time for me without word from him, or you. When did you get back? When did you drop him back at the hotel?'

'Whenever we got back. A little after 6.30, I think.'

'Two hours ago. I've tried the hotel several times,' and she flipped open her handheld with an aggressive wrist and punched a button. Jamil walked off, out of his room. The receptionist listened again, mumbled distantly and then put her through. It rang out, shrill and urgent to her ear, long enough for him to answer, wake from sleep, splutter from a bath or shower, but there was no connection.

Throughout her life she had found it hard to control her impatience. Weak parental indulgences, especially from her father, had allowed such impulses to scale when she was young and, even though she realised now that it was often a self-indulgent lack of willpower and finesse, she had often justified it by telling herself it was a strength. It was that strength she now let flow, although coursing through were the undercurrents of fear and desperation.

She followed the noise of Jamil's descent downstairs and paced the ground floor rooms until she found him again, doing nothing but facing a window that looked out onto the garden.

'I want you to take me to the hotel.'

'Sorry? Why?' He half turned to her but still would not meet her eye. 'No, I won't. He's your boyfriend, not mine. Your lazyboy in not returning calls. Your problem. I've just spent the whole day with him, thank you.'

Jayda was perceptive enough to realise that this was a bigger issue than the frustrations of her own controlling instincts. She counted to five, silently, and walked between Jamil and the window so that he could not ignore her. He looked detached, isolated in a weary serenity.

'Jamil, it's time we talked.'

'I don't want to talk.' His face was suddenly contorted and energetic in disgust. 'Your boyfriend is a jerk and not worthy of you. That is all. There is little else to discuss.'

'Well Jamil, that is your opinion at the moment. If I did choose him to marry, because he made me happy, would you still be so against him?'

Jamil snorted loudly and again turned away from her.

'You won't be marrying him. I guarantee it.'

'You can't guarantee any such thing if I decide otherwise Jamil.'

He continued to avoid her gaze, which she noticed as unusual, even in argument. Before she could decide whether a fight with him would be worthwhile a voice started calling her from elsewhere within the house. It was her father. No doubt he wanted to enquire about the Englishwoman who had rung but before she could talk to him, or decide whether she wanted him to have any intelligence, she needed to try William again.

'I'll drive there myself,' she snapped to his motionless back, too impatient to argue.

She went to the kitchen to see which car keys were hanging up and found her father there, recently come in and with jacket and tie already discarded and chair-draped. When he saw her his forehead raised eyebrows in inquisitive concern. The emotional default, springing from childhood, of needing support, changed her mind with the sight of his face framed in patriarchal gravity.

'Baba will you drive me to the hotel to find William? Jamil doesn't want to help.'

The question was unexpected to him but he nodded quickly, the intimacy of crisis welcome. 'Go to my car then. I will inform your mother.'

He was ten minutes. She sat in the passenger seat in the thickening darkness of the underground car park as night blanketed in. She thought about the Englishwoman and her cold, clipped voice, her fears escalating scenarios, her happiness and ambitions all, suddenly, fragile.

'Your mother has been told,' he said without looking at her as he turned the engine with seemingly the same flow of his hand as he had thudded his door closed. 'She will understand.'

As Jad drove steadily through Abdoun and towards Shumisani, crossing the suspension bridge as its floodlights flickered on for the night, emphasising the falling darkness, his eyes, in relaxed concentration and tactile wisdom, averted from her slumped, anxious posture. She wondered for a moment how much her father suspected, or even knew, given those last words about her mother. With her baba at the wheel the journey seemed to lose some of its strident urgency and with that she was able to tell herself that, most likely, William was more dozy than deceiving in being out of contact for so long and a jealous ex-girlfriend was no real threat to her future. It was probably some misplaced sincerity from William before their relationship had truly started, before he had begun to love her. Still, she could not control one of her legs, jiggling its nerves, vibrating her toes with tiny, restless, rapid bounces. Amman was a nearly dark and looming backdrop, crouched on either side of the wide road: black and orange, black and tar yellow, black and dim grey, thickening the hidden world beyond.

Jad rolled his car slowly up to the perimeter of the hotel's security cordon and gently stopped as two hot and badly tailored security guards approached, their jackets each bulging on one side. One swept the car's underside with an extended mirror and torch whilst the other mumbled 'erhalan' from an observing distance. Jayda tried to control her fidgets. After they were waved through Jad turned to her and quietly announced that it would be best if he stayed in the car. She held herself strong in the walk toward the lobby but looked back at him before going inside and through the entrance body scanner. He was on his phone, already talking.

It was as if she held her breath from the moment she walked under the entrance canopy until the first rap of her knuckles, satisfyingly loud, upon the door to his room. She exhaled with a burst of air that released the dizzy tension which had increasingly weakened her as the elevator lifted her to his floor. All would be well now. He would open the door and she would launch a harangue with words of demand and enquiry but also emotional relief. Words to demand apology, respect and explanation. He was going to have to pay for her worry but, as she rapped again on the veneer, she wanted to see him so much, her man and her love.

He did not answer or open the door. She stared at it blankly, looked up and down the empty, heavily carpeted bright corridor and began to ring his mobile. Placing her free ear to the wood with the other on her phone she strained for the sound of ringing within the room. There was nothing. Footsteps jerked her head back. It was a waistcoat-liveried porter passing by, balancing luggage. She hurried away, embarrassed.

The elevator descended, quietly whirring its machinery in an overbright, soulless efficiency that drained her to numbness and deadened any residual anticipation she may have had with its door-opening ping. Another round in the ring. She knew now, as she raised her chin to approach the front desk, that William's absence could only be because of the rupture caused by Cosy Cheshire. That woman must have spoken to William today, as well as her. He would only be avoiding her if there was a lie he wanted to avoid. He must have cheated on her. The receptionist, an impatient smileless man, looked up as she stopped opposite. Her throat rose in a lump with adhesive pain as she tried to speak and there was small wetness beginning to burn behind her eyes. She glanced to her feet, saw the lines on her skin stringing tension between shoes and jeans, and dabbed her face with a tissue. When she looked up the receptionist, a label pinned to his uniform naming him Nasir, was waiting blankly.

'Hello, I'm Jayda Talhoun,' she managed.

'Yes, I know.'

'Oh.'

'Madam?'

'My boyfriend, err, I mean,' Jayda spluttered. 'I mean, my friend, who is a man, who is visiting us.' It would be so much easier to say boyfriend or partner, but this was not London. 'William Clive is not in his room. Room 159. He hasn't, I mean, has he checked out?'

Nasir tapped his keyboard for a couple of long minutes. 'No, he hasn't.'

'Oh. Is there a message? He's here visiting us and he's gone missing.'

She disliked it how Nasir then held his gaze for a second beyond comfort before nodding and turning to a back room. There he consulted with an unseen colleague in a low murmour before gliding back, as expressionless as before.

'No, I'm afraid not.'

'Do you know what time it was when he came back this evening?'

'Err, no madam. We don't record that. He must have gone straight to his room. Shall I ring for you?'

'He is not there. I've knocked. When he comes in could you leave a message for him to ring me.' This was not delivered as a question. Forgetting the customary 'shukran' she turned and clicked across the marble to her father waiting outside, his fingers drumming the steering wheel.

Once he had been told, her father drove home much more forcefully than the journey there.

'Jayda, I'm sorry to hear that. It is, I suspect, something to do with that woman who rang for you today?'

Jayda stared ahead. Whatever truths were axiomatic, it was still too hard to start to speak.

'Did you speak to William after you'd spoken to that woman? You did speak to that woman?'

'Yes I spoke to her. But I haven't spoken with him yet.' She rushed out the words.

'I think I can guess what she said to you. Whatever her strange name was, I remember Julian Green mentioning her in a conversation I had with him earlier this week. He warned me that William had a reputation, that he was promised to this woman and perhaps two-timed her with you, or you with her, it doesn't matter. Now that he knows that you know this, he is avoiding you. Us. Me.' His fists were clenched to the wheel and heavy and tight with each necessary turn.

'It's not like that Baba,' she whispered, surprised that she could talk at all. 'I'm sure it's not. I just need to speak to him.'

'Let me tell you this. I suspect that you hope to marry him, this English boy. Your mother can tell. And, since he is over here it must have occurred to him too, but you must be certain that he is innocent of any of this. A man who cheats once will always be a cheat. Marriage is long and often hard and a cheating man who seeks distraction in infidelity is a certainty for unhappiness. Jayda, there is no honour in having children with a foreigner who does not love you enough to stay faithful to you.'

Jayda nodded. She realised this anyway but there was the shock of hearing it despite it being her father's place to speak. He repeated himself in much the same language, in a loop, several times, until they turned into their driveway.

'But what if he has gone missing and is lost walking around Amman?'

'That is not very likely Jayda, is it? He is not a child.'

'Kidnapped?'

'Again, daughter, not very likely.'

'He can't have just disappeared.'

'He won't have. Jamil dropped him off there only hours ago.'

'I don't believe it is very likely that he has just disappeared without talking to me.'

Jayda caught her father's eyes and the pain within her own made him pause in his seat with one hand on the car door, the engine subsiding.

'Well then, if you do not find him by lunchtime tomorrow you may contact the police. They can discover whether he has flown back to London or not. Most likely he is in his room, cowering and planning to leave.'

Jayda hardly slept. By the time she had returned with her father Jamil had gone out and she realised that he was in a longterm mood to be unhelpful. She was asleep when Jamil crept his return up the staircase but she had already spent two hours upon her bed, alternatively tearful and determined, repeatedly trying William's number until she had saturated her ear with the familiarity of the exact length of rings it took for his message to click into play with its warm intonation of the usual reception clichés.

There was a ratchet in her head, ticking tension in droplets and there was no-one to release it with. Worries layered themselves in coils within her stomach, making her clutch herself as if resisting a tide of physical pain. She wanted to talk but there was no-one to listen, or rather, there was no-one she could trust with her vulnerability. William himself had become her usual lightning rod of empathy for daily trivia. Her father was too opinionated, her brother stonewalling and unhelpful and the option of her mother did not occur to her, too precious as her mother often was, to be of help. There were girlfriends of course but Jayda had spent too long abroad recently and been in love with William too intensely to allow the privilege of such intimacies with any sympathising Ammani gossip.

By morning and more calls, to his mobile, the

reception and room, Jayda had accepted the huge shadow of something having gone very wrong into the absorption of her being. In the mirror, arms locked to the sides of the basin to steady herself, the worry within her face scared her.

'Yes, I understand Mrs Talhoun but…'

'Miss Talhoun. Jayda.'

'Miss Talhoun. But the Administrative Police will only launch a missing person's investigation if 24 hours have elapsed.'

'Yes, 24 hours normally, but this man is an Englishman, a foreigner. He doesn't know anyone else here apart from me and my family. He knew that we were meant to be out for dinner last night. Please, I mean, I just know that something has gone wrong.'

'Many things could have happened. Not necessarily bad.'

The woman constable at the other end of the line was trying to sound sympathetic and less bored than she felt.

'Please, I know something bad has happened. I've rung him over a hundred times and he normally always answers to me, even, even, when we are arguing.'

'Have you been arguing with him?'

'No.'

'Well, as I said, if he doesn't turn up by 6.00pm then I can help you.'

'Look, surely it doesn't look good if an Englishman

goes missing?'

'Tourists get lost all the time.'

'He is not a tourist. He's a guest.'

'Well, hmmm.' Something had finally got through to the policewoman, maybe the fear in her voice. 'Let me think. If he's English then I am going to have to inform the duty sergeant. I could talk to him to see what his preliminary thoughts are.'

'Please, shukran, shukran.'

'OK, what are your details Miss Jayda Talhoun?'

CHAPTER XX

'Do you mind if I smoke? I like to smoke in interviews like this.' The inspector's face revealed the lines of an habitually serious man but he framed a smile, wanting to start off in a relaxed manner.

'I don't mind.' Jamil could not help but frown. He thought it very odd that he was being asked.

'These are Camels. Quite strong. Do you want one? It might make you feel a little less tense. I suppose you smoke Marlboro Lights like everyone else your age.'

'I'll have one, shukran,' replied Jamil. He was nervous. He assumed that at some point soon he would offered coffee and would eagerly accept that as well. Three of them sat in a windowless, underground interrogation room in the Wadi Sar Police Station. The call had come yesterday, on the second day after William and he had been to Umm Quat. The inspector had rung him at the office and asked for him to come in for a chat. Jayda had done her bit the previous day. He had been avoiding conversation with her, which was becoming increasingly awkward.

'Yes, everyone gets tense in these situations so I think we should just be friendly, OK? It's like having your pulse tested, no? It runs faster because just being at the doctors makes one scared!' The inspector was the only one who laughed at his little joke. He exhaled a plume of smoke with luxuriant appreciation and continued, 'OK, let's begin. We'll keep to English. I am Inspector Mutasem al Husari and this is Rami Makdah of the Mukhabarat, who is here to observe. It is 2.23pm and we are in the Wadi Sar Police Station commencing an interview with Jamil ibn Jad Talhoun regarding the missing person William Clive. There is a recording machine between us on the table.'

The policeman bounced in his seat, eager to start. He was clearly comfortable, nested in his element and uniformed, despite the seniority of his rank. Dark blue epaulettes lopsided the shoulders of his crisp, white, short-sleeved shirt. The man from the security service crouched impassively in a dark suit. Both were moustached, tieless and unblinking. Above them the air conditioning was waving out a continuous chill, an additional detail that Jamil disliked but did not feel relaxed enough to mention. Was it necessary? Was he the only one irritated by its intruding whirr?

'Jamil, you'll be aware that we talked with your sister Jayda yesterday; so we know about the nature of her relationship with William.' The inspector looked to him for an acknowledgement so he nodded. 'So, how long have you known him for?'

'Just since he arrived in Amman really, although we met once in London earlier in the year.'

'What did you do with William when you went to Umm Quat the day before yesterday?'

Jamil, though hardly surprised, did wonder what

else Jayda had told the inspector, especially whether she had opined that he did not care for her choice in boyfriend.

'I was showing him the farm and the house. We had lunch.'

'What time did you leave?'

'Errm, about 4.00.'

'So, all day you ate food and toured the fields in the sun. What else did you do?'

'Not much else.'

'Are you sure? When did you set out?'

'Mid morning.'

'Yes, well, I suppose a couple of hours, one and a half hours, to get there? You left at 4.00pm, about? Sure you didn't do anything else?'

It was then, with the inspector's eyes impassive but searching for any hints discernable to his policeman's suspicions, that Jamil feared as to how much he actually knew or could suspect. There were, perhaps, vast chasms on either side of him, the dangers of inadvertent implications gabbled out of nerves.

'Well,' he tried to appear relaxed and drew in a deep drag to sooth the echoing pulses of his blood. 'We fired some rounds off in the orchard, for fun. Not for long.'

'You were shooting targets?'

'Sure.'

'What were you shooting?'

'A Glock. A Walther PP5. An old M1 carbine.'

'Shooting various weapons, I see. Where do you keep these guns?'

'In the armoury, underneath the house, at Umm Quat.'

'You have licences for all of these?'

'Tab'an.'

'I hope so. So, what time did you arrive back in Amman?'

'Around 6.30. Maybe a bit before.'

'Yes, hmm. Is there anyone who saw you there at the farm?'

'Mohammed Surash, the manager. Fatima, the housekeeper, his wife.'

'And did they see you leave?'

'Errm, probably no. We did not see them.'

'Didn't see them at all?'

'Oh no. Fatima made us lunch. Mohammed set up the firing range.'

'What time did you arrive?'

'I'm not sure. Around midday.'

'That must have been a long lunch or a long time on the firing range.'

Jamil felt caught out with an implication that he was not sure that he understood. He wanted to shrug his shoulders or say, 'I don't know what you mean', but he stayed still, apart from his knee pumping underneath the table.

'Jamil, you understand, a missing person, a missing Englishman, is a very serious thing.'

'Sure.'

'OK. Also, a matter like this must be of huge concern not only to your sister but for the overall reputation of the Talhouns.'

'Yes. Maybe.' He was not sure what that meant. Was he being threatened?

'So, Jamil, where do you think your sister's boyfriend is?'

'I don't know. Back at his hotel?'

'What did you talk about that afternoon?'

'Guns mainly. Farming. And other, inconsequential stuff.'

'Did you talk about Jayda? About his relationship with her?'

'No.'

Inspector Husari inhaled deeply and then, before he exhaled, stubbed out the cigarette on an ashtray between them. His eyes never left Jamil's.

'What do you think about him Jamil? Did you like him, approve of him for your sister?'

'I was getting used to the idea. I mean, I still am.' The sweat within his palms became too much. He stubbed out the cigarette, having hardly smoked it and rubbed his hands on his knees, rocking gently forward and back without realising its extent of motion.

'Still, it must be difficult to come to terms with. I suppose that a sophisticated family like the Talhouns might allow a marriage to a westerner? Or would it be better for a big business family to approve of an alliance closer to home? Jamil?'

'Well, I don't suppose we minded either way.'

'No? Jayda thought you might have argued with William about the suitability of the match.'

'Why? Why did she say that?' It seemed best to be defiant, to be able to have at least some influence over wherever this was going. He got his own cigarettes out.

'I put it to you that you did argue with him or he at the very least gained the impression from you that you disapproved of his relationship with your sister.'

Jamil fired his cigarette and was glad for the pause his lighter, stalling its ignition with flint static splutters, gave him. The inspector picked up a biro and began doodling lines on a pad in front of him that Jamil had not noticed before.

'Why do you think that? We got on fine.'

'Well, it might explain why he is no longer in contact with your Jayda, or anyone else in your family – if he felt that any prospect of a marriage or continued relationship was pointless.'

'Inspector, with respect, that is just not realistic. For one, we did not argue and even if we did, he would not have run away because of it.'

'Maybe that's right.' The inspector gave the knowing smile of a clever feline toying with a helpless rodent. 'So, tell me, have you any ideas – why has he gone missing? You must have some thoughts.'

Jamil then comprehended, or thought he did, that he was being gently prodded, not necessarily for sport because of who he was, though the lustre that he believed his name carried may well have stimulated jealousy in his inquisitor, but because the inspector appeared to want to prove himself, as if this were a game. His status was not being accorded enough respect but he could not think how to establish his rank and distance in a way that they would not have already anticipated.

'I told you, I think...I don't know.'

'Surely not?' Then, as if as a concession the inspector added, 'We have spoken, you are aware, with Jayda and your father already.'

'Yes.'

'So?'

'Well, if you have spoken with my sister and my father then you will no doubt have heard their theory that he has been discovered as a cheat, because of some Englishwoman ringing Jayda and saying so.'

'Yes, we have heard that. What do you think of that possibility?'

'It is, I suppose, possible.'

'No. That theory, I believe, is just not realistic.'

The inspector was now returning the same phrasing to him, gently mocking him again, he thought.

'Why not?'

'Well, it has been several days since you were at Umm Quat with William – three days actually and, unless he has done so in the past hour, he has not checked out of the hotel, has not returned there at all in fact, where he has left clothes, money and the like.'

'He hasn't left the country,' said the man from the Mukhabarat, his voice, reverberative and deep, cutting into the dialogue unexpectantly.

'How do you know that for sure? You don't.' Jamil felt that to be clever.

'Because we have this,' said the inspector. He slanted his right hand down to something he retrieved from a buff coloured folder on the floor beside him. 'For the benefit of the recording I mention that I have here, in a clear evidence pouch, the passport of William Clive.' He placed it on the table between him and his colleague. 'It was handed in to the reception desk of the Thabran Police Station by a member of the public two days ago, the day that William Clive was reported missing.'

'The day he was reported...' but Jamil did not finish his repetition. He was nodding to show his understanding.

'And we also have this,' continued the inspector, who could not suppress a smile flashed to both Jamil and his companion. Again he slipped downward to his right and fished up another pouch, 'a brown leather pocket wallet, with credit cards, belonging to William Clive, empty of cash, which was handed in at the same time.'

Jamil had nothing to add and the two men opposite him allowed a pause to develop, the inspector having reframed his face to an impassive solemnity. He could hear the soft whirr of the recording machine and wished, intensely, that he had some tactical ability to read their intent.

'So, Mr. Talhoun, since these items have been turned in we do not believe he has left the country.'

'Yes, I see that.'

They did not reply but shifted in their seats, as if uncomfortable but mainly allowing for the significance of recognition to clunk into place. This allowed Jamil to imagine that he could perhaps, somehow, outwit them. He wondered, blankly, as to how. The inspector raised his lips to speak but Jamil jumped in with, 'Have you told Jayda that you've found these things?'

'No. They came over to us this morning. You can tell her. Have you, err, have you spoken much to your sister about when you last saw William?'

'A little. She's very upset.'

'Indeed.' The inspector picked up and clicked the button at the end of his biro a couple of times. 'You were the last person that we know of who saw him and it would be interesting to understand how you spent the day with him.'

'I've told you all that.'

'There may be something you've left out. Everything is interesting to us.'

'Tshh, hang on – are you suggesting I'm in trouble here?'

'Are we?' The question was directed at him, jauntily, not expecting an answer. It served to unsettle him even more.

'Laa, I mean, why are you recording this? Why so formal if this is just meant to be, what did you say on the phone, "a discreet, friendly chat"?'

'Well, Mr. Talhoun, the matter is serious enough for us to undertake the correct procedures.'

'What correct procedures? I mean, if you are arresting me? Shouldn't I just shut up until I have a lawyer with me? You can't trick me like this. I came here today, freely, in the middle of my busy working day, for my sister, to help you find where he has gone and you treat me with all this formality, with a recorded conversation. It is as if I am under suspicion. It's ridiculous!'

'I don't believe that we tricked you at all, Mr. Talhoun. The tape is just a wise precaution.'

'Did you record my sister and father?'

'Ah, no. We talked to them outside the station.'

'Let me interrupt here.' The besuited security service officer's voice was still alarmingly rich and unexpected. He crumpled his frame forward to lean on both elbows across the table, ensuring that his point would dominate Jamil's attention.

'This is not some American police drama like you see on TV. If you co-operate with the way we choose to do things we will try to ensure that they are done discreetly without any avoidable embarrassment to you or your family.'

'I understand. I appreciate that.'

'Good. We just want to be able to rule you out of police enquiries,' regained the inspector, shifting himself as he glanced between his colleague and Jamil.

'So at this stage,' continued the security officer, 'we would appreciate it if you bear with us as the inspector takes you down whatever line of questioning he wants. No more talk of lawyers today, OK?'

As soon as Jayda could sense the morning's wakefulness creeping across her slumber she rolled further into her pillow, readjusted the warmth of her feet amongst the soft cotton of the sheets and urged herself back to sleep; for moments only, before she began to rise again to the surface where her anxieties, fears and difficulties awaited with the dull headache that she knew was crouched, waiting to faintly but continually throb, as soon as her eyes opened.

The thin vapid feeling that had emerged with her waking headache was still with Jayda in the early afternoon and all morning had been like that: failed attempts to find distraction from the shadow looming above her, a presence not seen when she turned to grasp an impression of it and felt foolish for doing so, but its weight pulsing and lowering by imperceptible degrees upon her. She knew she could resist it but was losing the will to do so. Ever since speaking to that Englishwoman a film of tears lay beneath everything but she had not yet cried. Events seemed too immediate and too unlikely to be real enough to accept any conclusions that could allow for grief.

By midday the sun had found its way through the large window of her room as a wide zoned spotlight. It was, as usual for the time of year before the coming autumn's thin blankets descended, shockingly bright. The colours of Amman reflected the glare: the buildings' pastel browns and sands, white stone, glistening polished glass and the vastly varied forms of advertising shapes and colours. The day was canvassed huge outside, beyond the walls of the garden compound and, above, clear, thick, blue and arched. The sky's purity pained her but the low humming bustle of the city battered her focus down and within, to more prosaic attentions.

The shakes from three quick coffees forced her to view herself in the mirror and she saw that her eyes no longer wanted to be brave. Maybe he had left her, without word, because of that bitch Englishwoman, because of fear of being caught as a cheat; maybe because of fear of marriage, of the counter-cultural mix that would have to be crossed, because of Jamil's contemptuous sneers; maybe worse, maybe he was lost to her, killed when lost. All of it too far away from reality but, with fists clenched and screwed into her eyes, tears eventually came anyway, hot and stinging frustration.

Suddenly she sniffed and raised her head. She had to be doing something, so she searched the clutter in her bag to check that car keys were there and tried to put some purpose into her steps as she came upon the staircase landing, not knowing where she wanted to be; but when her face hit the flood of sunlight from the atrium she shuddered still again, the intrusion of too powerful light clouding everything sepia, confusing her to the spot, knowing her tears were not finished yet.

'Right, Mr. Talhoun.' The inspector poised his pen over his notepad. 'Let's establish the timings again. What time did you collect William from his hotel?'

'About 9.30.'

'And when did you arrive at Umm Quat?'

'A little after 12.30 or so.'

'So, take us through what you did there.'

'I showed him the house. We smoked together on the terrace. Then lunch, as prepared by the housekeeper. We went to the orchard and shot various guns at a makeshift firing range we have there.'

'Why did you do that?'

'To get to know one another better, away from Jayda. She is not fond of guns.' He looked for understanding and the interviewers recognised this and gave brief nods, wanting him to give more.

'Targets?' asked the inspector.

'And the odd can and bottle.'

'For how long did you shoot?'

'I'm not sure. Quite a while. I'm very safety conscious and had to run through it all beforehand.'

'Are you proficient with firearms?'

'I was a captain in the 40th Armoured Brigade.'

'Yes, but would you say that you are proficient with weaponry?' This was the security officer, with an aspect of suddenly irritated exasperation.

'Yes, of course.'

'Did you spend all your time shooting?'

'Just about. We had to clear up of course.'

'Don't you have someone to do that for you?'

'I had given the farm manager the afternoon off. It was hot and slow work. We drove straight back to Amman.'

'Straight back, I see.' The inspector made a note.

'Why did you give your manager the time off?' dropped in the security officer again, who despite his seeming irritability was avian in attentiveness, as if seeking justification for his aggression.

'Well, I'm not sure. It seemed like a fair thing to do. It was very hot and I know that he had been working hard.'

'Did you not show William around the farm?' asked the inspector. 'I thought you said earlier that you'd toured the farm?'

'Oh yes. We did. In the car before leaving.'

'Is your vehicle appropriate for farm tracks?'

'It managed, yes.'

'What time did you leave?'

'A little after 4.00.'

'And arrive back at the hotel?'

'I told you. About 6.30.'

Another note was made. 'Did anyone see you with him at the hotel?'

'Err, maybe not. I didn't get out of the car. I just dropped him off.'

'Did you see him go into the hotel?'

'Errm, yes, I think so.'

'So, do you think that the security guards would remember you dropping him off?'

'I don't know. Maybe.'

'I'm sure that the hotel security cameras will be able to confirm the time.' The security officer's eyes never seemed to leave him although his voice, rich and laconic, now seemed more relaxed. In contrast, the inspector's attention bobbed between his notepad and his subject.

'Yes, errm,' Jamil rocked in his seat. 'I'm not sure. You see, I dropped him off outside the security area.'

'Oh, why did you do that?'

'It, umm, had been a long day. I just wanted to drop him off.'

'That is a pity. It would have been useful to be able to verify your story. Did a security guard, did anyone, see you drop him off?'

'I hope so. I can see that it would help you rule me out of things if we could find a witness who saw us, but I wasn't looking to be seen, you understand?'

'Of course we understand. Tell me, are you certain that you saw him enter the hotel?'

'I don't remember, but I certainly saw him move

towards the entrance.'

'Hmm, so now Mr. Talhoun,' continued the inspector as he lit himself another cigarette, 'you don't seem to be able to help us as to any motivation as to why William has gone missing and...'

'Why do you need motivation for that? You have his passport and wallet. He has been robbed on the street! You should be looking at CCTV across Amman, not asking whether I liked him or not or what I did or did not do with him on the farm at whatever time!'

'Thank you Mr. Talhoun. We are also doing just that. And we are talking to you.'

'And, Mr. Talhoun,' came on the security officer, 'we need to be making some progress. A missing Englishman is a serious matter affecting many things that you are not likely to be considering. This investigation is being monitored at the highest levels. We are all answerable to somebody and in this case I am answerable to my superior and my superior is answerable to Prince Rashid and the sidi is not known as a patient man. He is taking personal interest in this and he needs results.'

'Hasanan, yes, I am trying to help.'

'Good. So Mr. Talhoun, I need to ask you...' The inspector stubbed out and leant forward, covering his pad with his elbows. 'When you drove here today, was it in the same vehicle that you went to Umm Quat in?'

'Yes, it's a black BMW 7 series.'

'We need you to leave it here.'

'Why on earth?'

'Our forensics people need to go over it. To help put you beyond any suspicion. I'll have a constable drive you to wherever you need to go.'

'That is preposterous! If you are accusing me of something then say so. If you think I have killed him or kidnapped him then arrest me.'

'We have nothing on you at present Mr. Talhoun but as soon as we do, you can be assured, we will arrest you.'

Jamil stood up abruptly, repulsed.

'Keys please.' The inspector flung out his arm in demand and held Jamil's stare. The security officer leant back and smiled.

Jamil slowly withdrew the black fob from his pocket and handed it over. Then, as if to prove he had some control, he sat down again and lit one his own cigarettes. No one spoke but as he inhaled another line occurred to him.

'Laa majaal! You are tricking me again. If I were properly, legally advised you would not be taking my car. I change my mind. I'll have my key back. If my lawyer tells me that you can examine it then you may but not before then.'

'What have you to hide Mr. Talhoun? If you want us to put you beyond suspicion then it's best you co-operate. You can go and see a lawyer and he'll probably tell you, if he's any good, that you shouldn't be obstructive. In fact…' and the inspector arched himself back in his chair, warming to an idea, 'we will certainly be keeping your car. If you continue to insist that I return the key to you, I will arrest you, arrest you here and now. Then I can impound the car as evidence. Then you'll be legally entitled to a lawyer.'

Jamil let the cigarette burn between his fingers, its distraction quite gone.

'And if I do that Mr. Talhoun, it becomes public knowledge that you have been arrested. An arrest in a case like this is certain to be publicised widely. You might find that a little embarrassing.'

It was not just the strangeness of the situation that dislocated Jamil from his usual alertness but a cold, clarifying sense that whatever the end point which would be reached, it would be found regardless of his own input. It numbed him.

'So, to spell it out again, to minimise the damage to your family, you should co-operate with us.'

'Look, if you have his passport and wallet surely you must be suspecting some extremist religious group? Surely he has been kidnapped? You know, he left the hotel, wandered around, got a taxi somewhere, got lost somewhere around Thabran and was grabbed by an opportunist jihadist?'

'Obviously that has occurred to us and we are making appropriate enquiries,' said the inspector flatly.

'However,' continued his security colleague, 'it is unusual that we have not received any demands or propaganda. After two days, we would expect to.'

'If they weren't expecting to find him then they may not be fully organised yet.'

'Mr. Talhoun,' breathed out the security officer with an air of impatience, 'there is a good reason why you don't hear of terrorists and fundamentalists in Jordan – we don't have any.'

'Nonsense!' He almost shouted it and then composed a contemptuous stare to justify the outburst.

The intelligence agent held Jamil's eyes for a few moments and then shrugged his shoulders. 'Well, there are certainly not many. Maybe some sympathisers, but certainly no active groups. We have satisfactory control of that sort of thing. It is an unlikely area of enquiry.'

'Are you observant Mr. Talhoun?' asked the inspector.

'As much as I can be.'

'How much does Islam affect your life?'

'Allah is highest in my life.'

'Tab'an, as with all of us.'

Jamil paused and then saw they clearly expected more detail.

'And, Mr. Talhoun?'

'And what? I pray. I attend mosque. I try to observe the five pillars but that does not make me a kidnapping terrorist.'

'It might make it a little harder for you to accept the consequences of your sister marrying a foreign Christian.'

'That's just your circumstantial musing.'

'Which is good enough for us, for now.'
Jamil could think of nothing to say.

For some reason, unexplained by the receptionist, her
father was out of the office. So was Jamil. The only
place she could think of going to in the impatient
moment that she gave herself was the hotel. It gave
her a sense of purpose. A typical, mid-afternoon,
inexplicable jam of slow traffic belched her into anger.
She shouted and swore and sounded her horn to no-one
in particular, along with several others slugged across
an intersection. It made no difference to anything
tangible but cheered her up enough to feel, once she
parked beside a pharmacy opposite the security cordon,
that what she was doing was worthwhile.

The hotel was an imposing tower of sandstone,
glass and steel, curved into a cylinder and flecked on
the terraces of its base with incongruous palm trees.
Jayda stood on the pavement beside the driver's door
and tried to imagine William standing across the road
on that night. She saw the tired furrowing of his brow,
the squinting eyes and pink tanned hot skin, the roll
of shoulders in his gait, crumpled in his linen jacket.
Where would he have gone? She looked for a bar or
an arcade but it was an area of boutiques below offices
and she moved around on foot, circumnavigating the
hotel, ignoring horns and the heat, but nothing gave
her any clue.

The ballroom entrance was open so she slipped

inside. A large, empty, heavily carpeted entrance hall opened to the larger room, its vastness strangely empty with stacks of cheap gilded chairs and the wooden undersides of round tables rolled up beside. She had been to wedding dinners in similar ballrooms – would this one have held her own? Then, with a sudden horror that caused her to gasp, she realised that that thought used a past tense. She gulped and turned away with unthinking haste, back to the floor's empty lobby and its elevators. Before she understood clearly what she was doing she found herself rising to William's floor, nauseous in the throat and stomach, as if convulsed by horror, and heading towards some irreversible event.

Once again she stood outside his room in the windowless corridor, the carpet too thick, the halogens too yellowy and fading on the eyes despite their brightness. She rapped her fist on the door and waited. She knocked again, not wanting to take her eyes from its veneer. Her head bobbed tremors without her realising because her whole body was moving, shifting from foot to foot. She took out her handheld, flipped it apart and pressed his button. When it clicked to his message she could feel the tears descend again but managed to keep her voice firm and level when, for the first time, she left a message. 'I love you. William, please come back to me. I need you.'

'I believe it is also fair to inform you,' the security officer began in a tone of fresh efficiency, 'that we intend to visit Umm Quat tomorrow, so we'd appreciate the farm manager's and his wife's details.'

Jamil nodded.

'They can open the armoury for us?'

'Yes.'

'Good. To inform you of another thing, to leave you in no doubt as to how seriously this is being taken, the British Ambassador has been informed and he has requested the American Ambassador to allow us, the Mukhabarat, access to one of their satellites so we can see where your car went to two days ago, and at what times.'

Jamil's immediate thought was whether his face was as impassive as he was compelling it to be but then heat prickled within him and he sensed beads of sweat upon his brow. There was a darkness swelling somewhere nearby, as if above him, watching. He wondered if it might be his own fear. Or a Jinn, circulating with malevolent joy. Scrambling for reasoning he forced himself to the issue to realise that, whilst theoretically possible, such co-operation was unlikely for what was, for now, a missing person's enquiry. He felt an urge to say so with a sneer but instead the words which came out, hesitantly, were, 'That's possible? You can do that?'

'We can do that.'

'And you consider William Clive important enough to do that?'

'An Englishman who is in love with someone as beautiful as your sister,' rejoined the inspector, 'is not likely to disappear without trace deliberately, with his passport and wallet left on the street. From this morning we view this as much as a potential murder enquiry as a missing person's search. So, Mr. Talhoun, what are those numbers for Umm Quat?'

When he returned home Jayda was seated in the sitting room he kept off his bedroom. She seemed sullen and empty of purpose but for the presence of her listlessness waiting for him. Her face, full of exhaustion and enquiry, and the fact she was there told him that she still trusted him. Still, no doubt, found him difficult and irritating, characteristics given further impetus by his low opinion of her choice of lover, but despite arguments and temporary hates they had always supported one another and she looked up to him, as was natural for their ages.

He flung his leather jacket upon a chair and then sat on it, standing up, grateful for the jacket as an excuse but actually because he was nervous. He could not meet her eye.

'Have you just been talking to Inspector Mutasem al Husari?' From her tone, quiet but impatient, he guessed her ignorance.

'Yes. I gather that you spoke to him yesterday.' Now he would have to be the messenger. 'There is bad news Jayda.'

She raised herself, still seated, fearful like alert prey.

'They found his passport and wallet. He hasn't left the country, is not avoiding you. It must be that he is missing involuntarily or that he is dead.'

Jayda's head began tiny tremors.

'No, no, no.'

'And they seem to think me suitable for suspicion, which is absurd.'

A wave of sound rose within her, groaning from the depths. She stood up unsteadily and looked at him. 'I've imagined that but it is awful to hear it said.'

'I'm sorry Jayda.'

'I think I will talk to the inspector from now on.' She turned and ran from the room, leaving Jamil staring blankly at the doorway and wondering what the implications of that meant.

CHAPTER XXI

There was a breeze across the roof of the Sweifieh building, softly growing in increments as the daylight lost its power and Jamil was grateful for it as he greedily, frantically, sucked in the first drag of a second cigarette, even as his chest hurt from the many he had already inhaled that day. Each twitching nerve of his being throbbed with a dry craving for nicotine, their yearnings not so much addictive or automatic but a medicinal crutch for stress. The uncomfortable unfamiliarity of not knowing what to do was a bewildering predicament. It made him feel ill, with worry, with loss of certainty, with shame. If he had had a confidant he would have sworn, shown anger and complained of the irritations of being misunderstood but there was no-one and his handheld was on silent. He did not want to be disturbed because he was slowly reaching the futility of even denying to himself what seemed inevitable.

Tactical possibilities jammed into his consideration though, confusing any chance of true clarity of vision. He realised that the next action should be to talk to his father and persuade him to ratchet up his energy to find an appropriate lawyer and use their political influence to lean on the police somehow, but he was hiding on the roof of this building, hesitating and drinking. Such manoeuvring as that would all be sham and the truth of that stunned him into aboulia.

The building was a prestigious development that Jamil had actually built. His father had already bought the land and appointed an architect but Jamil project-managed the construction. He had been on site each day, looking for and discovering the workers' lies: too many bricks, too little insulation, too much glass, not enough marble and, throughout, the continual fight to grasp the trickles of a slipping timescale. An international fashion name now in the ground level shop with three levels of offices above, all separately let, were contained behind a sheen of postmodern sandstone, steel and glass. An 8% investment yield on development costs. Good enough to keep despite the temptations of its risen value. The loan diminishing each year. It was a concrete professional achievement and that must have been why, for the pride it raised within him, he came here at this time.

He took a slug of whisky from the bottle that he had snatched from the hallway drinks table. Then another, hardly noticing its taste but the strength of it gave him all the flavouring he needed.

The roof, though newer and higher than its neighbours, was as jumbled and dusty as a thousand others throughout the city. Flat, with a solid walled lip of a balustrade that hid the commonplace physical housekeeping of commercial property: whirring metal air conditioning chests, air vents thick and bowed in dull metallic curves, vast heat-baked water tanks, thin pipework of unknown utility, a bank of three rows of photovoltaic panels providing some electricity to the common parts, the tubs of some abandoned chemicals. Yet there was room to pace, so long as he minded his footwork. He soon found a rhythm, pacing from one wall to the other, around and between the clutter, trying to order his thoughts to find that clarity and those solutions. But his crisis was vast and too imminent and suddenly too close to analyse in perspective. Why had he done what he had done? It was, he groped, out of a feeling that might be love. Certainly he loved Jayda. He might not feel understood by her, not that he was understood or truly known by anyone, and he did not feel any intimacy of emotional closeness but she was his sister. Therefore there must be trust and love. He supposed that apart from with his mother, when he was a baby and infant, he had not felt or given love. Not unless it was defined by the gap that prevented its wholesomeness. The gap that, by its existence, defined his self-centredness, his reserve and that gap's leap, throughout his life, was what he had found so hard to close, to achieve the elusive connection to someone else without it seeming dishonestly false. The weird separateness of other people meant that he had always been aloof, surrounded by an impregnable boundary that yearned to be breached but, in an awkwardness that expressed itself in the physicality of a large gangly frame, had always remained intact, unaltered by experience. He had told himself his independence was a strength but the unarticulated fear, growing within a hidden cancerous camouflage, was that he was and had always been damaged, isolated and misunderstood. Was he evil? He shook himself free of the thought, creasing his shoulders in a bear-like roll.

He slugged more whisky. There was the honour of his family to consider and, with the most pious of intentions, there was the impulse of wanting to ensure that Jayda's children would be Muslim. He did not often drink but the chemicals surging within his head told him that he could gulp the entire bottle and would barely feel it.

He stopped suddenly, swallowed again and saw it all clearly. They had nothing on him. Their case relied on whether they were able to track his car's movements. The conclusion his bluster settled at guessed a 50% probability that they were bluffing him. But ruin lay with the alternative.

Although he had imagined killing William several times before, those had been fantasies of strength and of fighting. Holding his aim with the Glock had tired him and he had woken from his trance to the sight of pleading and fear on the Englishman's face. It was as if he had just imagined shooting him and then woke, surprised, to find himself with gun in hand and the opportunity isolated and unique, ahead of him. He was, again, surprised when William crumpled instantly and softly upon the soil and gravel, without any dramatic collapse or cry, or any discernable recoiling noise because he was not aware of actually firing. It was all a curiosity to him though seemingly, quietly, banal. He had waited a moment, staring at the crumpled body on the ground and wondered why it had structured itself in the way it fell. It was instantly annoying. He could not recall the fall. He almost shouted out loud for the man to get up, it seemed so improbable that he had actually been shot and, so stunned by what was before him, death, there was no reverberating echo of gunshot from the bowl of hills encompassing and swamping him, baked white in the sun. The instant seemed pressured yet extended, amplified but muffled and hazed and dislocated from reality. He had not even heard the shot itself, though afterward, seemingly long after staring at the collapsed body ahead of him, a clear, tiny metal chink came to him of an empty cartridge case bouncing upon stone.

He dropped the Glock to his flank again and absorbed the picture ahead. Windless, the brightness was constant though its dappled nature: angled pools of burning radiance through the fruit trees. The moment suspended itself, giving him pause to realise this evil but, far off, a vehicle's exhaust fired a splutter and continued. The strangeness of the moment lubricated itself to a gear reverse, into an affectation of normality. He decoupled the magazine, glanced down the breach and fired the pin safely to the soil. Turning to the trestle table behind him he placed both softly upon its surface and stretched his right arm, pulling away the previous ache. A small bottle of mineral water was lifted to the taste of thin, overly smooth metallic plastic. Only then did he turn to look again.

William's body was slumped on its side and twisted away from him, the result of its collapse. As Jamil crunched toward it he rapidly tried to compute what he needed to do next but it was not easy. A neutralising vacancy blanketed over him, detaching him from any fear, shock or horror at what he had done, almost absolving him of participation. There was a corpse in front of him, inanimate and strangely there, put there by another hand, incongruous within the fat, pierced light burning itself upon the tilled soil of his heartland. He stood over the body and imagined he saw blood draining from the already pale skin. The question was what to do, now that it was done. For all his military years he had never dealt with a corpse. Once, in Madaba after the bread riots, he had seen a corpse, like now; just someone slumped still and dusty but not one actually to handle. A discipline of sorts, though, clicked in. For all the urge he felt to look around him to see who was watching, he forced himself not to. He continued to stare at William, dead, a fly unbrushed upon his cheek crawling below the motionless open eye. It felt, standing astride the lumped body, as if he was being observed from somewhere elevated that he could not pinpoint but near. That, at last, made him move.

He returned the weaponry to the armoury in one journey but the heat made him pause and pant before cleaning and storing away. Next the trestle table, with each return step on the orchard's soil lightly sinking him, making his legs ache with the effort. He locked the armoury but rather than returning the key to the manager's house, climbed the steps to the house and left it on the kitchen table. A sweep of the pantry found him an old newspaper and a roll of pedal bin liners but he needed a spade and could hardly ask the manager for one. He checked for tools amongst the toys in the pool shed although he knew that nothing useful would be there.

Time was running out. It was 3.30 and he was at least an hour and a half from Amman. He had already resolved that he could not do the burying at Umm Quat; too obvious. In an instance of resourcefulness that pleased him he thought of using a saucepan as a digging tool so he ran back to the kitchen, grabbed one, then dropping it for a larger one, then clattering that down when he saw a large frying pan.

Despite the heat's thick quilt he pounded a quick, sweating pace to the top of the orchard slope, his frame giraffing in a jerky bob with each step until he stopped, cursed to himself, and swung around back to his car, his head bobbing again like a released trebuchet. The vehicle was oven fresh. Jamil squirmed on the leather as if in agony and started to breathe in short, frightened pants but concentration maintained the speed of his actions. He drove off the tarmac, tyre fibres softened in the heat, making the car's roll denser and somehow ominous, and onto the dust rutted familiarity of the orchard track. Juddering cautiously he descended with the trees on each side, past where he had stood to his left and, since there was no safe turning space, turned left into the parallel ride, stopping directly beside the targets. He moved quickly. Popping the trunk open, there was nothing in it save for a half empty bottle of engine oil. He spread the newspaper out, then a layer of bin bags, both slipping around, their molecules annoyingly inadhesive. Sweat broke over and through him, rising upon his back, under arms and forehead. He wiped his forearm across his brow to leave a glistening film upon its hairs and waited for his breathing to quieten, staring into the trunk until it levelled out and only then turned to face the corpse.

William's back was to him, legs curved and head slumped as if he was, uncomfortably, sleeping. There was, he then noticed, the bullet's exit hole bursting open like the crown of impacted liquid but seemingly without surrounding blood or burn. Jamil approached slowly. It seemed innocuous, as if the thing was incapable of serious consequence, almost accidental. He asked himself how he felt and felt nothing but surprise at this neutrality, curious as to why and yet pleased that he could be so cool, so confident of his reactions as to what needed to be done. The blood was on the other side. Why had he not seen it earlier?

He had not looked. The shot had entered the chest somewhere near the heart and blood, deep maroon and dried, stained a wide spread around and below the entry point. Dead before the ground, he must have bled out, slumped above, before the coagulants of the dying blood sealed the incursion.

The Englishman, pink and faintly tanned before, was now repulsively etiolated; death as a blanched pastel. The face was pressed upon the dust and gravel with its eyes frozen wide and expressed, not in the shock and fear of his futile pleadings nor any semblance of peace in death but with an impassive mannequin blankness. Flies crawled, flew and resettled to stop-start crawl some more. It looked uglier than Jamil was expecting. He had half-acknowledged the threat of William's looks in life: the boyish, clean handsomeness posed to suggest intelligence and reliability. But the man had been a fraud, venal beneath the veneer. The street-fight had proved that. The prospect of a marriage to Jayda proved that. He had deserved to be flung out. Jamil continued to stare. Yes, he conceded, to die was perhaps undeserved but the sin of murder was something that he could be forgiven for. His intention had not been fully clear to himself, even as he had stood there pointing the Glock at the Englishman. It had therefore been an accidental killing. So long as he covered up somehow and brazened some necessary lies there would only be Jayda's shortlived misery to contend with. He would make it good with her. He would find her a decent husband.

He straddled the corpse, for a moment truly pleased with what had been done as he nosed down upon it, then stooped and lifted underneath the arms. Heavier than expected, William was already stiffening. It was a reminder that time was slipping fast again and he jerked and shunted as quickly as he could, scraping themselves across the gravel. Something fell out of the jacket but Jamil moved on, with a final heavy curve hitting the car bumper with William's legs and rolling him down into the trunk with a thump. Turning immediately back to the orchard he saw a wallet upon the ground, splayed out. He picked it up and realised that the ground itself needed raking over. There was a trail of heel dug resistance which he spent a hasty minute kicking over. Over the spot where William had slumped he found blood on several stones and the surrounding dust so he theatrically span the throwing arc of a semi-circle, hurling them out above the tree tops and dispersed the soil with his feet.

The weight of the wallet in his hand made him wonder about some sophistication in a half-formed plan to be rid of the body and suggest a story. He had to regard the corpse again as he closed the trunk. It was ugly and shamefully there: white, bloody, crumpled. An evil, long prescient and suppressed but inadvertently arrived at with the squeeze of his trigger finger. The afternoon was still bright. The sky clear blue and flawless yet Jamil felt a darkness watching him, fleetingly above and behind him. Nervously alert again he burgled the pockets, twisting the bulk sideways to access, finding nothing until William's small maroon European passport joined the wallet in his hand.

He stood still, listening and hearing nothing but the heat. No answer came to him as to where to place the burial. He only understood that it should be away from the scene.

The car convulsed warily at low speed until he bumped back onto the forecourt of tarmac in front of the house and then, with escaping speed, past the manager's low, white home, billowing dust as it crinkled down the gravel track. He returned to the King's Highway and turned to Amman, hearing the thunk of the rolling corpse behind him as he accelerated into a curve, prompting him to turn on music, louder than he would normally bear it. Every so often, leading off from the straight tarmac were dirt tracks, usually at right angles, visibly leading nowhere for great distances. Sometimes, on the left, western side, low hills hid the route and down one of these he turned. A kilometre or so in, the ground seemed as stony, dusty and hard as everywhere else. A tented Bedouin encampment sprung up suddenly as he drove behind a hill; goats, sheep and children sprawled and, seeing him, jabbered excitedly, turning away or toward him in equal measure. A few children were running to his window, confusing him. He halted, shunted his car around in awkward turns and drove back. That moment decided he had run out of time to bury him so he drove to Amman, its suburbs and rush hour jamming the journey home, giving him time to try and think.

He did not sleep that night. The magnitude of what he had to do hazed everything else into an unreal periphery. Waiting until the early hours, his mouth dried painfully by too many cigarettes, he found a spade in Abdul's unlocked shed and drove north out of Amman, past Zarqa, past the civilising snake of orange highway lights to somewhere near the Syrian border. There he turned east down a side road and then south down a dirt track, unmapped and similar to a hundred others, stopping eventually in a shrub-bordered passing area at the base of some nondescript rising undulation. There was enough reluctant moonlight to work without headlights. At the base of a hill he dug for over an hour, frantically, until the grave was at the depth of his hips and the length and width to drop the stiffened body without forcing a crease. Doing so was awkward. The corpse was now rigid like an outsize plank of wood and he had to grapple with it, holding his breath against the dry dust and an odour of baked gaseous pungency. He dropped in the newspaper, bin liners and frying pan on top of the dark shape below. When the filling-in was done, he looked for stones and pebbles to camouflage the disturbed surface but there were very few about.

The light was suffusing a slow dawn when he drove back, his eyes stinging with fatigue, his head drooping until bounced up and shaken and slapped violently. When he reached the Abdoun mansion he tried to be as quiet as could be, in parking, replacing the spade and climbing the stairs. Tiredness, though, made him as clumsy as a drunk but he woke no-one. Sleep, when it came, did not come for long and his mind's rest was short, blank and gave no peace.

Despite his hatred of William when he was alive, he was self-aware enough to understand the evil that he had done and now felt afraid of the consequences for his soul. Behind all his ceaseless thoughts since those deeds was the knowing uncertainty as to whether he would ever be able to redeem himself in Allah's eyes, not by any confession, but through the good deeds he now had to achieve to save his soul. He drank more whisky, ceased his roof pacing and looked out across Amman; the sighing dusk fading a pinking, heated, rose light, lambent in its glitters from the glass of buildings and compresses of car brake lights. Heat still elevated in vision-distorting towers, though now diminishing in strength and fading behind the descending veils of half-night. He shuffled, suddenly lightheaded, to beside the parapet and glanced down at the street scene of shifting alternatives below. Amman, where he had been born, which had grown with him, where his future and his own death lay. He had assumed patriotism for his city instinctively without realising that he loved it, its clean lines and reassuring colours, its quiet, ceaseless, unassuming energy, rooted in stability. A crime-free prosperity. For all the snubs and frustrations, the social awkwardness he felt amongst the petty, money-obsessed shallowness of the predominant bourgeois that he had to mingle amongst, it was the homestead of his familiarity.

Foremost he thought of his father. The pain it would bring to him if he faced trial. The disgrace. Whether he was found innocent or guilty, jailed or executed, the very subject would tarnish such a stain upon him in his father's eyes that he would be banished forever, disowned and rejected without any attempt to understand. The blackness upon the family would last generations. It could ruin them forever if the banks turned, if the other commercial powers excluded them, if they eschewed doing business with the social pariahs.

More whisky, the bottle sounding a distinctive slop as he upended it for another slug. He may have spent his life independent, and brave to have been so, he thought; but the most hurtful part of this moment was that he was isolated. There was no-one to confide in or find advice from; no-one to even share a moment where he could sense some flow of sympathy or understanding returned. The only people he could think of, in default, were his family. And then he thought of his guilt. Whenever some shape of the truth of his situation formed he could see his father, pacing, apoplectic with frustrated confusion; his mother, quietly emitting misery and Jayda, drained by tragedy, ghostly and lost.

Alone, now out of cigarettes, inebriating himself as if it were a disliked but virtuous medicinal, the day's warmth escaping rapidly from the conquering chill of descending darkness, the wind's lifts intensifying slowly, he continued to stare over the front of the building, peering below at the strangely unreal smallness of the street level people, then jerked himself back to spin about and thump his feet to the rear parapet, to overlook the partially surfaced and dust-fringed delivery yard, empty except for the caretaker's pick-up, parked beside by a clumped rising slope of another abandoned plot of real estate.

He stumbled on something as he leaned into the view, swaying too forward in a drunkard's roll. The wall's lip hit his knees and he flopped over the edge, too quickly to scream. Moments before he had been scrambling to decide something, anything to give himself compass. The indecision he had been facing was as frightening to him as the prospect of the murder being discovered. Not knowing what to do was what had led him there, to this roof, anyway. Being unused to drunkenness he wanted to peer over the sides by way of establishing his physical limits, so that his mind could work within concrete boundaries. He had been considering kneeling to pray to find peace, even though he was just out of time for the sunset salat, but the moment was not right to pray for forgiveness. He was too drunk. There was the amorphous invisible darkness again, present somewhere near.

He was drunk and suddenly falling, arms outstretched ahead, legs kicking the air, head strained up to see the ground approaching. Before the slam of his death he was surprised at how much he managed to think. Predominant, of course, was the motion of his falling and the accelerated chill of exaggerated convulsions waving through his limbs. But he did not fully notice that. He thought of Jayda and how he loved her, how he had done this sin because he loved her, how his hate had been born of piety and goodness. He saw her face and whispered 'sorry'. The next thought he had was one of relief. The black tarmac was going to impact so fast that surely there would be no pain. Then he realised that he should, perhaps, repent, atone, say sorry aloud again to make it real but there was no moment left to mouth any word.

CHAPTER XXII

Cosy slipped a receipt into one of her liveried plastic bags. She was so pleased with designing the bags herself. It gave her more pleasure than the overpriced shirt a supplier had made for her with her label. These she handed it over with the best smile she could manage, given her usual dehydrated mid-morning headache.

Once that purchaser had left there was only a European couple browsing before the shelves. At least they seemed European: both were slightly dark-skinned and affluently dressed, too obviously in faux British country style, in London. Cosy enjoyed her observational skills, especially when eyeing punters in her shop. She could not help but give the air between them a single disapproving sniff and was about to slide over for amusement, to patronise them as best she could whilst seemingly being solicitous when the entrance chime went off again.

A slim Arab woman stood inside, poised still beside the door. Cosy could tell she was Arabic by the white headcovering she wore, framing the face incongruously like a nun's habit. At least it seemed strange to Cosy, even in the West End of London. She did not often regard things beyond her perception of how the world should be. The headcovering, however, was no real protection from the day's grey brumous drizzle.

Assuming that the woman was misplaced Cosy, prickling indignantly that her shop was being inappropriately visited, advanced from behind her counter with a frosty, 'Can I help you?'

The woman did not reply. Her suntanned visage glared a knowing hatefulness and Cosy realised who she was as soon as she caught her eye. Or rather, she understood a moment later as soon as she had been struck. Jayda's clenched fists uncurled to air and she slapped Cosy's face with an open palm, with as much sweeping force as her arm could project.

Cosy shrieked, then gasped, moving her head aside and looking downward. With her other palm Jayda slapped from the underside, bringing Cosy's face level again and stunned into a momentary, frightened silence.

With trembling composure in the stinging, warm aftershock on her hands, Jayda unravelled the nijab from her head, revealing it to be a shawl. Then, from measured rehearsal, she shook her hair back into its habitual balance.

'How dare you! Who the hell are you?' regained Cosy.

The European couple were silent, frozen into mawkish observers.

Jayda ignored the tone of the exclamations. 'I wore the headdress so that I would need no introduction.'

For the indignity she felt, from the natural violation of being unexpectedly struck, there was within Cosy an inchoate recognition of crude justice catching up with her. She stood in front of Jayda, panting and suddenly embarrassed at the presence of the other customers.

'Leave now!' she said, but she said it to no-one in particular and Jayda did not move. The Europeans shuffled and, hearing this, Cosy turned to them and repeated herself, slightly louder. They left, hasty with their heads down and looked back from the other side of the glass door before moving off, words rising between them.

Cosy eyed them away, as if waiting for a clear stage but she had no idea what to say next. Jayda was more confident.

'Did you ring him?'

'Ring who?'

'Don't be stupid. Ring William. Did you ring William after you spoke to me?'

'I, well, no. I tried to but, errm, he did not answer.'

'Same day? Did you try him on the same day?'

'Yeah, I think so.'

'You did not speak to him after speaking to me? You haven't spoken to him since?'

Cosy nodded. 'That's right.'

'What's right?'

'I haven't spoken to him.'

'OK.' Cosy glanced behind her at the glass door and noticed its sign. She walked across wincing involuntarily as she passed Jayda, half expecting to be hit again. As she flipped it over to 'Closed', Jayda snapped, 'Tell me, for how long and when were you in a relationship with William?'

Cosy stood in silence, feeling it to be one of those moments which embarrassment would quickly filter into memory's oblivion, especially if she did not answer. She had no intention of replying but had not any idea how to steer this confrontation to its end. Then Jayda looked about to speak so Cosy surprised herself by mumbling, 'Not really.'

'Not really?'

'But he behaved very badly and I felt that you needed to be warned.'

'Well. I haven't seen him since we spoke on the phone either. He's missing, presumed dead.'

'Oh. How?'

'My brother is also dead. He jumped to his death from a roof. So they assume that he killed William.'

'Oh. That's awful. I'm sorry. But he's officially just missing though? He might come back?'

'Whatever.' Jayda walked to the door, turning as she opened it and in a voice of suddenly cracking emotion declared, 'I loved William and I loved Jamil.'

Cosy stayed standing there, stared at Jayda pass from sight and continued there for some minutes, numb, until she realised that her shop was still announcing itself as closed.

That was a Monday so that night Cosy, with no distracting alternative offered, found herself at home in her dark house, isolated under the hum of the bathroom light, with a belly full of vodka and tonic, her grandfather's old cutthroat razor in her hand, opening the many times healed cicatriced weals on her forearms; the blood oozing gleefully in deep velvet runners down her smooth pearl skin, her breath caught and held in heart-thumping anticipation from the first incision to the spring of the blood's release.

Soon she would bandage her arm and lie fatigued upon the bed's sanctuary, alone with lightly stinging throbs pulsating from the wounds, grateful that the pain connected her to her sense of the world, forcing a perspective of her own mortality as she would then, inevitably, puzzle about the Arab woman and William Clive; a man who, when she concentrated enough to recall his face, she could not now remember why he was once so important to her. She had moved on from the sharpness of her craving for him but nonetheless, with solitude and bleeding cuts easing her through it, she was, this night, suspended in a sordid emptiness by the finality of William gone. Jayda, she realised, was now also lost in the grooved emptiness of elliptical emotion; both of them fringed, illogically and unavoidably, with guilt.

CHAPTER XXIII

Jayda had arrived home in the early hours, the RJ Heathrow flight being later in than usual. It was mid-morning when she rose and drove to her father's office, eschewing a breakfast with her mother in a perfunctory manner that mirrored her alternating black and determined mood. She took her mother's car, having asked for it in an unpleasant snap that she immediately regretted but could not say sorry for. So as she was leaving she twisted herself back in the kitchen to squeeze her mother's hand and, before anything more was said, ran to the garage.

The basement parking underneath the office block was thick with shadow and she halted in a delivery bay beside the lift shaft, too unsure to manoeuvre the car around the chipped concrete pillars into a designated space. Pressing the engine button to off she held her hands in her lap for minutes until her breathing quietened, her head down with eyes closed. When she thought that she might be ready she raised a hand, watched it and saw it wobble faintly. With the air-conditioning off with the engine, heat rapidly cloaked around her even in this shadow and the vehicle lost its sanctuary comfort, urging her out. The lift clunked open and the office boy slunk out carrying something, halting and surprised when he saw her. She got out, the heat even thicker as she stood up and, ignoring her witness, walked past him into the lift.

She expected to be shown to her father as soon as she presented herself to his secretary but had not accounted for her unannounced arrival clashing with his appointments. He had someone with him. The rumble of two voices, his the deeper, came through into the reception area where she sat, impatient and uncomfortable, with coffee, water and dead magazines. She did not know how many worked at the head office but, certain that the tragedies were universally known, she imagined that they all, at least twenty or so, found an excuse to stride or meander through that space during the long minutes she sat there.

She recognised Khalifa al Khaldun, the Finance Director, as he came out from behind the closed door. His face altered to one of sympathy when he saw her and he was clearly about to say something measured and sympathetic but she burst past him before he could, before she would be forced to cast herself into an appropriate response, before the secretary could intervene to announce her, and snapped the door to her father's office behind her.

'Jayda!' She knew that he would exclaim her name like that with an outstretch of arms, moving from behind his desk to greet her.

They kissed the ritual turning of cheeks, hugged affectionately for longer than usual and then sat opposite each other in the black leather armchairs. Jad's slumped posture indicated that he welcomed her unannounced visit but wanted to pause. They both examined the rings of exhaustion and doubt below each other's eyes until it became necessary for one of them to speak.

'I was out at a dinner last night so I was not home when you rang your mother from Heathrow.' He gestured with a hand to give her room to start but she said nothing. She could not think how to. He continued, 'I would have told you to stay in London. To finish your studies.'

'I can't.'

'You should finish your studies. It is not good in life, not finishing what you have started. You have no doubt done a lot of work already, so don't waste it.' He took a cigarette packet from his jacket but hesitated, rolling its angularity in his big hands. 'Besides, it would do you good to be away from here for a while, to forget what happened.'

'I left London because I am reminded more about it there, about this naqba, the awfulness of what happened, much more than I would be here. I met William in London, fell in love with him there, argued with Jamil when he last came over there and am reminded of the past there every hour of every day.'

She drew breath. Jad adjusted himself in his seat, silent for her clear rejoinder.

'And my future is here.' She hard-eyed him with all the apprehensive determination that had ruminated and hesitated within her over several days. 'Here with you. Helping you run these businesses. Proving myself. Giving me a purpose and a way out of this endless, descending grief. Learning from you.'

Jad now withdrew a cigarette from its packet but spent time tapping it against its box and then placing it, as if it were already lit, between his fingers. All the while gazing at his daughter, clearly troubled.

'It is not seemly for a young woman of your rank to be dirtying her hands with commerce,' but he was now avoiding her stare and his tone did not find its usual warming confidence. 'It is inappropriate and you are already provided for, so there is no need.'

'To which I say, "So what if I am provided for? I want to! I want to prove myself in your world."'

'Jayda, you have not been prepared for…'

'And you will need me.' She had just interrupted him, something she had probably never done since childhood, so she continued, as strongly as she could. 'You are in your late fifties and you smoke too much. Fiesel is a boy and your health may be in trouble long before he joins the business, if he even wants to. For the sake of dynastic insurance, you need me.'

Jad met her eyes for a moment and then, instead of arguing back he gave a tiny nod. He seemed elsewhere, his sightline moving beyond her shoulder to the sheening surface of the office door beyond. She had said her piece quicker than she had imagined she would and now fell silent. He allowed the moment to expand, until, 'I don't understand why, Jayda. Why did he jump? He must have been guilty of murder. I was going to tell him that night not to do anything rash, that we'd find the best lawyers and perfect his story. There must have been some sort of accident which he did not think he could explain. He would not have killed him just because he disapproved of the match you'd made? Jayda?'

'I just don't know, Baba,' she whispered.

He jerked his head away from her gaze and she saw a film of wetness around his eyes. He sucked in breath to control himself and felt the stability of his emotions tremble with the underlay of bewilderment that had been agitating to the surface ever since it all happened. With the sight of such unfamiliar suffusing and barely controlled grief rising within her father, Jayda's own eyes sensed the pinpricks of tearful relief gather within her but she knew that if she cried now she would lose momentum and possibly lose her argument forever. Outside a cloud shifted with speed and the office darkened everything a momentary grey; then the room swelled with light again, and brighter, as if the sun were throbbing louder. Facing the wall of glass in front of her that revealed Amman, with her father's hunched shoulders darkened to shadow, the resurgent brightness made it harder still to hold back the tears that wanted to commune with his grief. But that was not what she had travelled for. It was annoying that tears were still so close. She needed to grasp her emancipation. Who would she be crying for? Herself? She had wept copiously in the immediate aftermath but the time for that was past. Sorrow was struggling to break through and would, given time. She had not grieved fully. There was no William to focus on. There were the unresolved questions to put to Jamil, still immediate, still unanswered, allowing nothing else but their constant demanding. Had he killed William? Why? Why? Would she be crying for Jamil? Maybe. Would she join her father now in tears? He was hurt and she loved him still but to show her weakness would allow him to regain his strength.

'Baba, I came to a realisation in London that I must move on from William and dedicate myself to this family, this dynasty and business, not my own, now that Jamil has gone.'

Jad finally replaced the cigarette in its packet and dropped it on the coffee table between them.

'Were you going to marry him?'

'I would have done. I loved him. He loved me, I know that and he was preparing himself to ask.'

'You would have wanted to live in London?'

'Probably. And here. I could never leave here.'

Jad sighed. 'I would have accepted it. I would have been troubled by doubt but I would have accepted it.' He was frowning at the space between them.

She thought for a moment that she should use this to confront him somehow but did not know how to make her point. Something about why should she need his acceptance for her choices. The intensity of this intimacy however, almost never before achieved, was unnerving her but the pause now and the pauses just past were capable of being interpreted in different nuances that she was uncertain of. They elevated the situation into something too precious to be despoiled by a cheap debating point. 'Did you see his sister in London?'

'No.'

'Why not?'

'She is coming here anyway. I'll see her plenty then and things might be clearer.'

'You should have seen her.' His voice held a hint of disapproval.

'I couldn't Baba. I couldn't face her yet. I went for a different purpose.'

He narrowed his eyes.

'I saw that woman who rang. I confronted her. I, well, I don't think she was any threat to me. She was just jealous. William had spurned her for me.'

Jad stayed silent, waiting for more.

'I need to know,' she added.

'That I approve of. You know, I would have allowed you to make whatever love match you wanted because I wanted to indulge your happiness and because I still had Jamil.'

'I can be as good as Jamil, even more so.'

'Maybe, maybe not. You have no experience. You are a girl.'

'Being a woman is not relevant in business.'

'I did not want this for you. I wanted you to marry into a good, local family and have the joy of children.'

'I want that as well Baba, eventually, but for now

I need to be someone else.'

He took out and finally lit his cigarette, rushing the movements. Then, speaking quickly, barely suppressing emotion, 'Go and see Khalifa. He is going to visit all our properties over the next few days. Perhaps you can accompany him and start learning. Go. Leave me now.'

She stood up and saw red rims around his eyes as he exhaled deeply, smoke clouding as a shield, and moved to him a hesitant step as he slowly raised himself. She moved to kiss him in thanks but he waved her away and turned his head, inhaling but then exploding an ugly splutter as the smoke met an uncontrolled wave from within. A part of her wanted to watch this vulnerable exposure but she had just won and could not trust herself not to cry if she remained any longer. She said, 'Shukran,' slightly louder and more wavering than she intended and turned away. As the door gently closed behind her Jad slumped to sit again, stubbed out the cigarette in an ashtray, placed his face into his palms and released his pain, bursting in convulsive sobbing waves, his eyes trying to squeeze out the tears so that he would not have to cry for too long.

About the Author

Johnny Leavesley is a lawyer, businessman, husband and father of five. His work has taken him to many parts of the world and Jordan in particular. He served for six years as Midlands Treasurer of the Conservative Party and is High Sheriff of Staffordshire in nomination for 2015. This is his first novel.